Parallels
of Murder

A Bekbourg County Novel

Bekbourg County Novels

PARALLELS OF MURDER

A Bekbourg County Novel

Sherrie Rutherford

Venice, Florida, USA

ISBN: 978-1-7345992-5-1
Library of Congress Control Number:
2023919936

Venice, Florida

*Dedicated to all those who have supported
my efforts over the years.*

Prologue

January 27, 1925

Dizzy Matthews had just hung up the phone with the dispatcher. "Hell and damnation," he swore as he took a long draw from his cigarette. In the past five hours, he had smoked over a pack.

"What's happening now, Boss?" asked the young currier they had nicknamed "Bones" due to his tall, thin-as-a-pole frame.

Dizzy was the railroad's operator. "It ain't good. I hope like hell Number 2 can make it in. It's already two hours late, and this storm is getting worse. Temperature's droppin' like a rock, and that slush on the tracks is startin' to freeze. Not only that, the snow's pickin' up."

The ticket agent walked in just as Dizzy was finishing. The operator's office in the depot was filled with cigarette smoke. Even though the room was warm enough, he lumbered over to the pot-belly stove and shoveled in a couple more pieces of coal. "It better make it in. Don't want to think about two-hundred people being stranded out there in this weather."

"Hell, I don't know what we're goin' to do with all

those people if they do make it here. If the weather lets up, the train can probably make it on to Cincinnati, but if not, they'll have to stay here overnight."

"I thought you already sent Bones over to the hotel to tell 'em about the possibility."

"I did, and I've already got people 'round here lined up with horses and sleighs and wagons to take 'em to the hotel, but they can't all sleep there—not enough rooms." Dizzy took another drag. *"But I ain't goin' worry 'bout that. That's the hotel's problem. I just hope like hell Number 2 can make it in."*

A few hours later, Dizzy and the freight agent, ticket agent and Bones were sitting around Dizzy's office drinking coffee and commiserating about the worsening weather conditions. Over the past hour, the snow had started peppering so that they could not see the freight house across the rail yard, and the temperatures were plummeting. "I ain't never seen it this bad," groaned the freight agent who had only joined the group in the last few minutes. "This is a damn blizzard. What's the latest from Dispatch?"

Dizzy stuffed out a cigarette and lit another. "It's down to half speed. Last report they thought it might be here in 'bout thirty minutes, which makes it four hours late, if nothin' happens, but I ain't got a good feelin'."

Three long, two short rings—Bekbourg's phone signal—abruptly interrupted the conversation. Dizzy looked around at the men. "Hope this ain't more bad news." He yanked up the receiver, "Matthews here." The men stayed quiet as they listened to Dizzy's end of the conversation. They could not tell exactly what was going on, but from Dizzy's side: "You're shittin' me." "Holy hell!" and "How the hell can it get any worse?" it did not sound promising. Dizzy started making notes and repeating what he was hearing: "Two hundred passengers, thirty-one in first-class, six train crew, and twenty-two employees from the dining car, sleeper car attendants, mail car and luggage. Got it." Dizzy put down the pencil to take a puff when his eyes got big. He grabbed the pencil. "You got to be kiddin'. . . . Yeah, I've already got men lined up to take everyone to the hotel. They're goin' to handle it from there. I'll let 'em know."

"What was all that about?" asked the ticket agent when Dizzy hung up.

"We got a damn mess on our hands. Dispatch says Number 2 should be arriving in 'bout forty minutes, if we're lucky. But it's bad, boys. The freight train down the line heading west toward Cincinnati was tryin' to clear the track so Number 2 could get by, and the track switch got stuck and it's derailed." Swearing erupted around the room.

The freight agent looked at Dizzy. "How long's that goin' to take to clear up?"

"Don't know. They'll have to get the hook brought in to move the cars off the track. Hell, that could take a week. But that ain't all the sunny news. There's a break in the track up east of here near milepost sixty-six, so

*they can't take the passengers back east without that bein'
fixed. Bottom line—they may be stuck here in Bekbourg
for a week, depending on the weather." He inhaled, and
stuck out his lower lip to let the smoke rise. "We'll have
to line up about three or four firemen to stay on the
engine to keep the steam up. We can't have the train
freezing up. We should also call in some car men to see
that the cars don't freeze up after the passengers unload.
We need to move the train down near the coal dock so
they don't run out of coal and water."*

"Can of worms," muttered the ticket agent.

*"Sure is." Dizzy puffed again. "We'll get all the
passengers transported to the hotel. At least it'll be warm,
and they'll have some food. The hotel owner will have
to figure out what to do with all the people. The train
crew members are all from Bekbourg, so, if they can
get to their homes, they have a place to stay. The train
employees will probably stay on the train." Dizzy wrote
something on the paper where he had been tallying the
number of people on the train and ripped if off. "Bones,
run this over to the hotel and tell 'em you need to give
it to the owner himself. Make damn SURE he sees this
last part," Dizzy said, pointing to what he had just jotted
down. Bones' eyes grew wide. "Hurry. Time's wastin',
and that hotel owner is goin' to have his hands full."*

*As Bones stuffed the list in his shirt pocket, grabbed
his coat and hat off the hook and started to dash out,
Dizzy shouted, "Also, assure the owner the railroad will
pay for its services." Dizzy took another puff as Bones*

ran out the door. "That hotel owner is goin' to drop a load. I sure as hell am glad it's not me dealin' with all those passengers."

The ticket agent stood. "Yep, that's a lot of people to have to find lodgings for, and they ain't goin' anywhere it looks like for a week."

Dizzy nodded, "Yeah, but that ain't all. Two of the passengers are a Russian Count and his wife."

The ticket agent's eyebrows shot up. "An honest-to-god Russian Count—you mean like a king or something?"

"That's what Dispatch said," affirmed Dizzy.

"Holy shiiiit!"

"Yep, that's 'bout the sum of things," Dizzy nodded as he lit another smoke.

Chapter 1

"Hey, Pal. How's it going?" Lucky asked when Sean answered the phone. Prior to Sean Neumann's retirement from the Marines, Sean and Lucky Brennan had worked together when Sean's investigations cut across civilian lines and involved the FBI. Since joining the Bekbourg sheriff's office, Sean had partnered with Lucky on other criminal cases arising out of the small town.

"You know about alligators?"

Lucky laughed. "Know all about them swimming around my neck."

Sean smiled. "What can I do for you?"

Lucky's voice turned serious. "Sean, I hate to spring this on you, but I need you to come up to Columbus tomorrow."

Sean knitted his brows. "What's going on?" He knew Lucky would not ask if it was not important.

"I really can't go into it over the phone. There's someone you need to meet."

"Sure, Lucky. I'll get there about ten o'clock if that works."

"That's fine, Sean. See you tomorrow, and thanks."

The following morning, Lucky's assistant escorted Sean into a small conference room in the FBI's Columbus office. Lucky rose and greeted his friend. "Sean, I appreciate you driving up on this short notice." Lucky stepped back for Sean to meet a man of average size dressed in a gray suit. His dark hair had started to gray, but his mustache showed no signs of graying. "This is Elias Chabert. He is in the FBI's attaché's office in Paris."

Sean's thoughts leaped to "CIA" as the two men shook hands. Elias peered hard into Sean's eyes. "Lucky has told me about your distinguished career, both with the military criminal investigative division as well as your time as sheriff." The men broke the hand shake, but Elias continued his scrutiny. Sean was also sizing up Elias. "It seems remarkable that a man of your capabilities would land in a small town."

"I grew up there. I didn't intend to stay when I returned after retiring from the Marines, but things happened, and I ended up staying."

Lucky moved toward a chair. "Sean had joined the sheriff's department and suddenly found himself investigating a mass murder and drug cartel. He not only solved both cases but met a woman who is now his lovely wife."

Elias and Sean both took seats. "Ah, should have known a woman was the reason for you making such a small town your home."

Sean glanced at Lucky wondering who this man was and the reason for the urgent call to come to Columbus.

Sensing Sean's curiosity, Elias' thin lips puckered

as he continued to gauge Sean. Sean could return the stare as long as the Frenchman. Finally ready to proceed, Elias leaned forward. "Lucky assured me you can be counted on to honor a duty of confidentiality and that you would be at the top of his list to investigate a rather daring smuggling ring."

"I'm glad Lucky put in a good word for me, but I am not interested in taking on an assignment anywhere else. My responsibilities are to the people of Bekbourg."

Lucky's impatience with Elias thinned. "Sean, hear Elias out." Lucky was thinking Elias had put on enough theater and needed to either confide in Sean or leave. When Elias had told him what he thought might be happening around Bekbourg, Lucky did not hesitate to think of bringing in Sean. This was Elias' case, so he waited to see what the agent decided.

What in the hell is Lucky trying to pull me into? Sean thought as he looked between the two men.

"I must insist you keep what I am getting ready to tell you in strictest confidence."

Sean glanced at Lucky. "I have no intention of becoming involved in an investigation outside my duties as sheriff."

Lucky trusted Sean to do what was right. He nodded toward Elias, who in turn looked at Sean, "We have reason to think an international criminal or crime syndicate might be targeting Bekbourg, or could already be operating there."

For the first time since sitting, Sean stirred as he

leaned toward Elias. "If that's the case, I need to know *everything* you know. If any of the citizens in Bekbourg are in danger or if there is a crime going on in my jurisdiction, I want to know."

Lucky smiled to himself. Even the pompous Elias attempted to conceal the intimidation he felt from Sean. Lucky had seen Sean in action and knew Sean's intensity. *When Sean decides to flex his authority, common sense should dictate you don't stand in his way,* thought Lucky as he waited for Elias' next move.

"Yes, I see your point." Elias then opened up. He explained that, over the past two decades, Interpol had been tracking a criminal element that brokered stolen paintings, antiques and jewelry across Europe. Interpol's investigation had not uncovered anything about the criminals themselves. They did not know if there was a central organization that ran the ring, or if there were multiple theft rings or even if it was just an individual at work. What they knew was that private collectors and museums had been the victims of theft, and the stolen articles never surfaced. Among the targeted items were jewels and artifacts belonging to Russian nobility. "Obviously, only legitimate collectors and museums report thefts, and so we do not know the extent that illegitimate private collectors are victims themselves."

Elias told of a wealthy businessman from Dallas, Texas, who had acquired a collection of jewels once belonging to European nobility through the black market. About ten years ago, he was approached by a dealer who had come upon a broach believed to have belonged to one of the Czar's sisters. On a trip to England, she had taken her jewels out of Russia before the Czar's demise, and once the Bolsheviks took control of the country, she lost her financial means. A few years after the revolution, out of necessity, she sold the broach. It disappeared from the public eye, and no one ever knew what had become of it. When the Dallas businessman heard of the broach, he wanted to add it to his collection and arranged to purchase it from the dealer for a small fortune. When they met to transfer the broach, both were shot dead. "We learned the details from the man's wife, who reluctantly admitted to the plan and even about his collection of other jewels. What we think happened is that this jewel thief we have been tracking somehow learned of the transaction and ambushed the men, killed them, and stole the broach. The killer may be a collector and may have kept the broach for himself—or herself—but more likely, they sold it."

"What has this got to do with Bekbourg?" asked Sean.

Elias pulled a copy of a newspaper article from a folder. Uneasiness seeped down Sean's spine. "I understand this story was written by your wife, Cheryl Seton." Sean recognized the article but continued his silence. "This is a picture of the Russian Count, Zakhar Voskoboynikov, and his wife, Elizabeth Griffiths." Elias pointed to a necklace worn by the Count's wife, which Sean had never taken notice of until now. "From experts on the Czar's jewelry maker out of Paris, this necklace is believed to have been made at the Czar's request. Possibly for his wife, but we do not know that. It was never seen in public before or after this picture, which was taken in Bekbourg. When this picture surfaced, we sent an agent to talk with Elizabeth's granddaughter, but she knew nothing about any jewels the Count had given her grandmother."

"I'm still not certain why this picture might be a connection between Bekbourg and an international theft ring."

"This is the last sighting of the jewels. Your wife's article was published the third week of August—about six weeks ago. It's had time to get out there. This photo could draw a thief or collector to Bekbourg to see what they can learn about the jewels."

Silence filled the room until it was broken by Elias. "Sean, I don't have to tell you that criminals in the underworld are ruthless. If you notice anyone new around your county who might seem suspicious, let Lucky know immediately. Interpol has been trying to get a lead for years—just a name might give them the break they have been searching for."

"So, you think Cheryl's article might attract an international theft ring to Bekbourg, but you don't have any idea who the players might be?"

"We need a break, Sean. Your wife's article might turn out to be an enticement if it's been picked up by the criminal element which follows rare artwork, artifacts and jewels."

On his ninety-minute drive back to Bekbourg, Sean reflected on their conversation. Bekbourg—population around five-thousand—in southeast Ohio was in the heart of the rust-belt. Unlike some of the cities in the Midwest region of the country, it had not only survived the economic devastation but had reinvented itself as a tourist destination and was on the upswing. Yes, the town was doing well, but what was the likelihood an international theft ring was working out of his small town? It almost stretched the imagination that Cheryl's recent article about a Count and his wife being stranded in Bekbourg eighty years ago would trigger something like this. Stranger things had happened—he knew well—and he would stay vigilant, but this seemed to be an exercise in futility.

Chapter 2

Bri marveled as she took in the foyer and the grand living room off to the side. "C.P., this is magnificent. I never dreamed this old mansion could be restored to its former elegance in such a contemporary style."

C.P. Traylor had grown up in Bekbourg County, Ohio. After graduating high school, he took a job with the local railroad as a means to finance his education. His college education was interrupted when he was drafted and assigned to the U.S. Army Railroad Corp. After his discharge, he completed his college degree and started moving up the corporate ladder. He eventually reached the executive ranks within the railroad conglomerate. His name was recognized throughout the railroad industry. While he had a reputation of being hard-nosed, he was held in high esteem because of his overall expertise and for being an innovator in introducing technology into the railroad operations. After retiring from the railroad, he accepted a position reporting directly to the Secretary of the Department of Transportation in Washington, D.C. He fulfilled his commitment there, and then his life went full-circle when he returned to Bekbourg with the intention of acquiring the city's railroad that was on the chopping block by its owners. His unceasing vigor had Bekbourg's citizens applauding the boom to the area from his fight to prevent the WVB&C Railroad Company from shutting down. But his ambitions did not stop there. He was in the process of starting up a twenty-five-mile scenic railroad from Bekbourg to just north of a state park to bring tourists back and forth. Most recently, he had announced the purchase of the Grand Hotel in Bekbourg, which had been shuttered since the late 1930's—except for the GilHaus, the city's most upscale restaurant located on the hotel's first floor.

This evening was to celebrate the completion of the restoration of the old Schriever mansion—C.P.'s new home. C.P. smiled and looked over at Mary Zimmstein, his friend and hostess. Bri spied the warmth between them as their eyes touched. "Thank you, but it was Mary who pulled this off. She had the vision and worked with the contractor to transform this grand dame into what you see."

Mary beamed. "Now, C.P., you know most of the credit lies with you." She turned to their guests, Bri and her husband Max. "It was C.P.'s idea to update its features with a contemporary flare, and the architect he hired from D.C. took it from there. I just offered suggestions here and there."

Bri joked, "I can guess which one of you is responsible for that beautiful fall display out front. I can't imagine C.P. putting up a scarecrow and all those pumpkins."

C.P. chuckled. "She thinks of everything."

As she motioned them through the foyer toward a large conservatory overlooking the back grounds, Mary said, "We are pleased you could join us this evening. Let me show you to the refreshments. Please feel free to move throughout the house. We will be showing people around, but you do not have to wait on us. The cellar is just that—the cellar—so there is nothing to explore below this main floor. On this first floor, C.P. has an office area and exercise room, which is on the far back side of this floor," she said pointing toward a hallway leading to the right. She smiled. "Of course, he has a theater room on the second floor where he can watch his sports shows. The master suite is also on that floor—as well as a small kitchen and sitting area. Although a couple of guest suites are on the third floor, the construction crew is currently renovating the guest house in the back where guests can opt for more private quarters if they prefer."

Max laughed. "C.P. sure knows how to do things first class."

Bri spoke up. "Yes, but Mary, we know he relies on you, and this project's success could not have happened without you."

Mary's fleeting wistful smile did not escape Bri's notice. It was obvious to those around Mary and C.P. there were deep feelings between the two, but they remained just friends. Both people were private when it came to personal matters, so it was unclear to Bri why their relationship had not evolved. She had some theories, but in her mind, the two belonged together, and she hoped whatever obstacles there might be, they could be overcome.

As they approached the bar, Mary introduced them to a couple who had catered events for her parents for years. They had driven down from Columbus as a favor to Mary, because they knew how important the evening was to her—she wanted C.P. to be pleased. Mary excused herself to return to greeting other guests. As Bri and Max stood off to the side enjoying hors d'oeuvres and a glass of wine, Max commented on how the open house brought back memories of their open house for the B&B about fifteen years earlier.

They each had successful careers in Cincinnati when they heard of the small town in southeast Ohio that was developing into a tourist destination by capitalizing on its proximity to rivers, a lake, state park, and national forest. They took a leap of faith and quit their jobs, moved to Bekbourg, and purchased a dilapidated boarding house in the downtown. Bri and Max restored it and opened a bed and breakfast, which had turned into quite a profitable venture. Next door, they purchased the building where Max initially opened a coffee shop. Due to its success, he expanded its operations into a popular bistro. Max and Bri felt they had landed where they belonged and had worked with other community leaders and volunteers to make Bekbourg a better place. Bri had been elected mayor and promoted several successful pro-growth initiatives.

As the evening progressed, many of C.P.'s and Mary's friends stopped by to visit and admire the stately mansion, which was in Highland Heights—an upscale residential part of downtown that was slowly seeing a revival. They took small groups around and explained the history as well as the renovations.

C.P. and a small group of men were standing out back on a slate patio near a firepit. C.P. was explaining that the next task to tackle was the grounds. Mary was working with a landscape designer, and they hoped to get started with those changes in early spring. He was not going to install a pool, but a fountain was in the works.

"What about that old guest house?" Sean asked, looking at the small two-story structure in the back corner.

"Just got started on that. I wanted to get the house completed first, but with that now finished, Cole's men recently started working in the basement area to shore up the foundation. The first and second floors are going to need updating, but structurally, they're in pretty good shape. That project should be finished by summer," C.P. told them.

"You've been at this for a while, haven't you?" another man asked.

"Yeah. Starting with bringing in the architect, it's been going on nearly two years. When I first got here, I rented a room in Bri's B&B, which took its toll on my waistline." The men chuckled. "I then rented a house not far from the train station until this was finished."

Max asked, "I know you were traveling a lot. You

see that changing?"

"I hope I can spend more time here now that I closed the deal on the WVB&C. I'm working to get the scenic railroad going, a museum set up in the depot, and the Grand Hotel renovated and opened."

Milton Grant smiled. "Yeah, C.P., you sure keep us busy at the newspaper writing about all the great things you're doing around the area." The men laughed in agreement.

Bri saw Cheryl Seton walk in the front door and sided up to her, assuring Mary she would show Cheryl to the refreshments. Cheryl was the owner of the local newspaper, the *Bekbourg Tribune*. "I saw Sean earlier with C.P."

An automatic smile lit Cheryl's lips when she thought about her handsome husband, the sheriff. "Yeah, I had a couple of things I needed to take care of, so he got here before me. This is incredible," she commented as they walked toward the conservatory.

"Grab some refreshments, and I'll show you around. This is a real showcase."

Cheryl had just been handed a glass of sparkling water when they heard, "Darlings, how lovely to see you."

They could not contain smiles as they turned to see their friend, Dillie Beaumont. They exchanged hugs— each balancing their drinks. "This home is absolutely marvelous," exclaimed Dillie as her free hand motioned around the room causing her gold bracelets to jingle. "Mary and C.P. have created a masterpiece."

"I was just getting ready to show Cheryl around. Would you like to join us?"

"I would love nothing better, darling. Where do we start?"

Bri opted to start on the third floor and work their way down. Dillie had recently moved back to Bekbourg after living away for about thirty years. She had purchased the old Schumacher cigar box factory and turned it into an avant-garde artist gallery. Dillie was a long-term guest at Bri's B&B while waiting for her own grand old mansion in the downtown area to be restored. "Dillie, we look forward to seeing your new home, too," Bri said as they reached the second floor landing.

Dillie's eyes twinkled, "Yes, darling, another perfect opportunity for a soiree. Frederic absolutely loves planning parties for every occasion. I have no need to ask him where he stands on planning the gala for my home opening. He knows my mind better than I do."

The three women laughed in agreement. Frederic St. Fleur, Dillie's personal assistant, capably saw to her business and personal matters.

The three women ultimately ended their tour in the kitchen as Bri had planned. She loved cooking and did not want to rush as they admired the huge area and its state-of-the-art appliances. "I love the bold contrast in here," Cheryl observed as she looked around. "Every kitchen I see anymore has stainless steel appliances. Mary opted for black cabinets with white appliances, and it's great."

"I especially love this." Bri was looking at a massive china cabinet at one end of the kitchen. The women walked closer to admire the piece.

Dillie rubbed one of its doors. "There were some gorgeous pieces left in the house and guest house that Mary thought C.P. should keep and work into the décor. This is an original piece from when the Schrievers first moved in here."

Cheryl said, "I thought I saw a few antique pieces. You're right, she knew exactly how to work them in with the contemporary furniture she chose. It's all perfect."

Dillie was close friends with Mary and C.P. During the renovations, Mary had invited her to walk through the house on occasion to see the remodeling efforts and the various furniture items as they were delivered. "This home is simply magnifique! All that is missing is Mary moving in."

Both Bri and Cheryl whipped their attention to Dillie. "Do you know something?" Bri asked simultaneously with Cheryl's "Is something going on with Mary and C.P?"

Dillie sipped her martini. "Darlings, I wish I could share such delicious news, but unfortunately, I know nothing. What I do know is they look at each other with such love in their eyes. I even said to him one evening when we were having drinks at your lovely B&B that Mary was most definitely interested in him."

"What did he say?" Bri asked. Bri was a romantic at heart. Cheryl smiled to herself as she looked at

Bri in her flowing smock and long wavy hair. Cheryl suspected Bekbourg was the only city in the country with a mayor who was a prized pastry chef and looked like a hippie from the 1960's.

"The poor dear! Despite our friendship, he shied away from the topic. He made reference to not thinking it was fair to Mary with the age difference. I naturally poo-pooed such nonsense and assured him that love conquers all. I suggested he should let Mary be the decider."

Cheryl was intrigued. "What was his response?"

"Typical. He immediately changed the subject and poured me another martini and himself a double of Max's fine scotch."

If anyone could get C.P. to talk, it was Dillie, thought Cheryl. Nothing about Dillie would ever reveal she was approaching sixty. During her years in Europe, she had acquired an accent somewhere between French and Eastern European. She carried charm and elegance with a natural beauty. She was glamorous and always stylish—tonight she wore designer black satin leggings and a colorful sequin tuxedo with gold stilettos. Her platinum blond hair hung just below her shoulders despite having jeweled pins containing its curls. Her bangles danced, and her jeweled rings glistened as her graceful arms moved with animation when she spoke.

"So, you think it's him who is hesitating?" Bri was surprised.

"I assured him it was quite debonair for men to have much younger companions, but I could tell he was uncomfortable talking further about the matter. I respected this and changed the subject. Frankly, darlings, I have known many couples where the age difference is much greater than theirs, which is a mere fifteen years." Dillie waved her free hand at her shoulder and added, "Sometimes, it is the woman who is older, by several years I might add, but again, who should care?"

Bri looked around to make sure they were alone. "I wondered if it might be Mary who was holding things back. Not because of the age, but because of what happened with her husband, Jeff Thompson. Maybe she thinks that would be a stigma, and she doesn't want C.P. to be embarrassed."

"Mmm. I had not considered that. But if that is her reason, she should immediately dismiss it." Dillie was confident. "Something like that would be trivial to a man like C.P."

"I agree," said Cheryl. "She had nothing to do with that, and look what she did to compensate for his actions. Her foundation has helped so many people around here. She didn't have to do that. She could have stayed in Columbus and turned her back on Bekbourg, but she didn't."

Dillie paused. "My best guess is that it's C.P., and it's the age. We can only hope they come to their senses." Dillie's eyes sparkled. "As you know, darlings, I've been married five times. I simply do not believe in procrastinating when it comes to love."

Cheryl and Bri laughed as Dillie's lips turned up in a familiar mischievous smile.

Chapter 3

Cheryl was standing at the counter waiting on a coffee order when Andrian Kray entered Max's bistro. "Hey, Cheryl, how's it going?" he asked as he walked up to put in his coffee order.

C.P. had hired Andrian a few weeks prior as an archivist to go through the railroad files and assist in establishing a railroad museum in the train depot. Cheryl had gotten to know him when she was researching an old train bridge collapse in Bekbourg. She greeted him and asked how he had been.

"Can't complain. I've been meaning to call you. That story you published a while back about the Russian royalty getting stranded here during that blizzard was interesting. That's the type of thing that might be good to include in the railroad museum. I've been looking into that event. I was thinking we could work together and compare notes. I've found some things in the WVB&C's files about that particular train stop. If there's more in the newspaper's records, it might be helpful in putting together a complete picture of what was going on at the time. Let's face it—it wasn't every day a member of the

Russian imperial family came here." They both laughed. "I think it would be interesting to see if we can find out who they spent time with and what they did while they were here. Russians aren't put off by winter weather," he smiled. "Maybe the Count did outings with some of the men. I suspect the women found ways to entertain his wife—those types of things. People who visit the area might find the story interesting."

"That's a great idea," said Cheryl as the barista handed her the coffee.

After she paid, she turned to Andrian, "It's funny you raise this, because a retired professor who is an expert on Russian history is coming here to talk to me."

Andrian blinked. "Oh. What's that about?"

Cheryl sipped her coffee. "I'm not sure. He's coming by this afternoon. If I get the chance, I will ask him about the Count and see what he knows about him." Cheryl glanced at her watch. "I need to run, but I'll call you to get together about this."

"Sure. Who knows? As we rummage through these old files, we might learn about other famous people who came to Bekbourg on the train we can spotlight in the museum, too."

Cheryl nodded as she turned to leave. "Yeah, it's amazing what jewels these old files hold."

Chapter 4

When Cheryl walked into the *Tribune's* building, the receptionist had the phone pasted to her ear and a pencil twirling in her free hand. "Yep, we'll be sure to have something about it in the morning's edition." Blinking lights lined the base of the phone. "This phone's been ringing off the hook," Patti groused as she pushed a button to disconnect and left her finger hovering over another flashing button. "Was Milton able to reach you?"

Cheryl started to pull out her phone, but remembered she had left it on her desk. "No. Why?"

"He took one of the reporters with him. We got a call saying that they had found a dead body at C.P.'s place."

Patti had been the receptionist at the newspaper for years. A colorful beaded eyewear retainer shimmied along the sides of her face leading to the bright red glasses plopped atop her unruly bleached-blond mop. Phone slips were semi-stacked across the front of her desk by reporter, and yellow sticky slips and papers were in no discernible order to a casual observer. The phone rang again. "*Tribune.* Hold please," she barked and pressed the hold button without giving the caller a chance.

Cheryl did not wait for Patti. As she hurried toward her office, she yelled behind her, "I'll call Milton and see what's going on."

"Good idea." Patti cradled the phone on her shoulder and raised her voice. "Don't forget your meeting with the professor this afternoon." The phone was ringing again as Cheryl reached her office.

Milton picked up on the third ring. "Hey, Cheryl, guess you heard about the dead body found at C.P.'s?"

Milton Grant was an old-style newspaper reporter, who was like a father to Cheryl. He had taken her under his wing as a young reporter and taught her the ins-and-outs of investigative reporting. When she told him about the opportunity to purchase the *Bekbourg Tribune*, he retired from a newspaper in Cleveland—where he was a household name—and moved to Bekbourg to help her run the *Tribune*.

"That's all Patti told me. What's going on?"

"The construction crew working on the guest house out back of C.P.'s mansion was digging in the basement. I talked to the two workers themselves who found the remains. They saw what looked to be an old rag and kept digging—not thinking much about it. But they soon discovered it was a blanket or something wrapped around something. Charley said they weren't sure what to do, because neither of them had a good feeling about it. But they knew they wouldn't know until they looked. He pulled at the blanket and saw some old clothes and pulled back more and saw a skull. Stopped right away and ran to call Cole Fischner, owner of the construction company.

"Cole didn't want to call the police or C.P. until he checked it out himself. Didn't take him long to get there. And sure enough, it was a dead body. Charley said it looked like men's clothing, so I'm suspecting a male, but we need to wait for confirmation. Sean's here along with a couple of his deputies. C.P.'s here, too. No one knows much at this point. Sean's asked the state forensic techs from Columbus to come get the body. The only thing they all are saying is that it's been there a long time."

"Any idea on the cause of death?"

"Not at this point. That's why Sean asked the techs from Columbus to get involved. It's especially interesting since the property was owned by one of the most influential people in Bekbourg for years, and this body could have been put there back then."

"Very interesting, Milton. Have you had a chance to talk to C.P.?"

"Yeah. Said he didn't know a dead body came with the deal."

Cheryl grinned. "I guess you've already got someone looking into the history of the house?"

"I just sent Jake back to the paper to start digging through our archives to see what we have. We don't know when the body was put there, but we'll include some general information about the house and the owners in the write-up. If you get anything from your husband, you'll let me know?"

Cheryl laughed. It was a running joke between the

two. Sean was just as closed-mouth on his investigations with her as he was with anyone. "Don't hold your breath on me scooping you."

Milton shook his head. "Won't do that. Martha's not ready for me to kick the bucket just yet."

They both were laughing when they hung up.

Chapter 5

Cheryl walked into the conference room where her receptionist had shown Dr. Dimitri Shlykov. He stood and extended his hand. "Ms. Seton. The pleasure is mine."

Cheryl smiled as she looked down to meet his alert dark-blue eyes. "Dr. Shlykov. It is nice to meet you. Please have a seat. Did my receptionist offer you something to drink?"

"Yes, and she is getting me hot water for my tea. She was not familiar with Russian tea. I gave her an extra tea bag and suggested she try it."

Cheryl had just enough time to observe the older gentleman with thinning silver hair, goatee and round, wire-rimmed glasses before Patti hustled in with a mug of hot water. "My deepest gratitude, Patti. I assume you have no objections to me calling you by your first name?"

"Suits me fine," she grinned. "I've been called by many names."

"All saintly, I'm certain." He looked at Cheryl. "I knew the minute I met Patti, she and I were kindred spirits. Her desk looks like mine."

Patti laughed as she moved toward the hallway,

"Let me know if you need anything."

He took his time stirring the tea before laying the plastic spoon on a paper towel supplied by Patti. "A couple more minutes before the tea is properly steeped. In the meantime, I am aware of your admirable reporting on the Pinkston murder case a few years ago. My understanding is that you were a reporter for the esteemed *Cleveland Presenter* at that time. I assume that explains what brought you to Bekbourg, but becoming the owner to the *Bekbourg Tribune* is remarkable. You are to be congratulated on such a lofty accomplishment. Do you mind if I call you 'Cheryl'?"

"Please. Are you still teaching?" Cheryl found it interesting he had researched her.

"I am no longer affiliated with a university as a lecturing professor. I wanted more freedom to select my engagements." He caressed his goatee. "At my age, it was time to do something else. I retired from the university three years ago and returned to Cincinnati where I spent my youth. I still lecture at universities both in the U.S. as well as across Europe. I also find I am in demand to speak about my expertise on Russian history by government officials as well as with security and military officials. Frankly, I am busier now than when I was on the university staff." He told her he had retired from an east-coast university that was renowned for its Russian studies.

He sipped his tea. "I came across your article on the Russian Count spending time here in Bekbourg and found it fascinating. Let me say that had I known about it earlier, I would have already reached out. You see, my assistant saw the article when it was picked up by the Cincinnati paper and clipped it. In all the demands, it slipped his mind to raise it with me. I was in Europe at the time. I found it in a stack of papers he had put aside for me during my absence. It's probably best I didn't learn of it during my obligations for a museum in Austria. It certainly would have been a distraction to think of a member of the Russian royal family walking these very streets!"

Cheryl nodded. "I was surprised when I came upon the story in our files. It is remarkable. How can I assist you, Professor?"

He dresses like a professor, although a dapper one, Cheryl mused. His tweed sports coat hung flawlessly from his slender shoulders, and his bow tie displayed colorful pheasants.

"Naturally, as an expert on Russian history and its aristocracy, I am curious." His eyes twinkled. "Ah, I'm getting ahead of myself as I am apt to do when I learn of an undocumented event regarding the Russian imperial court. I am, of course, interested in learning what I can about Count Zakhar Voskoboynikov's time here. I was wondering what might be in your archives. Also, the library may be a source of information about his time here, but can you think of other places we might look? I want to learn as much as possible about the man—his hobbies, what he did in his spare time." He chuckled, "even his tastes in foods."

Cheryl laughed. "So, you are familiar with him?"

Dimitri held out his hand and tilted it back and forth. "I have heard the name, but since he was not in the Czar's direct line, I never researched him, but I intend to."

"Whatever happened to him?"

"Unfortunately, he died young. It wasn't too long after his time here. He's buried in Elizabeth's family plot in Rhode Island."

"What happened to his wife?"

"She went on to marry again and had a daughter. Elizabeth died several years ago. I'm afraid that's about all I can tell you now, but Jeffrey and I are both researching his background. I hope to know more soon." He smiled and took another sip. "If there are any photographs of him or his lovely bride, of course I would be most interested in viewing those as well."

Cheryl considered how they might be able to assist each other. "Before I published my story, I did a thorough review of our files, but it's possible I missed something. I will be happy to see if there is anything else in our files. I would appreciate your expertise on the Russian family, and maybe you can help me put this in historical context about what was going on in Russia at the time."

He savored the tea before he spoke. "Absolutely. Most of my acquaintances accuse me of talking too much about what I know. I will be glad to share my knowledge." He smiled, "I would hope you would be generous and give credit to my contributions in your news articles."

She smiled. "Of course. It will add gravitas with my readers that I collaborated with an expert on Russian history and the imperial family."

"Did you come across many photographs of the Count and his wife?"

"No. I found the one I published in a file along with the copies of the old articles. The file was labeled: 'Count Voskoboynikov and wife January 31, 1925.' I don't know how the picture came to be in our files. It's possible Schriever or the newspaper hired a photographer for the gala, or it's possible the hotel or someone else hired a photographer for the event."

"That's odd that there would only be one photo of the imperial couple."

"It wasn't the easiest thing to take pictures back then. Also, the couple may not have wanted much publicity." It dawned on Cheryl how little she knew about the couple. "The articles written at the time didn't contain any interviews with the couple. There were mentions of social engagements involving the Count and his wife, which I included in my story."

"I see. Would it be possible to see copies of all the articles about the Count and his time here during the snow storm?"

"Of course. I'll have copies made for you. Like I said, I don't think there is much else in our files here, but I will check."

"Well, if you need an extra hand in reviewing boxes, my assistant is available. He is quite good at research."

He shuffled in his seat. "I have commitments after the first of the year, so I am interested in starting work here as soon as possible. I am going to return to Cincinnati and have my assistant prepare us to return to Bekbourg and settle here while I research this. Perhaps you would be so kind to give me the names of possible places we might stay?"

With the holidays approaching, she could understand why he wanted to get rolling.

"Since I published the story, I have learned there is a community of Russians who live in Cincinnati."

"Indeed, your information is correct. My family tree is Russian. That is how my parents came to live in Cincinnati."

"There is someone else here who is interested in the Count. It might be helpful if all three of us are working on this."

Dimitri's head tilted, "Oh?"

"The man who recently purchased the WVB&C railroad which runs through Bekbourg is planning to open a railroad museum in the old depot. He hired an archivist to research the old railroad files, and one of the things he is doing is looking for items of interest to be displayed in the museum. I talked to him today about coordinating efforts on the Count's stay here. He thinks visitors to the museum will find the story interesting."

The professor's shoulders relaxed. "I see. Yes. I think most people would find that interesting. Perhaps my assistant can work with him as well. I had not thought of the railroad files, but that could be an important source of information. I should speak with him and see how we might work together—if you would be so kind to plan on making the introductions when I arrive back here."

"Of course. His name is Andrian Kray. Do you mind giving me your assistant's name and contact information? I will pass his name on to Andrian, and I'll also call him with information about Bekbourg that might be helpful during your stay here."

When Cheryl mentioned Andrian's name, she noticed the professor's eyes flicker. She started to ask if he knew Adrian, but before she could, he said, "His name is Jeffrey Blankenship, but contact me please. Here is my card. He will be busy preparing our lodgings and organizing research necessities. Now, I have taken enough of your valuable time. I need to return to Cincinnati for a dinner engagement this evening."

Cheryl quickly made a list of places around town they might want to stay and handed it to him. "Any of these places would be fine to stay at, but the B&B has delicious pastries, especially the scones."

"Ah yes. I saw the B&B down the street as I came into town. That would be convenient."

He slipped the paper in his pocket. "Thank you for meeting with me on such a short notice. I feel we have made a lot of progress today. I look forward to this project." He moved toward the doorway. "You mentioned that the archivist was hired by the new owner of the railroad. Has the archivist been here long? I thought if he has a love of history, we might have something in common and he could show me around Bekbourg. My interests lie in Russian history, but history of any sort whets my appetite," he smiled.

"I think Andrian would be happy to show you around. I don't know how much he has learned about the area because he has only been here a couple of months, but he has been working his way through the railroad files, and they contain history about the railroad and the town."

"I look forward to our association, Cheryl. I can show myself out."

Cheryl heard him talking with Patti as she returned to her office. *Interesting,* she thought. *I wrote the article as a human interest story. Little did I know it would engender so much interest!*

Chapter 6

It was late afternoon, and the remains had been loaded for transport back to Columbus. Sean returned to the old Schriever mansion to talk with Ronnie Vin, the state's forensics expert, before she left for the day. She told him her team would be back tomorrow, but she was not sure how much more they would find. The guest house had been roped off with crime scene tape, and Sean would need to tell C.P. to hold off on the construction until they completed their investigation. She showed Sean a revolver found alongside the body. "It's too early to tell the cause of death, but we know he was wrapped in a blanket and buried there. He's in dress clothes. And, Sean, given the state of the materials on the blanket and the clothing, this could have happened as much as a hundred years ago. It's hard to say until we complete our analysis."

Ronnie told him she was likely going to ask the FBI's crime lab to review the remains, because they had the equipment that could best pinpoint the time period. More research into the revolver was needed as well, and the FBI's expertise might come in handy there, too.

Sean told her he would call Lucky, whom she knew. After Ronnie left, Sean went to speak with C.P. to tell him about the delay in having the workers back on the property. "No problem, Sean. Just let me know when it's okay. Any idea how long the body has been down there?"

"We'll know more after the crime lab completes its work. Ronnie is going to consult with the FBI and get their assistance. But to your question, this is speculation on her part. Keep it under your hat until we know, but she said it could have been there as much as a hundred years."

"You think you'll ever be able to identify the body?"

"I don't know, but I'm going to try. One thing I feel pretty comfortable in saying is that even if Ronnie is off by a couple of decades in her timing, if foul play was involved, the perpetrator is not alive."

Chapter 7

Sean arrived home before Cheryl and took Buddy, the overzealous chocolate Lab, for a jog to the park. With Buddy, it was never a jog in the traditional sense, because he lunged at squirrels and sniffed every hydrant along the way. When he and Buddy returned to the duplex where he and Cheryl rented one side, he knew Cheryl was home from the way Buddy bounded toward the kitchen where she had started dinner.

Cheryl's eyes twinkled as her six-four husband walked into the kitchen in his jeans and OSU t-shirt. "You and Buddy arrest anyone on your rounds to the park?" she grinned as he took her in his arms.

"No. Didn't see any crimes being committed, so we thought we'd come here and watch from the porch. Never know when someone might commit a crime in front of the sheriff's home."

Cheryl giggled at his dry sense of humor and kissed him. She pulled away from his strong arms to stir something on the stove. As he started setting the table, she asked, "So, what's this all about with a body being found at C.P.'s new house?"

Sean briefed her on what she had already heard from Milton, but he went on to explain. "The basement is a cool, dry area. There doesn't appear to have ever been any water in there. Ronnie told me we were lucky that the remains had not been more compromised."

"Did DD come, too?" Dennis Douglass was the state medical examiner.

"When I saw that the remains had been there a long time, I just called Ronnie's office. I left it to her to see if she thought DD's help was needed."

"Makes sense—like you always do." Sean shook his head as Cheryl grinned. Sean had given Milton a statement for the newspaper. "Anything off the record I should know?"

He laughed, "No."

She made a zipper motion across her lips as her eyebrows shot up with humor.

"Okay, off the record?" She gave him an exaggerated yes nod, and he grinned. "It appears to be a man."

When he didn't volunteer anything else, she turned back to the stove. "Well that's something from the close-mouthed sheriff."

Sean laughed. During his twenty years as a Marine, he was a criminal investigator in an elite crime unit. He had not been ready to retire, but severe injuries sustained in an ambush left him no choice. He had returned to Bekbourg to heal, both mentally and physically, and was offered a deputy position from his high school friend, who was the sheriff. Sean was easily elected sheriff when time came. Not only did the citizens have confidence in his integrity and credentials, but it did not hurt that he was quarterback of the high school football team that had won the state championship. That alone hoisted him into a celebrity status around Bekbourg.

"What I think makes this all the more mysterious is that Harry Schriever owned the house then. He along with Gregory Geisen pretty much ran the town. The high school is even named after Harry, Schriever High School," said Cheryl.

"Once we have a more definitive time period on when the death occurred, I'll have a deputy comb through the police files to see about missing person reports and incident reports, and maybe you could have someone look through the newspaper files."

Cheryl walked over and put her arms around him, and he pulled her close. "Of course. See how a lawman and a reporter can make such a great team."

Sean's eyes warmed. "I already knew that. My investigative skills led me to that conclusion shortly after we got to know each other." He leaned forward and kissed her lips. He still found it hard to believe that this beautiful, vivacious woman had come into his life. She was tall and slender and looked like a model—who could grace the cover of a sports magazine. She had changed into leggings and a sweatshirt after returning home from the office. Her long dark hair was pulled back in a ponytail, and her face radiated vitality. "Maybe we can short-circuit dinner?" he suggested as he embraced her tighter. There was no mistaking his desire.

Cheryl giggled and gave an enticing wiggle. "Let me get this dinner finished so we can do just that."

His smile grew. "Okay, now that we've got that settled, tell me about your day since there won't be time for talking afterwards."

Sean loved hearing Cheryl's laughter fill a room as it had just now. She told him about the visit from the professor. "He and his assistant are coming to Bekbourg to research the Count. Dr. Shlykov is an expert on Russian history."

This is interesting, thought Sean. He wanted to inquire without raising Cheryl's suspicions, which was not easily done. "Well, it's not the first time one of your stories attracted outside notice. What did you say his and his assistant's names were?"

Cheryl's purse was nearby, and she grabbed a business card. "He gave me this, and I wrote his assistant's name on the back. After talking with him, I'm hoping to learn more about the Count and his wife—do a follow-up story."

Sean pulled a beer from the refrigerator and poured sparkling water for Cheryl. "Well, the Czar's family, especially how their lives ended, holds interest for a lot of people. I'll be interested in hearing what else you learn."

Chapter 8

Cheryl opened a folder where she had filed copies of the five articles published in the *Tribune* in late January and early February, 1925. She decided to reread the articles to see if she had overlooked some information or might get new ideas on how to learn more.

The first article's focus was on the blizzard.

Blizzard Wreaks Havoc
January 28, 1925

A blizzard, the likes of which no one around Bekbourg has ever seen, brought nearly two feet of snow and paralyzed the region on Monday. The severely cold spell for the two weeks leading up to the blizzard froze the ground and caused the snow to accumulate at a record pace. At the height of the storm around 4:00 p.m., nearly white-out conditions existed. The heaviest snowfall lasted about ten hours. We can only hope that the temperatures start to warm soon. The high yesterday was eleven degrees below zero.

According to Mayor Goehring, "The good news is that our public utility services in town have not gone down." He told our reporter that the local phone exchange around downtown is still working, but the lines connecting Bekbourg with other towns and cities are down. Gas service for those who use gas to light their homes is still operational. Electric service around the city is still working, but for rural areas that have electricity, service is down. There is plenty of coal, and the railroad is opening its coal dock so those who are running low can go there for coal. The city has a stockpile of firewood behind the county storage warehouse at the western end of Front Street for any residents who find their supplies are running short. The Mayor also issued *a statement thanking the people who have cleared the sidewalks in front of their businesses and homes and hope more people do that.*

    There were two-hundred passengers on the Number 2 heading to Cincinnati and on to Chicago when the train got stranded here in Bekbourg. The WVB&C's Operator, Dizzy Matthews, said it could have been a lot worse if the train had not been able to make it to Bekbourg. "It was dicey, but our engineer was determined, and the train arrived safely." When asked how long the train would be stationed here, Dizzy said that a freight train derailed west of here because of the weather, and it could take up to a week to clear the tracks. Turning the train around to head back east is not an option until the broken track is repaired. "Train personnel are working to clear and repair the rails, but it's going to take some time. Our goal is to have Number 2 on its way within a week."

*Both Dizzy and Mayor Goehring
applauded the owner of the Grand
Hotel, Hugo Marschall, who they said
found lodgings for all of the two-hundred train passengers. According to the
Mayor, the Grand Hotel's Mr. Marschall
sprang into action and got the hotel staff
cooking extra food and sending curriers
to local establishments. Marschall also
enlisted the sheriff's help in sending out
his deputies to knock on doors of local
residents to see if they might be willing
to let passengers stay with them. The
Mayor told our reporter, "The generous spirit of Bekbourg's citizens again
came to the rescue. The two downtown hotels and boarding house could
not accommodate all the passengers.
Local residents opened their homes
and welcomed strangers by providing
shelter and food."*

Another article was published in the *Tribune* the
following day.

Russian Royalty in Bekbourg
January 29, 1925

Soon after the passengers from the stranded train began arriving at the Grand Hotel two nights ago in need of shelter and food, rumors began circulating that a member of a royal European family was on board. Mayor Goehring confirmed to our reporter that his Highness, Zakhar Voskoboynikov, and wife Elizabeth, an American, are now guests of one of the families here in Bekbourg. According to sources, the Russian Count and his wife were traveling to Cincinnati to visit family.

Our reporter has been able to confirm that Mr. Dizzy Matthews, the Operator for the WVB&C, sent word to Hugo Marschall, owner of the Grand Hotel, that a member of the Russian royal family and his wife were passengers. Arrangements were made to meet the Count and his wife at the depot when the train arrived and whisk them to a private home. Private carriages and sleighs have been seen around town and in Highland Heights, but no public sightings yet of the royal couple.

The temperatures are now up to five degrees below zero. In the meantime, those entertaining the royals have wasted no time in getting back into their social activities.

Chapter 9

Cheryl called Andrian to set up a time for them to get together and also tell him about the professor's interest in the Count. Katrina (Kat) Clark could not help but overhear Andrian's side of the conversation—not that she wanted to tune it out. Even with his back to her, she could tell something had dismayed him.

"What was that about?" she asked as she continued her survey of the box's contents. Kat was a bookkeeper hired by C.P. to inventory the assets of furniture, equipment, fixtures, tools and other miscellaneous items stored, for years, in the old depot, other sheds, and buildings belonging to the WVB&C railroad. Most would likely be committed to disposal facilities or junk collectors, but C.P. wanted a thorough accounting of the assets before deciding on the next steps. Also, some things might be of value to the train museum he had planned for the old depot. Because Andrian was responsible for reviewing all the old company records and archived files, he and Kat often found themselves working in the old depot.

Andrian turned back to the boxes he had been reviewing before Cheryl's call and shrugged. "That was Cheryl

Seton. We talked yesterday about coordinating our efforts to find more about the time the Russian Count was stranded here due to the snow storm. She was calling to set a time."

"It sounded like someone else is involved?"

He shrugged, still with his back to her. "Yeah. Some professor who lives in Cincinnati saw the article. He's some expert on Russian history."

"Mmm. That was in the early 1900's, wasn't it?"

"Yeah."

Kat eyed him as he pulled another file from the box. "Isn't that the time period of the boxes you've got stacked up in the other room?"

"Yep."

Kat knew from experience Andrian quickly grew annoyed if she drilled him with questions. She knew he had tagged her as a nosey body, which she was, but she tried to refrain from being obvious. She allowed quiet to settle around the room while she logged entries on her laptop. Calculating enough time had passed, she attempted to be casual. "Do you think you've found all the documents for that time period?" When he did not reply, she sighed, "I know from my work around here that things were not kept in the greatest of order and are spread all over the place. That warehouse is a mess."

"I don't know."

"Are you going to take Cheryl up on her offer to help?" She was wondering if that was what had irritated him during the call. She could tell something had altered his mood, although that was not hard to do since he was a moody person anyway.

He jerked his head up and started plowing his hand back and forth through his short dark hair. "I need to think about it. I'll talk to C.P. about it. I don't think he would have a problem if she is helping to put together information about the Russians being here. With her newspaper files, it might be worth doing."

She ventured further. "Did Ms. Seton say something that upset you?"

"No! Why?" he turned and frowned at her.

She shrugged. "I don't know. You seemed agitated on the phone, and even now."

Andrian went back to his documents. "I don't know where you got that idea. Anyway, I need to get through these boxes before the end of the day."

He wished she would spend more time working in the warehouse. For one thing, he wanted his privacy. For another, he did not want to do anything that might inadvertently encourage her with thoughts of a relationship. When he first moved to Bekbourg, she hinted at going out. Even though Bekbourg was a small town and he had not met many people, he had no desire to hang out with Kat. Her nosiness was damn irritating, and growing more so by the day. Somewhere along the way, she had not learned that curiosity could kill the cat. Anyway, as soon as he finished his mission in Bekbourg, he was out of here. In the meantime, Cheryl's news that Dimitri Shlykov, the professor, was interested in the Russian Count could complicate things.

Chapter 10

The professor worked out of a turn-of-the-century two-story brick home he had purchased in Pleasant Ridge when he returned to Cincinnati. His office at the back of the house provided Dimitri with privacy from his assistant and quiet from the neighbors walking around the neighborhood.

Jeffrey Blankenship, his assistant, had a desk in what once had been the dining room at the front of the house. He heard Dimitri enter through the kitchen entrance and continued working on research notes for Dimitri's meeting with other scholars planned in Denmark after the first of the year. Dimitri poured himself a vodka and came into the living room and sat in his favorite chair. He beckoned Jeffrey to join him. Jeffrey knew the professor's moods, and the look on his face spelled displeasure. He poured himself a whiskey and sat across from the professor. "How did your meeting go in Bekbourg?"

As was usually the case when it was just the two men, Dimitri's charismatic façade faded away. "You told me you didn't want to distract from my lectures and engagements, but failing to tell me about the article about the Russian Count sooner—really, Jeffrey. You disappoint me, again."

Over the years, Jeffrey had tired of Dimitri's surliness and started asserting himself against the professor's condemnations and condescending remarks, but only to a limited extent. He did not want to lose his job just yet, because he had plans. Unbeknownst to Dimitri, he had accumulated a small nest egg. He just needed to bide his time a while longer, and he could retire to a quiet life in Panama. "What difference does it make, Dimitri? You could not have interrupted your lecture series."

Dimitri's eyes hardened. "I'll tell you why. That damn Bolshevik has a head start on me. Well, us, since you are going to be looking into the matter. This may be the biggest story in years coming out of the Russian revolution, and I want to be the one to publish it." Dimitri handed Jeffrey the paper from his pocket. "Here is a list of motels Cheryl Seton wrote down. See if you can make reservations at Bri's B&B. It's first on the list. You can find something on the list for yourself." Jeffrey got the hint, which was fine with him. "You need to get us stationed there as quickly as possible. I mean days, Jeffrey. Now, I've got some research of my own I need to get started. I'll let you know what needs to be done."

Jeffrey scanned the paper Dimitri had left. Motels were listed, and in Dimitri's handwriting, some other notes. However, one name, Andrian Kray, jumped out. Cheryl must have written his name along with, *Archivist – WVB&C Railroad,* and a phone number. A heavy check mark, clearly Dimitri's doing, was beside the name. *Interesting,* thought Jeffrey.

Dimitri touted himself one of the world's foremost experts on Russian history, particularly for the period beginning in 1547, when Ivan IV assumed the title of Tsar, through the fall of the Romanov rule in 1917, ending with the assassination of Russia's last Czar. The professor was ruthless in the academic world, and while he was well known around the world for his in-depth knowledge on Russian history, Dimitri had made enemies for stealing ideas and undercutting colleagues.

Jeffrey had majored in Russian history. All through undergraduate, he worked night shift as a janitor making minimum wage at a chain restaurant. That job enabled him to scrape by, but just barely— eating mostly popcorn and peanut butter and living in an attic room in an old house shared with six other students. During his junior year, he became friendly with the secretary of the department head. They occasionally hooked up for the night. Seeing how little he had, she arranged for him to take leftovers from the weekly faculty luncheons. During his senior year, he applied for the Master's program in Russian studies and a teaching assistant position and was granted both.

The teaching assistant's position nearly paid enough for him to not have to work, but he still took odd jobs. Then, one day at the conclusion of the meeting with his thesis committee, Professor Dimitri Shlykov asked to speak with him privately. Whether Dimitri knew of

Jeffrey's financial hardship he did not know, but he asked Jeffrey if he would be interested in doing research for him for a book he was writing. He told Jeffrey he would pay him for his efforts—a modest sum, but enough that made Jeffrey jump at the chance. By the time Jeffrey had defended his Master's thesis, Dimitri's book was published and had received accolades throughout the academic circles.

Coming out of the Master's program, Jeffrey had no job prospects. He could not get a job with the government, and no corporations were interested in hiring someone who had a degree in Russian history. He needed to pursue a doctorate degree if he wanted to teach at a university, and he had absolutely no desire to get a teaching certificate for high school employment. So, Jeffrey was grateful when Dimitri offered him a full-time position to work for him as a research assistant. The pay was not great but enough for him to make it, but only because Dimitri offered him a room in his house as part of the package. That certainly beat living in the roach-infested attic room.

Although working with the temperamental Dimitri was difficult and, most of the time, quite trying, Jeffrey found the work interesting. Years passed, and the pay improved slightly. He had always been a loner, and despite having gotten an education, Jeffrey had never been ambitious. He took the easy way out by settling as Dimitri's assistant, but he had enough to live on with his frugal lifestyle, and so he stayed. Even in Cincinnati, where Dimitri moved after retiring from the university in Maryland, Jeffrey lived on Dimitri's premises—a one-room apartment with a small kitchen and bathroom above Dimitri's single-car garage.

He figured he knew almost as much about the Czar era as Dimitri. After all, he was the one who did the research and penned the materials for papers and books that never bore his name. Dimitri was too vain to share the limelight, but Dimitri would give him a paltry bonus each time he published. On the few occasions Dimitri had needed Jeffrey to accompany him on a trip, he at least paid Jeffrey's expenses.

Jeffrey drained the remainder of his whiskey and slumped into his desk chair to call the B&B to check on lodging arrangements for Dimitri. He made reservations for himself to stay in the old motel on the outskirts of Bekbourg's downtown. Dimitri would not care as long as he was at his beck and call, and the place was cheap. He knew Dimitri would not have included him on the trip if it was not for the tedious work like slogging through courthouse and library records, and whatever other local research might be needed. Dimitri researched only what he wanted kept close-to-the-vest. Dimitri was good at shielding his confidential work, but sometimes, Jeffrey had prevailed in finding Dimitri's secrets.

Chapter 11

Cheryl continued her reread of the articles found in the *Tribune's* archives. Day three after the train was stranded brought another front page article in the *Tribune*.

Russian Count and Countess
Welcomed in Bekbourg
January 30, 1925

Bekbourg's own royalty have welcomed the Russian Count and Countess with open arms. By all accounts, the Count and Countess are newly-weds. Count Zakhar Voskoboynikov and Elizabeth Griffiths, heiress of the Griffiths textile manufacturing fortune out of Newport, Rhode Island, were traveling to Cincinnati to visit her aunt and uncle when their train was stranded due to the blizzard. Rumors have it that Harry Schriever was having drinks with Hugo Marschall when a curvier from the WVB&C came rushing in with news that a Russian Count and his wife were aboard. Schriever reportedly sprang into action and told Marschall that he and Kathleen would host the couple. Schriever's private driver and valet were waiting at the station when the train pulled to a stop. After conferring with the conductor, the royal couple was escorted into a private carriage complete with fine wine, cigars and warm blankets for their comfort as they traveled the short distance to the Schriever home. A second carriage followed in due course with the couple's luggage and the Countess's personal maid.

Since being settled, the Count and Countess have been welcomed with open arms by Bekbourg's finest families. Accompanied by Schriever, Gregory Geisen, Konrad Schumacher, and Mayor Goehring, the Count has been seen leaving the downtown in horse-drawn sleighs for hunting trips. Other notable passengers on the train include Mr. Clayton McClellan, owner and president of York-Cal Steel Company, and his wife Beatrice. McClellan is another frequent guest on these outings. The Count purportedly told the Mayor he felt at home in the snow and freezing temperatures, prompting the Mayor to respond that Bekbourg was glad to oblige.

While the men have spent their days hunting, the women have entertained Elizabeth with teas and lunches. The Countess has certainly impressed with the latest of European styles. Known for her wit, Grace Geisen is quoted as saying, "We ladies here in Bekbourg are now reevaluating our wardrobes in light of the beautiful clothes worn by the Countess." The Countess was seen in the Grand Hotel for tea wearing a velvet red jacket with fur collar and large fur cuffs and a matching pleated, fitted skirt.

Private dinners are being hosted by the first families of Bekbourg, but there was an appearance of the royal couple last evening at the Grand Hotel at the invitation of its owner, Hugo Marschall, for drinks and hors d'oeuvres. The Count was seen wearing a single breasted dark brown wool suit. The Countess was stunning in a satin skirt and matching blouse, long strands of pearls and short boots with a mink coat.

A little bird said that a grand gala has been planned for tomorrow night in honor of the Count and Countess, but details are hush-hush. More glitz and glam for Bekbourg, you can be sure.

Chapter 12

Jeffrey left a note on Dimitri's desk advising him that an open-ended reservation had been made at Bri's B&B through the end of November. The owner, Bri Sanderson, would work with them beyond that date to the extent she could, but she was mostly booked between Thanksgiving and New Year's.

Dimitri leaned back in his chair to consider how best to play his time in Bekbourg. Being the owner of the town's newspaper, Cheryl Seton was an influential player around town. She had mentioned knowing the new owner of the railroad, C.P. Traylor, who obviously was someone with whom he needed to acquaint himself. That damn archivist, Andrian Kray, would not lift a finger to help him, unless his boss, C.P., so instructed him. He knew about Andrian. Yes, he needed to get an introduction to C.P. soon. Of course, getting to know the mayor also had its advantages and should be easy enough—given she owned the B&B where he would be staying. It was helpful to know people who could open doors, if needed.

Chapter 13

Cheryl finally found time to reread the last two articles published about the Russian couple's time in Bekbourg.

A Ball fit for a Count
and Countess
January 31, 1925

The ball last night at the Grand Hotel was the biggest shindig anyone around here can ever remember. The Countess was stunning in her Grecian style dress in silver metallic. Who could have missed the magnificent necklace? No one, I dare say. The Count added to the glamorous pair in his tails and white vest and white tie. The distinguished men and women who attended the gala were decked out in their finery as well—nothing too good for the honored couple.

Hugo Marschall arranged for local musicians who perform at special events to entertain throughout the evening. The Grand Hotel's head chef brought in cooks from our local restaurants to assist in preparing the foods and drinks. Additional staff were hired and trained by the maître d himself to serve throughout the evening. The Hotel hired local men as bellmen, who lined up to escort the guests and literally rolled out a red carpet through the front doors that was borrowed from the theater for the occasion.

Bright lights could be seen shining through the Hotel's windows and music was heard playing until around five o'clock in the morning. Apparently, no expenses were spared to entertain the royal pair, which has brought European grace and style to our town.

Cheryl studied the photo she found in the newspaper's archives, which she had published alongside her article. The Count was a slender man, striking in his confidence and intensity. A widow's peak drew attention as his thinning dark hair was brushed away from his face. Elizabeth wore her youth with assuredness, having obviously been raised around affluence and opportunity. The sapphire and diamond necklace was unnecessary to the fashion of her attire but made a statement, for sure, of wealth and status.

Until the train's departure three days later, the story about the ball was the last mention of the royal couple's time in Bekbourg.

Bekbourg Bids Adieu
February 4, 1925

Who would have thought that a blizzard would have brought magic to our small town of Bekbourg? Our town has been delighted by the honor of having Count Zakhar Voskoboynikov and his lovely bride Elizabeth in our midst. The excitement has electrified our town in ways not seen in a lifetime—if ever. We now bid farewell to this royal couple and to all the other passengers as Number 2 was finally cleared to depart, with several stops—including

Cincinnati—where our sources say the royal couple will disembark—and then on to Chicago.

Our reporter arrived early at the station in hopes of glimpsing, and speaking with, the Count and Countess, but the Count was already settled into Harry Schriever's private train car. The Countess was seen speaking with Harry Schriever on the platform before boarding the car. Leave it to Schriever to make his private car available for the rest of their journey into Cincinnati. Others were then allowed out of the station to board.

Schriever gave a statement to our reporter that the royal couple was grateful for the hospitality extended during their stay in Bekbourg and had made many new friends. "They plan a visit in the spring on their return trip, and we look forward to seeing our friends again then."

Other passengers spoke of how they enjoyed the generosity and friendliness of the people of Bekbourg. Mayor Goehring said, "The people of Bekbourg stepped up under diffi-cult circumstances and took into their homes and businesses strangers who they could now count as friends. That's what we do here in Bekbourg. We stand proud and strong and will always extend a welcome hand."

Chapter 14

Cheryl brought Andrian a couple more photos of the Count she found among others in a box. They were taken from a distance of him and other men preparing to go on a hunting trip. He told her he had not discovered anything else, and they turned their attention to reviewing boxes he had pulled from the side room. Occasionally, they would talk about a document or something related to the operation of the train or the schedule, but nothing pertinent to the Count and his wife was there.

Being the impatient type, Kat did not think they were looking in the right places. She had reviewed enough of the train records to know there had to be more. It was not her project to be reviewing information about the Count's visit, but she wanted to help. An idea came to her to look through some of the financial records. While Andrian and Cheryl continued to sift through the dusty boxes, she left and went to a storage room in the old railroad office building and started looking based on calendar years.

After Kat left, Cheryl noticed Andrian loosened up some and talked more. He asked her about growing up in Bekbourg, and she told him she was born there and

lived there until she was fourteen years old. She did not
see the need to elaborate on what prompted her mother
to move them to Cleveland, but she told him about their
time in Cleveland and how she ended up being an investigative reporter for the *Cleveland Presenter*, a small
evening-edition newspaper with a heavy focus on investigative reporting. He had never heard about the mass
killing that had brought Cheryl back to Bekbourg. She
explained about meeting Sean during the investigation
and ending up making Bekbourg her home.

"What about you, Andrian? Where did you grow up?"

"I grew up in Cincinnati. I have an older brother who
lives in Houston. He's an accountant for a large drilling
company there."

"Do your parents still live in Cincinnati?"

"No. They moved to Englewood, Florida. My grandfather was always kind of sickly. He had lots of stomach
problems. He moved in with us after my grandmother
passed away. I was about seven. Grandma worked as a
seamstress for one of the big stores there. It was hard
for Granddad to keep a steady job after a while, but he
did the best he could. Both my parents worked, so my
brother and I spent a lot of time with Granddad. Anyway,
my dad thought the warmer weather would be good for
them and Granddad. I think it was, but Granddad died a
few years ago."

"My mother and I lived with my grandparents
before we left Bekbourg when a horrible thing happened.
I was very close to them, but especially my grandfather.

It sounds like you were close with yours?"

"Yeah, I was."

After a few hours, Kat came across some files. Then, something jumped out at her. A file of passenger manifests. She whooped, "I found something!" when she realized she was looking at a passenger list for the very train that had brought the Count and his wife to Bekbourg.

She whizzed into the depot where Cheryl and Andrian had been working. Cheryl was packing up a box, getting ready to leave.

"Where's Andrian?"

"He left about an hour ago. He had an appointment."

"Well, I discovered something I think you both will like." She waved some papers. "It's the passenger manifest for those people on the train that the Count was on."

Cheryl walked over. "Let's have a look."

They reviewed two lists. One was an official-looking manifest of first-class passengers. The second was hand-written and looked to list everyone who was on the train. At the bottom of that one was a listing under the notation "railroad" of the employees on the train. Cheryl pointed to the top portion of the hand-written document under the heading "first class." "You're right, Kat. Here is Elizabeth Griffiths' name—and the Count's name. Their names show up on both."

Kat looked at the list. "He had a long name. The railroad company didn't abbreviate it. My mama told me when people immigrated into the United States, the immigration people used to shorten the longer surnames, which they usually kept in their new life in the U.S."

"That's right. That's one of the reasons it's sometimes hard to trace ancestors. The names were changed once people entered the U.S., and knowing what the surnames were back in Europe could be a challenge." Cheryl smiled, "I suspect it never dawned on the Immigration service to shorten the Count's name."

She asked Kat how she was able to locate the passenger list, and Kat explained that during her past reviews of boxes containing financial documents, she had come across several documents related to ticket sales and decided to look.

"Well, I'm glad you did. Would you mind making a copy for me?"

"Not at all. I'll go ahead and make Andrian a copy and Jeffrey, too."

"The Professor's assistant?"

"Yes."

Cheryl was surprised Kat knew the professor's assistant. She had not met him, and Andrian had not mentioned working with him. "Has he been here looking through the train records?" asked Cheryl.

Kat's eyes popped wide and a blush rose on her cheeks. "No, not here, but I met him when he first got to Bekbourg, and he told me he was researching the Count for the professor."

Cheryl nodded. "You might also make a copy for the professor. I suspect he might want it."

"Good idea. I'll give it to Jeffrey to give to him."

Chapter 15

Dimitri reserved a large table at the GilHaus for his dinner companions. C.P. was there along with a friend, Mary Zimmstein, and Cheryl, Sean and Bri had also come. Max was unable to attend because of a rehearsal dinner at his bistro. Dillie Beaumont was also there. He had met her at the B&B and found her fascinating, especially when she told him she had met a Romanov descendant during her time in Europe. He would like to spend more time with her, but she was leaving soon for a trip to Greece.

Throughout the evening, the topic discussions changed, but toward the end, C.P. said to Dimitri, "Cheryl told me you might have an interest in working with my archivist to see if we have any records of the Russian Count's time in Bekbourg."

"Yes. My specialty is Russian history, particularly during the time leading up to the 1917 Revolution. I would like to think the arrangement would be mutual. Perhaps I can share my insights with your archivist for your train museum."

C.P. nodded. "I'll tell Andrian to expect your call."

"Thank you. My assistant's name is Jeffrey Blankenship. I'm sure Andrian will find him helpful."

Sean, who had been listening to this exchange, said, "Cheryl's article was published the third week of August. I guess I'm a little surprised you are just now looking into this. Aren't you concerned someone could have beaten you to Bekbourg?"

Dimitri chuckled, "Excellent point, Sheriff. Indeed, academia can be very cutthroat. Unfortunately, even if I had known, I could not have gotten here any sooner because of a commitment in Austria. Also, because I didn't know, I did not send Jeffrey earlier. After returning to the states, I saw the article in a file Jeffrey had prepared for me and contacted Cheryl right away."

"With all the traveling you do, does Jeffrey jump-start projects for you?"

"Only if I first approve it. He may not be aware of papers and research that's been published or what I may be planning, so it is important we coordinate before he starts something new." Dimitri smiled at Cheryl. "It was indeed my good fortune to meet with Cheryl as quickly as I did. She was helpful in giving me a list of places where we could stay while we conducted our research, which accelerated my ability to settle in."

Bri was happy to help them. "Your assistant is welcome at the B&B, Dimitri, if he changes his mind. We have an opening until the week of Thanksgiving."

"Thank you Bri, but Jeffrey prefers things quiet when he works, so he chose a motel outside of town."

He smiled. "And away from me. If I'm close by, I have a tendency to drop in with thoughts and research ideas, which can be disruptive. Of course, once he tastes one of your pastries, he may well change his mind."

There was consensus around the table that Bri's pastries were a big draw. As the dinner wound down, C.P. reiterated his support. "Professor, I travel some, so Andrian is your best point of contact on your research. He's often in the depot during business hours, so feel free to stop by or have your assistant drop by."

Chapter 16

Andrian was reviewing a box of documents when Kat walked into the depot. "Morning, Andrian."

He didn't look up. "Morning."

She stopped and looked at the box. "That doesn't look like things relating to when the Count visited. Not even the same decade. Is Cheryl not coming today?"

"No. She had some other things she needed to do. Anyway, I think she's about ready to give up on finding much here in the train records."

"Oh. Well, maybe after what I found, she might change her mind."

Andrian looked up. "What did you find?"

She picked up papers and brought them over. "I made you a copy, too. It's the passenger manifest for the train that got stuck here during the snow storm. We found the Count's name and that of his wife."

He appeared more shocked than pleased. "Where did you find these?"

She turned to head back to her table. "Oh, ask me pretty and I might tell you."

She intended a joking tone, but Andrian was not in

the mood. "What are you doing looking for this anyway? This is something C.P. asked me to work on with Cheryl. I'm not in the playing mood, Kat, and I don't appreciate your attitude. I need to know so she and I can see if there's more information."

Kat narrowed her eyes. "Ha! You're the one who's not a team player, Andrian. I thought I might know where something was because of some boxes I came across a few weeks ago before all this started. I went and found this, and you're acting like I've done something wrong."

Andrian did not want to get on Kat's bad side. She had found this, which might prove helpful, and there might be other documents somewhere. "I'm sorry, Kat. I got some disturbing family news yesterday evening. It's been on my mind." That was not the truth, but he needed to come up with some excuse.

"Oh, is that why you didn't return after your appointment?"

Another lie. "Yes. So can we start over?"

"Sure. What was the family news?"

"I really don't feel like talking about it. You understand—I'm sure."

"Oh, okay. If you ever want to talk to me, I'm a good listener."

She would be the last person he would confide in. "Thanks. So, you found this. Where did you say it was?"

"In some boxes in the storage room in the main office."

Because those seemed to be accounting and

financial records, Andrian had never considered looking through those boxes. He needed to check them out. "Well, good thinking. You said Cheryl was happy to see this?"

"Yes, I made her a copy as well as copies for the professor and his assistant, Jeffrey."

His eyebrows shot up. "Where are those copies? I will give them to the professor when I see him."

"Oh, I already gave them to Jeffrey."

"What the hell? Why did you do that? When did you see him?"

"I saw him last night at dinner." She fidgeted and rubbed her arm. "I knew C.P. said you were to work with them on this, so I gave him copies."

"That's right, Kat. I am working with them on this. I need to keep a list of things I give to them so I know they have everything, and I don't duplicate things or forget to give them things. If you find anything else, you need to give it to me so I can add it to my log. I'll take care of getting them copies."

"Okay. Well, you can add this to your log. I need to get to work. Want a cup of coffee?"

"No."

She walked into the small kitchen area to put on a pot to brew. He could tell she was mad, but Andrian was furious. *Dammit! Why can't she mind her own business? And, why in the hell was she having dinner with Dimitri's assistant?*

Kat and Andrian worked in silence the rest of the morning. Around lunchtime, there was a knock on the door to the depot and a tall, gangly man of middle age entered. Both Andrian and Kat looked up. "Jeffrey, what are you doing here?" Kat asked as she walked toward him.

"Hi, Babe. I thought I'd take you to lunch if you don't have plans," he said as he looked at Andrian. "Are you Andrian?" he asked as he stepped forward to shake hands. "I'm Jeffrey Blankenship."

Andrian shook his hand, "You're Dimitri Shlykov's assistant?"

"Right. I think we're supposed to be working together on finding information about the Russian Count and his time here in Bekbourg. Kat tells me you've not found much, but if there is anything I can help with, or information I can share with you, I'm at your service."

Andrian's eyes flickered. "That's right. Cheryl Seton, the owner of the newspaper, and I have been reviewing the railroad files. We haven't come up with much at all here. Frankly, I'm not sure there's much here to find. Kat told me about the passenger list." He glanced at Kat. "I looked at it, but other than a list of passengers and the train's origin and destination, and stops along the way, I don't know that it holds much value." Andrian had looked at it and hoped the others did not notice what he had.

Jeffrey smiled at Kat. "I haven't had time to look at it, but I will." That was a lie. After she left his motel room, he had poured over the list. He noted a handful of Russian surnames. Were they the Count's valet, body guards, assistants? He would be tracing the names to see what he could learn. Jeffrey studied Andrian. *Could this be the man Dimitri had called a Bolshevik? He doesn't look very Russian, but perhaps he inherited features from other nationalities in his family line. It may behoove me to get to know him better. He might be useful.*

"Andrian, you are welcome to join us for lunch. I thought we'd go to Frau's."

Andrian shook his head. "Thanks for the invite, but I've got some catching up to do."

"Okay, some other time." Jeffrey turned to Kat. "Ready?"

"Yeah. I'll just grab my bag."

After they left, Andrian walked over to the window and watched them walk up the street. He noted Jeffrey's car in the parking lot. He wondered what Kat was doing with Jeffrey. It did not go unnoticed Jeffrey had called her "Babe." *I need to be extra careful from now on around here. I don't want to leave anything lying around. Hell, Kat may be spying on me and passing information to that damn professor or his assistant.* Andrian's grandfather had warned him to be cautious about anyone wanting to know about Count Zakhar Voskoboynikov. He had also warned him specifically against associating with the professor.

Chapter 17

C.P. reserved the corner table for his dinner with Mary. As she sipped her wine, he observed her elegance and attractiveness. She was petite with a round face and layered hair that fell around her neck. He appreciated that nothing she wore was ever overstated, from the muted fingernail polish and lipstick to the more subdued clothing colors like beiges and soft pastels. She typically wore a pearl necklace and modest-sized earrings. Mary was a private person but early on in their friendship, she confided about the tragedy of her first husband perishing in a private plane crash. She and her young daughter Rachel had moved to Bekbourg when she married an influential public official. Despite the tremendous humiliation that followed his sudden downfall, she held her head high and rebounded. In the aftermath of that fiasco, she and Rachel had moved back to Columbus where she enrolled Rachel in school. After a time, Mary returned to Bekbourg and founded a foundation, "Bekbourg Gives," as amends for her ex-husband's deplorable and criminal behaviors. She began commuting between Columbus and Bekbourg. As it was a ninety minute drive, she often stayed in Bekbourg three or four days a week. Her parents cared for Rachel when Mary was away.

Mary never shared the extent of the shame she felt by her ex-husband's actions, but C.P. knew it must have been overwhelming. For thirty years, her grandfather ruled the state house. When he decided to step down, he founded a law firm, Zimmstein & Zimmstein, along with Mary's father, which was hugely successful and powerful throughout Ohio. C.P. admired Mary, but more than that, along the way, he had fallen in love with her. During the open house of his new home, it felt so right having her there as a partner entertaining their guests. With her eye for details, everything went off without a hitch. They were frequently seen around town at social functions and dining venues and were each other's social companion. He thought perhaps she shared similar feelings for him, but she was not the type to take the first step in a relationship. She was of the old school in that way, which set right with him. Despite his feelings for her, he had reservations about taking their relationship to the next level. He was fifteen years older, and that seemed insurmountable. Not that there were any obstacles between them in that regard. He prided himself in staying fit, both physically and mentally. But he knew as time went on, that could change. How easy it would be now, in this elegant setting at the GilHaus, where they had dined together for the first time, to tell her his feelings. If only he could pull the trigger.

His thoughts were interrupted. "C.P., this French

wine has a rich flavor. I like it very much."

"I thought you would. I know you lean toward dry flavors rather than sweet wines, and I asked Gill to stock a few bottles."

"Speaking of Gill, you must be pleased he has decided to continue operating the GilHaus."

"Yes, I am. I assured him when I bought the hotel I didn't want any change in the operation of his restaurant. When he sold me the building, he was more than happy to sign a lease for the restaurant operations. Gilbert Geisen did the town a favor when he purchased the old hotel in the 1950's. Even though he never operated it as a hotel, his maintenance kept it from going into further decline. The restaurant here has served Bekbourg well, and he saw to the upkeep of its original features, such as the glass chandeliers, ornate crown molding and walnut hard-wood floors."

"I have mentioned this to you before, but the hotel desk in the lobby area is exquisite."

C.P. smiled. "It really is. It is one of a kind. It's my understanding it was made in Europe and brought over in pieces and assembled here. They spared no expense on that. It's made of walnut and twenty feet wide. I really like the high back panel with the old fashion nooks for mail and keys along the back."

"Yes—and the white marble desk top is quite beautiful as well."

"Mary, I'm really happy you have agreed to oversee decorating the hotel. You did a great job with the house.

Everyone really likes it. I know I should have said it before, but I really appreciate all you do for me."

Mary's face brightened. "Thank you, C.P. I am honored you trust me to do these things, and I am very happy you asked me. It is something I love doing. I think we make a good team."

Mary could never bring herself to be forward with a man in that regard, but sometimes she wondered if she should gently nudge C.P., at least to see if he felt something beyond friendship toward her. Her mention just now that they made a good team was as bold as she dared. She hoped he might take that as a hint she was interested. She was in love with him. They were compatible in their interests, and their time together was fun and comfortable. He was a successful businessman with a vision and zeal for new opportunities and developments. It was amazing what his entrepreneurial pursuits had brought to Bekbourg. Even though he was tough-minded when it came to business, people liked C.P. What convinced Mary he was the man she wanted in her future was his generosity in donating his talents and resources. He was instrumental in getting a memorial built in town to honor veterans, and he had donated substantial sums to her foundation and other causes. In his short time back in Bekbourg, he had become an icon and statesman. Her family liked and admired him—including Rachel.

It had not escaped her thinking that perhaps it was her fault C.P. had not expressed more interest. When she first met him, she was rebounding from a nightmare with her second husband. C.P. may have mistaken her hesitancy for there being no interest in a romantic relationship. But she had tried, as she had just now, to signal her feelings, but so far, to no avail. "Maybe it's just not meant to be," she thought.

"How is Rachel?"

Mary smiled. "The school is having a fall dance this weekend, so she and her friends are excited, and she's already talking about the Thanksgiving break."

"That's good. What are your plans for Thanksgiving?"

Mary was hoping they could be together again this year for the holiday, "I'm glad you asked. Mom asked me to invite you to join the family for Thanksgiving again. It will be like last year with my brother and his family, Mom and Dad, and Mom's sister and her husband and their children and grandchildren. But Rachel told me she would not mind coming to Bekbourg for the weekend. She likes it here and enjoys spending time with her friends she was in school with before we moved back to Columbus." *I want to be with you on Thanksgiving. I hope you understand Rachel and I would also be happy to celebrate Thanksgiving here with you.* She smiled and added, "If you want, I could try out that new kitchen by making Thanksgiving dinner here."

C.P. chuckled. "That's a tempting thought, but I enjoyed being with your family last year. Tell your mother I would like to join them for Thanksgiving."

Mary was happy. They would be together for the holiday, and either Columbus or here was perfect.

"Mother will be delighted you are joining us." Their drinks were refreshed, and the waitress brought them a menu. Mary had been curious about the remains found in the guest house's basement and asked.

C.P. shook his head. "Cole was joking the other day. He asked if I wanted him to dig up more places around the property. I told him to keep the digging to only what was absolutely required." Mary laughed. "Anyway, Sean's people removed the police tape, so Cole has started back work. Sean's trying to find out who it might have been, but that could be a challenge given how long ago it happened." C.P. joked, "At least I'll have a story to tell about the place."

Mary grinned and agreed. They enjoyed their dinner and conversation. He was leaving tomorrow on business, and she knew she would not see him for a few days.

Chapter 18

Sean drove to Columbus to hear what was learned about the remains. What Lucky and his forensics expert, Tate Jackson, had to tell him about their findings heightened the mystery.

Tate was able to pinpoint the period of death to be in the mid 1920's. The body had been wrapped in a hand-stitched quilt—likely from the early 1900's based on the fabrics and dyes used during the time. He placed the victim's age to be in his late thirties, and his height at five-feet-seven-inches. No abnormalities or indications of bad health were evident.

Evidence of the body suggested Eastern Europe. The clothing remnants suggested materials produced in Russia during the late 1800's and early 1900's. While the materials in the clothes were not entirely conclusive, Tate was confident the boots worn by the deceased had been manufactured in Russia. "The Russians used a type of oil in tanning leather extracted from a type of Birch that was located in the Siberian region. This is consistent with the leather from the boots he was wearing."

"So, you're saying this man could have been from

Russia?" asked Sean. He wondered how it came that a Russian was buried in the guest house of Harry Schriever.

"That's what my analysis shows, Sean," responded Tate. "There was nothing found on the body to identify the man. We found a wallet in a jacket pocket that had $26.00 in U.S. bills, which was nothing to sneeze at during that time, and what may have been a train ticket, but it's hard to say due to its decay. The threads of the jacket had deteriorated but—get this—Russian rubles had been sewed into the lining of the jacket. The Imperial ruble was replaced around 1922. The rubles we found were part of the newer currency, so we know he had to have died after 1922 or 1923."

Lucky spoke up. "We know the victim was shot at least twice, we suspect from the same gun, but the bullet wounds were not from the gun found with the remains. We got lucky and found bullet fragments inside the ribcage area. It looks like they were from a low-caliber gun, something like a twenty-two. We also found a hole from a bullet in the front of the skull." He pointed toward his forehead. "Whoever shot him in the forehead meant it to be a fatal shot. If we had to guess, this was likely the kill-shot. We didn't find evidence of heavy trauma on the remains, so if there was a scuffle or fight, there's no evidence to support it."

Tate added, "Like Lucky said, the victim didn't die from gunshots from the Mauser, which was the pistol found in the grave. It would have done a lot more damage."

"As Tate mentioned, the victim was wrapped in

a quilt. Whether or not that means he was killed in a bedroom, we don't know, because the blanket could have been carried from where it was kept, like a bedroom, or laundry area or hutch, to the victim. There are lots of possibilities. Hell, it may have been brought in from somewhere else. As to where he was shot, that's anyone's guess as well. He could have been shot in the basement, but that seems unlikely because why would someone go to the trouble of wrapping the body in a quilt before burying the body there?"

"Good point," thought Sean.

"We cannot determine if he was killed in the guest house. He could have been shot in the mansion itself, or even somewhere else on the property. I guess it's possible he was shot somewhere away from the property, but that seems unlikely to me. There were lots of other places around Bekbourg to dispose of a body if the killing didn't take place on the Schriever property. So our theory is the body was wrapped in the quilt and moved to the basement in the guest house where it was buried. Now, it's hard to say if more than one person was involved. A strong man could have managed by himself based on the size of the deceased, but there is nothing to indicate how many people were involved."

Tate added, "It was a shallow grave—about four feet, so the remains went undetected all these years until the workers started digging."

"Yeah, and if that hadn't happened, it may have never been discovered." Lucky took a sip of cold coffee and looked at Tate. "Want to tell him about the pistol found in the grave with the body?"

"Sure. The victim had a shoulder harness, which was empty. So, it's possible the Mauser was his and was thrown into the pit where the body was buried, but there is no way of knowing. Whoever buried the body threw the gun into the grave. The Mauser still had a round in the chamber and two in the clip. We know with certain the Mauser was not the murder weapon."

Sean was familiar with the German-manufactured Mauser handgun. They were manufactured around the late 1800's to sometime up to the 1930's and used in Europe by military as well as civilians. "With it being German-made, how likely was it that a Russian would carry that gun?"

"They were a German-made arms and popular throughout Europe," explained Tate. "The British, in particular, liked the Mauser, but so did the Russians. Hell, a Mauser was used in the execution of the Czar and his family."

After they wrapped up, Lucky invited Sean to his office. "I didn't want to say anything around Tate about the international thief Elias is investigating, but this seems damn coincidental with the timing of the Count being in Bekbourg and this man being shot."

"I agree, Lucky. The Count was staying in the guest house. Also, the Count was Russian, and the man appears Russian."

"The man could have been a bodyguard, a confidant or friend."

"Or a thief or spy," offered Sean. "He didn't have any identification on him, and a secret police from Russia would have tried to keep his identity secret. He sure as hell would not have wanted the U.S. government to know he was in the country. At the time, the Bolsheviks were in pursuit of members of the Czar's family, especially if they thought they had something that belonged to their country. He could have been part of the Bolshevik secret police pursuing the Count."

"What do you know about the Count—other than he was stranded in Bekbourg because of a snow storm?"

"Not much, but Cheryl has been researching the Count and his visit there. I'll see what she has learned and where that takes me. I'll also have our files researched to see if there were any missing person reports back then or anything else that might shed light on this. Say, have you all found anything out about the professor or his assistant?"

"Not yet. I'll let you know if something shows up. Have you picked up anything suspicious about either man?"

"I haven't met the research assistant yet. The professor is convincing on his purpose for being in Bekbourg, but hell, we know that's not worth anything. I'll keep you posted on any developments."

During his drive back to Bekbourg, Sean decided to issue a statement to the local media. In that, he would release the fact that the victim was a male, in his late thirties—with a height of five-feet-seven-inches. Estimated death occurred in the mid 1920's by gunshot—a handgun. He realized that no one alive today would have first-hand knowledge, but if they knew of anything that might be related, to please contact the sheriff's office. Sean was not ready to release information that a German-made pistol was found in the grave or any details about the man being Eastern European and likely Russian.

Sean had some ideas on who he might talk to around town who might know something. Also, he would double back with Cheryl and ask her to review the newspaper archives about missing persons during the mid 1920's.

His thoughts were interrupted when Alex called and told him about a call that had come in from Cole, the contractor doing work on C.P.'s guest house. When the workers got to the site this morning, they could tell someone had been in there overnight. Nothing was missing, but some old wood cabinets and boxes in the basement—likely there from early times in the building's history—had been moved around. Some dirt was found on the steps leading up to the kitchen and a little on the stairs leading to the second floor. "It looks like whoever it was moved around inside. Nothing we could use to take impressions from. The basement floor is plastered with foot prints and all sorts of impressions," Alex told Sean. He also told him that since C.P. was out of town, Cole was the one who called the station. "Since nothing appears to have been stolen, Cole thought it could be teenagers snooping around. There was a window that was unlocked, so we think that's how they got in. Cole didn't think it was worth checking for fingerprints since there have been so many workers all around. He is going to instruct his men to make sure all the doors and windows are locked up from now on."

In light of the conversation he had just had with Lucky and Tate, Sean found this development interesting. *Why would someone be snooping around the guest house? It could be a thief scoping the house out for a future job. Or, Cole could be right about it being teenagers. Since the intruders had gone to the basement, maybe they were into the supernatural and drawn there because of the remains found there. Some folks in Bekbourg were into that sort of thing. But, what if the break-in has something to do with the Count's stay in town? If Elias is right and someone thinks royal jewels are here—or at least a clue to their whereabouts—then that could explain the break-in. But, eighty years of missing jewels in Bekbourg—how likely is that?*

Sean called and asked Fred, a deputy who handled the files and evidence room, to see if he could find any records about missing men from 1923 until 1930. He also wanted Arlo and Syd to ask some of the old-timers around town if they knew something about the mid 1920's that could be helpful. He was going to ask their friend and landlord, Kye Davis, if she knew anything. Jules Leroux, a retired railroad engineer, whose family had a long history with the railroad, might know something as well.

Chapter 19

Cheryl and Sean rented one side of a duplex owned by a retired high school teacher, Kye Davis. Kye had become like family to them and dog-sat Buddy when they were away. Sean was not hesitant to express his appreciation for Kye's instruction during his high school English class. Not only was she well-respected around Bekbourg as a teacher, but she carried with her knowledge about the history of Bekbourg.

During dinner at their home, Sean asked Kye if she knew anything about what went on when the train was stranded in January 1925.

"Why yes, dear. My great aunt was working as a desk clerk at the Grand Hotel when the train got stranded. The hotel's owner certainly had his moment of glory during that time. He single-handedly orchestrated getting lodging for all those people on the train in just a few hours' time." Kye's eyes twinkled as she grinned. "I know I shouldn't repeat this, but all the employees called the hotel's owner Hawk Hugo—behind his back, of course."

"Why that nickname?" Cheryl asked hiccupping with mirth.

"They said he had eyes like a hawk. Dust or lint or specks could not escape his notice—nothing could. He was an absolute tyrant. He was French and had a pencil-thin mustache. He'd snap his fingers when he wanted something done and had a bell to summon the bellhops. His employees were scared to death of being fired, but the hotel was first-class during its time."

"Hugo knew a Russian Count was on the train?" prodded Sean.

Kye grinned. "Oh, yes. I heard the story so many times from my great aunt I can almost recite her story verbatim. The train people had sent word the train might be stopping for the night because of the storm, so Hawk Hugo was already flitting around the hotel giving orders. Hawk liked to hobnob with the bigwigs when they were around, so he was in the bar room with some men when a boy from the railroad ran into the hotel asking to see Hawk. The currier shoved him a list and told him the train could be stuck here for a week and accommodations were needed—as it was arriving in half-an-hour. It was when the currier told him a Russian Count was on the train with his wife that Hawk really started buzzing. Now, Harry Schriever was never a man to let an opportunity escape, so when he heard the boy say that a Count was on the train, he literally jumped out of his seat, told Hawk the Count and his wife would be his guests, and left to make preparations. The story goes that Geisen, who was there, wasn't happy Schriever beat him to the punch, but he was mollified when he realized he could host a steel magnate and his wife.

"Anyway, Hawk Hugo rang a bell, and all the employees within hearing distance came rushing into the lobby. The train operator was having all the passengers transported to the hotel first, so plans had to be made about where they would stay and transportation arranged for those who couldn't stay in the Grand Hotel. Hawk knew people would be hungry, so he got the kitchen to prepare a huge amount of food to feed them when they arrived at the hotel. According to my aunt, he was giving orders left and right. Hawk sent runners to the boarding house, the hotel at the other end of town, the sheriff's office and all the livery stables. The sheriff dispatched deputies to find residents who might be willing to put up passengers. It wasn't easy getting everything organized in the middle of a blizzard, but it all worked out. Hawk did a good job, but his obsession with organization was temporarily thrown into chaos."

Cheryl was laughing. "That's amazing, Kye."

"It was something. Harry Schriever took charge, like he was so capable of doing, and headed home to get things arranged for the Count and his wife. Later, when the train pulled in, he was standing on the platform to welcome the Count and his wife with his own staff to handle their luggage and transportation to his house. According to the stories going around, he even offered that he and his wife would move into the guest house so the Count and his wife could have their entire house to themselves, but the Count declined and ended up staying in the guest house. Mrs. Schriever had a feast ready for them upon their arrival. With Schriever taking the reins, it was all seamless for the Count and his wife."

"Sounds like it," agreed Cheryl.

"Those people who couldn't be put up in the public accommodations were placed in homes around town. Some of the passengers weren't English-speaking, but Bekbourg had people living here from different parts of Europe, so it all worked out. People around town talked about it for years. As time went on, the story faded. For those of us old enough—like me—who had heard the stories, your article brought memories of stories we have heard."

"Were the Count and his wife frequent guests at the hotel?" Cheryl asked.

"The Count was. He'd join the men in the bar in the afternoons. You know, the Count only spoke Russian and French. The owner of the steel company who was on the train knew French, and he would interpret. The hotel also had someone who was able to interpret, but I don't know who that was. A funny story was that Harry Schriever was overheard telling the Count he intended to get a personal tutor to instruct him on speaking Russian. Not to be outdone in their friendly rivalry, Gregory Geisen said he planned to learn both Russian and French."

"Did your great aunt ever talk about a hotel vault?"

Both Cheryl and Kye looked at Sean. Kye replied, "Yes, as a matter of fact, she and Hawk Hugo were the only two people who knew the combination."

"Did she mention if the Count ever put valuables in it?"

"No, she never mentioned that."

"Did she ever talk about someone missing around that time or sometime in the late 20's?"

"Let me think, dear." Kye got up to get plates for a coconut cream pie she had brought. "Nothing stands out in my mind, but if I think of something, I'll let you know."

Cheryl looked at Sean, "The *Tribune* is running your news release about the remains in our next publication. That's around the same time the Count was in town, and he was staying in the guest house. I wonder if they could be related."

Kye spoke up, "But, dear, surely someone like Harry Schriever would have known about someone being shot on his property. I can't imagine him not reporting a shooting to the police, much less allowing someone to be buried there."

"That's a good point," Cheryl said in concentration. "What if Harry didn't know? What if something happened involving the Count and he kept it hidden? Maybe someone tried to rob the Count. Or maybe, they just wanted to see a real-life royal and startled him."

Kye was skeptical. "There had been a blizzard, so it wasn't all that easy to move around for a common thief." Kye paused. "I guess people knew the Count was staying in the guest house, but I can't imagine someone breaking into Harry's property. Harry was well respected, but one thing I remember my great aunt saying was that he was a ruthless business man and no one around here wanted to cross him. That would include a thief and a curiosity-seeker."

"Mmmm," Cheryl uttered as she helped Kye put dessert and coffee on the table.

Sean smiled to himself. He could see his wife's mind churning. She suddenly straightened. "There were a lot of passengers who got off the train and were staying in the downtown area. Maybe they knew the Count was there and thought there might be something to steal from him, and one of his bodyguards shot them? I have a manifest of the passengers who came in on the train. I had focused on confirming the Count and his wife were on the train, but with this news, I need to look through it and see if anyone looks suspicious."

Sean grinned. "I don't know how you can tell something like that from a list, but I would like a copy of that list."

Cheryl joked, "Ah-ha! See! Even you are thinking like me."

They all laughed. She got him a copy the next day.

Chapter 20

Dimitri invited Cheryl and Sean to join him for drinks at the B&B, but Sean had a conflict.

After chit-chatting, Dimitri smiled. "My dear, I apologize if this is old news, but I have learned that the Count was a distant cousin to the Czar. The Count's father was a second cousin."

"No, I did not know that. What about his mother?"

"She was part of the French royalty. It was very common for royalty to marry royalty from other countries. Strategic alliances, not unions of the heart, ruled the times. The Count's mother died from an illness before the revolution, and his father perished in a conflict defending the monarchy before the revolt itself."

They discussed the history Dimitri had uncovered until he changed topics. "I am enjoying my time here in Bekbourg. I haven't had much time to get to know its history, but Harry Schriever certainly was important to its growth."

"Yes, he was. Harry Schriever started the Bekbourg Springs Milk Company in 1892. For decades, he was one of the local businessmen whose companies brought prosperity to the region. When World War II broke out, he kept his company afloat through sheer determination and ingenuity. Despite the economic downturns that ultimately lay waste to so many manufacturing companies in the Midwest, the milk company not only survived, but still employs a lot of people around Bekbourg. He is legendary here, not only because of what he accomplished through his business pursuits, but also because of how much he gave back to the community. To this day, people around Bekbourg know who Harry Schriever was."

"It's interesting that a small town like Bekbourg could have such important people in its history. Now, like many people here, I'm intrigued about the dead body found in C.P.'s guest house. It was built by Schriever, wasn't it?"

"Yes, it was."

"I know there were bootleggers and gangsters back then. Is there any reason to think Schriever had illicit business dealings and had something to do with it?"

Cheryl raised her glass to her lips. "I see you're also researching Bekbourg's royalty."

"Touché." Dimitri toasted his drink. "I thought it would be interesting to know who the Count spent time with. He seemed to have formed a friendship with Schriever—so much so that the Count and his wife were planning to stop here on their return trip to Rhode Island."

"I don't know how the two are connected — Schriever having illicit business dealings and forming a friendship with the Count. I've never heard anything suggesting Harry Schriever was engaged in underhanded or criminal activities. If he had been involved in things like that, there would have at least been rumors over the years."

"Ah, well, I was just curious. It's too bad Sean couldn't join us. I'm sure he has his hands full, and it can't be easy to investigate a crime that happened so long ago. I was curious if he has learned any more information on the man or what happened."

"I wouldn't know."

"So, there's no pillow talk?"

Cheryl did not like where this conversation had turned. Why was the professor researching Schriever? She certainly did not appreciate being pumped for information about Sean's investigation and Dimitri's insinuation. "No. Sean is a professional. We respect each other's boundaries."

Sensing he had offended her, he added, "Ah, poor taste on my part. Forgive me, my dear. I was simply curious about the mystery."

Cheryl shrugged it off, but it left a sour taste with her. She had intended to ask Dimitri what he thought about the manifest, but she soon left instead.

Chapter 21

Saint Petersburg, Russia 1913

"General, your son is here."

The General continued his attention to the document lying on his gilded gold-leaf desk. "Send him in."

"Yes, General."

The seventeen-year-old Zakhar Voskoboynikov entered and stood straight before his father's desk, waiting acknowledgment. Not for the first time, Zakhar observed his father's receding hairline. His father was fastidious in his dress, including the manner in which he maintained his thick dark mustache which curled upward. Zakhar hoped to one day reach a general's rank as he admired his father's double-breasted uniform trimmed out in metal buttons, sash belt, shoulder straps and piping around the collar and cuffs.

Several minutes of quiet passed as the boy wondered why he had been abruptly summoned.

Finally, the General laid down the pen and raised his hard eyes to his son.

"You have been well, Zakhar?"

"Yes, Papa."

The General continued his assessment and then instructed him to sit. Zakhar saw a flicker in his father's eyes. "You are going to Paris tomorrow. Mikhail will accompany you. There, you will continue your education."

When Zakhar heard the words he was going to Paris, his first thought was his father was sending him for a short excursion to his mother's birthplace, but when he heard he would continue his education there, his eyebrows raised. His reaction did not go unnoticed by his father. "It is best you leave for now. Unrest is growing in our country, and this movement by the Bolsheviks appears to be growing stronger. The possibility of war seems to grow each day. Mikhail will see you through this. When this is all past, you can return, but not before.

Zakhar did not want to leave his home. Of course, he had visited Paris, the home of his mother and her nobility, but it was daunting to consider leaving all that was familiar. He ventured the only persuasion that could possibly change his father's mind, "I hope to enter the military service and follow in your footsteps. My training is going well, Papa. Will these plans affect my ability to enter the service?"

"That has all been arranged. The Czar is most fond of you. You will remember the present he gave you for your sixteenth birthday?"

Of course Zakhar remembered the jeweled cigarette

case the Czar had given him. His parents were most pleased by such an elaborate showing by the General's relative. "Yes, Papa, I will always cherish the case. While I was most honored by the gift, it is you I think he wished to compliment. He trusts you, Papa. You are a trusted confidant."

The General sighed. "I wonder as to the effectiveness of my counsel."

"The Czar has approved of my delay in his service?"

"Yes. I used as my persuasion your affliction with pneumonia. He did not press the issue. Like I said, he is fond of you."

Without expression to his father, Zakhar was displeased he had been exempted from military service, particularly on what he considered a bogus health reason. Yes, pneumonia had plagued him throughout his life, but he had regained his strength.

The General put his hand on the papers. "Mikhail will see to your well-being. Should you not be able to return, you will have access to a vault in Switzerland to see to your comfort."

Mikhail was his father's uncle and had been ever present in their lives as Zakhar grew up. "Will he return to the Motherland?"

"I think not. His years are growing numbered, but his health is such that he will be with you for a while. Now, there is much to be done before dawn when you depart. See that you are ready."

"Yes, Papa."

"Be well, Son. We will look forward to the day we are again united."

Even as Zakhar agreed with his father, he was skeptical that day would ever come.

Chapter 22

"Hi, Jules. How are you doing?" asked Sean as he sat down at the table.

Jules Leroux had followed in his father and grandfather's steps as a railroad engineer. He had recently retired from the WVB&C and was embarking on his next phase. C.P. had hired him to be a steam engineer for a scenic train that would transport tourists on a twenty-five-mile excursion between downtown Bekbourg and a state park in the Lake Peatmont region north of town.

"Fine as you can imagine, Sheriff. You are a busy man lately."

"Thanks for coming in early to talk with me. I have some questions you might be able to help me with. It's in regards to the railroad back in the old days."

"As always Sheriff, I'm at you service." A waitress rushed up and refreshed Jules' coffee and poured Sean's.

"I assume you read Cheryl's article about the 1925 blizzard and the train that got stuck in Bekbourg for a week?"

"Yes, I did. It was a splendid piece. She was right on."

"There is something you might have some insight

on. I guess it was lucky it even made it into town."

"You're right. The snow was coming in heavy, and the temperature was dropping so rapidly that there was the chance a rail could break or the train could get stalled. In fact, a rail did break. That's the reason the train got stuck here. In those days, the steam engines were a lot heavier than the diesel locomotives of today. They had to pound through the snow, so there could be derailments. Out west where they had really deep snows, they had special engines that would clear the rails through the mountains. Still do."

"I'm trying to find out if there were any unusual things that happened on the train. Maybe you were told things about that train that we don't know about."

Jules sipped his coffee. "In fact, Sean, I do. My grandfather liked to talk about the blizzard. He was the fireman on the train, and his brother, my great uncle, was the brakeman. He told of a strange incident involving a drunken passenger. There were two men sitting at a table in the dining car who were foreigners. They were wearing suits made of a rough material that looked plain, unlike anything ever made in this country. They could speak very little English. Grand-papa described them as Russian or from Eastern Europe. This drunken passenger was picking a fight with them, making fun of their clothes and the fact they couldn't speak English. He was telling them to leave the dining car. Unfortunately, the poor men couldn't understand what he was saying, but they understood his tone. He apparently got under the skin of one, but his compatriot kept him in check. Well, the dining car captain thought things were getting out-of-hand and went and got my great-uncle to handle things. When he couldn't get the drunk to leave the dining car, he gave him a good whack upside the head with his Billy club and dragged him back to a car and cuffed him to a seat."

"This was during Prohibition. Where did he get the alcohol?"

"He must have brought it on the train with him. My great uncle found a bottle in his coat pocket." Jules grinned. "He didn't think it was a good idea for the drunk to have it, so he did a good deed and took it. Called it good shine."

Sean's lips twitched. "Did anything happen to the drunk? Was he arrested?"

"Naw. When the train arrived, he was taken with the other passengers to the hotel. By then, he'd slept it off. That's about all I know, other than my grandfather and great uncle said it was the worst blizzard they had ever seen. What made it so bad was how quickly everything froze up, and the railroad came to a complete halt. Unfortunately, a freight train down near Chillicothe derailed over a bridge where the track had frozen and broke. The train went into the creek, and it was several days before they could go out and see how bad it was. Took another few days to get it pulled out of the way and the track repaired. It was about a week before they could get that line back in service.

"Grand-papa used to tell how coming down the

line to Bekbourg you could see nothing in front of you because of the snow. They were worried they couldn't get through. That would have been a real disaster. Luckily, the passengers got to Bekbourg and the town found places for the passengers to stay. A lot of railroaders were called in to keep the train from freezing up. They had to keep the fire going in the engine and the steam flowing back through the train."

"You know anything more about these two foreign men?"

"Well, from what I know, when they got off the train, they went up to the hotel with the other passengers. I was told they didn't say much, but they appeared capable of taking care of themselves. My great uncle thought the drunk would best be advised to steer clear of them after he got off the train. Turns out he was a salesman going to Cincinnati. My great uncle never heard they crossed paths again."

Sean asked him about the passenger list Cheryl had given him, and Jules told him what he could.

After Sean wrapped up his questions, he changed subjects. "How is the transition of C.P.'s owner-ship going?"

"Smooth as silk, Sean. With my help, C.P. has made a smooth transition to keeping our beloved railroad open, and he's moving right along with our scenic railroad. That is where my real love is. We've got one old steam engine lined up and looking for a second for a backup to finish out our authentic train."

Someone suddenly yelled out from across the dining room as he headed toward their table. "Jules, are you under arrest? Sheriff, I can't imagine why Jules would be going to jail. Whatever it is, he didn't do it."

As Chaw pulled out a chair, Sean looked at him. "No, but I came to talk to you, Chaw." Chaw was a retired railroader, and he along with other railroaders showed up most mornings at Frau's for breakfast to share old stories and discuss the latest news.

Chaw harrumphed as he settled into his chair. The waitress appeared to refresh Jules' and Sean's coffees and splashed some in Chaw's cup. She asked if they were ready to order. "Can I get you your breakfast, Sean?" Jules offered.

"I can't believe it. Jules is going to spend some money," Chaw joked.

"No thanks. I'm on duty. I got to get going. Thank you, Jules." To the two men, Sean said, "Keep in touch."

After Sean left, Chaw asked, "What was that all about?"

"Nothing much. Just wanted to see what I knew about the blizzard in '25 when the train got stuck here for a week."

"And of course, you knew everything about it."

"I make it a point to know the history of the Bekbourg railroad."

About that time, Dusty and Mule Head joined them. "I just saw Sean leaving. What was he doing here? I haven't seen him here for a while." Dusty liked to keep up with things. When Chaw retired, Dusty had become the conductor. Mule Head had retired a few years earlier on disability.

"He was talking to Jules about the '25 blizzard," Chaw answered as he motioned for the waitress.

"You mean about the article his wife wrote?" asked Dusty.

"Was that it, Jules?" asked Chaw.

"A little bit. He just had some questions about the train. I told him how lucky we were it made it here."

Mule Head snorted, "Well, that sure was nothing like the blizzard in '78. Now, there was a blizzard."

They looked at him. "How would you know? You were just a kid," egged Chaw.

"All I know is it's gone down on record as the coldest and most severe blizzard in Ohio history."

"Well, they didn't have all that fancy weather equipment back in '25, so they didn't know how bad it was. But I tell you, '25 was right up there with '78—probably worse since they didn't have the machinery to clear the rails like they did in '78. Lots of people froze in '25. The railroad was shut down."

"Well, the railroad was shut down in '78, Jules."

"Yes, I know, but it was shut down before any damage occurred, and as soon as the blizzard was over, they were able to clean everything up and resume operation. Back in '25, it was shut down because of broken rails and derailments, and it took weeks after the thaw before they were fully operational."

Dusty added, "All I know is they didn't have school for over a week. We were all froze in."

Jules could top that, "Downtown Bekbourg was lucky, because its utilities managed to stay on, but the outer reaches and other areas weren't so lucky. Some schools were closed for over a month in '25. Everything froze up—even the plumbing. It took a long time to get back to normal."

"'78 was still worse," Mule Head persisted. "That was one of the snowiest winters in Ohio."

Chaw had something else on his mind. "Hey, Jules, what's this I hear? I heard some interesting rumors about who is going to be working on the scenic railroad."

"What are you talking about, Chaw?" Jules asked as he took a sip of coffee.

"I hear old Dollar Bill is coming back to work as a conductor on the train."

Jules enjoyed playing coy. "Where'd you hear that, Chaw?"

"Well, his sister still lives in town, and she was telling my wife he was moving back to Bekbourg. He's been working at some amusement park on their train ride and really got tired of it. He's ready to do something else. He's been wanting to move back here."

"Well, you heard right. If we can work it out, he'll be coming back and helping me out with the train."

Dusty was poised to pop a strip of bacon in his mouth. "I've heard some interesting stories about Dollar Bill. How'd he get his nickname exactly?"

"His name 'bout says it all," hooted Chaw. "For years, he had this policy where he wouldn't spend more than a dollar for a meal when he was on the job. And, he was strict about it." Chaw snorted, "Not a penny more. At first, I guess a dollar was enough. But, as prices got higher over time, it got to the point where about all he could afford with that dollar budget was coffee and the free crackers they offered. He'd put ketchup and mustard on the crackers to spice them up." The other three men were laughing. "Hell, with coffee being thirty-five cents back then, he was still under budget. But in the mid 70's, coffee prices started to sky-rocket. He had to make a budget adjustment. He went all the way to two-dollars."

"You got to be kidding," Dusty howled.

Chaw shook his head. "Nope. When the restaurants finally told him he couldn't keep eating their free crackers by the dozens, together with coffee prices continuing to spike, he upped his budget by another whole dollar bill."

Mule Head stabbed his egg with a fork. "Well, I guess we'll find out what his budget is now when he moves back here."

Jules grinned. "That we will."

Chapter 23

Paris and England 1914-1924

During the next two years, Zakhar settled into a new life in Paris. Many doors were open for him—given his noble mother had married into the Russian imperial family. His Uncle Mikhail had channels through which he was able to know of the political unrest in Russia and information about the family. He tutored Zakhar on the ways of the world and brought him into manhood.

In the spring of 1914 before the War broke out, Mikhail entered Zakhar's bedchamber and dismissed the house maid—whom Zakhar fancied for the night. "Zakhar, be ready to travel to Geneva tomorrow. We have important business to which we must attend."

Zakhar rolled over and scowled. "What is so urgent? I am to attend a ball tomorrow night."

Mikhail was quick to dismiss the frivolity of a ball with a string of expletives. Seeing his nephew's grin, he reprimanded. "You must not provoke your uncle."

"Why am I leaving for Geneva tomorrow?"

"I received an urgent missive from your father today.

We are on a mission for the Czar."

Zakhar sat up in bed.

*His uncle turned to pour wine and sat in a chair.
"I'm glad I have your attention."*

*"Now, you wish to keep me in suspense," Zakhar
bantered.*

*"I wish time permitted such. The threat of war
is growing graver, and the swell of the Bolshevik is
undermining the security of the country. The Czar
commissioned jewelry to present to the Empress on her
birthday. The jeweler has completed the work, but the
Czar is concerned that the delivery might be intercepted.
Your father assured the Czar he would handle the matter
on his behalf." Mikhail savored the wine as Zakhar rose
from the bed and began to dress. "We are to appear
at the jeweler's home at dawn and get the jewelry. We
will take it to your father's vault to be held until further
instructions."*

*"You make this sound so simple, Mikhail, but we do
not have the funds to pay for such expensive jewelry."*

*Mikhail sipped his wine and stood. "I still look for
adventure at my age. Happily, we do not have to find
ways to pay for the Czar's extravagance. He paid for
the jewels when he was last in Paris. We do not want
to draw attention to ourselves as we travel, but I have
taken precautions."*

*The jeweler had disguised the jewelry as pack-
aged coffee. They did not unwrap the disguise for fear
of breaking a seal applied by the Czar's jeweler. It was*

Zakhar's first trip to Geneva. His uncle showed him how to access the vault. Since his mother's family had provided housing and provisions—neither Zakhar nor Mikhail saw any reason to take any of the gold stored in the vault.

Zakhar completed one year of education at the university before the start of the War. He was able to complete a second year before his uncle relocated them to a relative's estate in the countryside of England hoping to escape the ravages of war. There, Zakhar spent time honing his skills in polo and hunting, but unwelcomed news from Russia found its way to Zakhar and Mikhail as his father's predictions became reality.

Zakhar received word his mother had succumbed to pneumonia during the winter of 1915, and his father had been killed in battle a year later. Unrest and political strife metastasized throughout Russia. Mikhail lamented the simmering revolt in his homeland. "Even the name of Saint Petersburg has been changed to Petrograd," he bellowed one evening to his nephew. "It is too bad your father is not there to counsel the Czar. The advice from those buffoons surrounding him is weakening him and undermining his influence. I fear the worst for our Motherland."

Those members of the Romanov family, who were lucky enough to escape, made their way to other countries. The February Revolution of 1917 brought the abdication of the Czar, and the October Revolution of

1917 saw the Provisional Government toppled by the Bolshevik revolutionaries. Zakhar despaired he would never again return to his homeland.

After the War ended and things had returned to semi-normal, he and his uncle relocated to Paris. At the insistence of Mikhail, Zakhar completed his education. He was introduced into society by his mother's family and eagerly embraced its pomp and circumstance. The distressing news from Russia had taken a toll on Mikhail's health. His contacts had all but dried up, but what little news he heard was dire. He repeatedly warned Zakhar that extended members of the royal family were at risk by the Bolshevik agents who had been dispatched to locate riches and jewels belonging to the royal family for return to Russia. "They will not hesitate to kill you, Zakhar. You must exercise caution." The warning fell on deaf ears as he continued his passions of hunting, womanizing, and polo.

Chapter 24

Cheryl stopped by the depot to talk with Andrian. He was organizing old photos of the train and crew as well as passengers. Kat was reviewing old ledgers at her desk off in the corner and listening to the low hum of a radio. She and Cheryl exchanged greetings, but Kat went back to her ledgers.

Cheryl walked over to Andrian's table and looked at the photos. "Those are interesting pictures. Are those from the mid 1900's?"

He kept shuffling the pictures as he talked. "Yeah, I found them in an old box in the telegrapher's storage area. I keep coming across things. Because there are so many things of interest, it's going to be a challenge to decide what to put on display in the museum. I've been thinking about rotating the exhibits to use a lot of the things I'm finding. That way, the museum won't go stale."

"That's a good idea," Cheryl said—watching the pictures as he flipped through them. "Have you come across any pictures for the train that was stranded during the snow storm?"

He stopped. "I found a couple of things you might

be interested in." He walked over to a box and pulled out a picture. "I was going through a box I had stored in there." He jerked his head toward the room where boxes were stacked, "and I found this. I'm pretty sure it's the Count's wife."

Cheryl studied the young woman in a fur coat and hat with leather gloves and ankle boots. She was standing on the train platform looking into the camera along with a man and woman. "Yes, that's Elizabeth. She's with Harry and Kathleen Schriever. I haven't seen this one. I wonder where the Count was?" She turned the picture over. "I don't see any writing on the back as to who took this. Do you have any idea?"

"I assume Schriever had a photographer there. I guess it could have been someone with the WVB&C."

"You mind if I get a copy?"

"No, not at all."

Cheryl walked over to the copier in the corner. When she returned, she said, "It's interesting that the body they found in the basement of C.P.'s guest house could have been placed there about the same time the Count was in town."

Cheryl noticed Kat had stopped working and was intently listening. Andrian, on the other hand, returned to his pictures, "I don't really see how they could be connected. Do you?" he mumbled.

"Well, I don't know."

Andrian shrugged. "I guess it's possible, but will they ever find out who it was? Anyway, here's something else I found." He pulled out a folder from under a stack on his table. "It's the train schedule. I've made a copy in case you want one. The Count and his wife were en route over thirty hours when they finally arrived here."

"Geezz. That was a long ordeal."

"Yeah, it was." He walked around his desk. "Anyway, we've been at this a while, and that's all I've found. I think we've run up against a wall. If I find anything else, I'll let you know. If I don't get focused, I'm not going to meet C.P.'s deadline for opening the museum."

"Of course. I've looked everywhere I know to look in the newspaper's archives and haven't found anything else." Cheryl again thanked Andrian and bid him and Kat a good day.

Cheryl was not surprised Andrian was ready to move on from the project. His interest had quickly waned. And, from what she knew, he had not been working with Dimitri or his assistant. Cheryl had not even met Jeffrey, but she knew he existed, because Bri mentioned him stopping by the B&B to see Dimitri. In any event, she felt she had learned about all there was from Andrian and Dimitri, and it was time to let her investigative skills take her to the next steps. She was going to go to Cincinnati and see what she could learn about the Count's time there. She also had learned that the Count's wife had a granddaughter, who she hoped to interview.

After Cheryl left, Kat watched Andrian continuing to plow through the box and wondered why he had lied to Cheryl about the photos.

Chapter 25

Spring 1924

Elizabeth Griffiths was the daughter of a wealthy American industrialist. When Elizabeth was twelve, her mother passed away from an illness. Her father relied on his sister, Josephine, who was childless, to oversee Elizabeth's education and introduction into society. He had spoken with Josephine about taking Elizabeth to Europe with the hopes of her marrying into a title. Elizabeth respected and loved her father and did not want to disappoint him. He arranged to take her to Europe, along with Josephine, to see that Elizabeth was properly introduced into the upper echelons of European society. Unfortunately, he died unexpectedly in a riding accident, leaving Elizabeth distraught. Her Aunt Josephine and uncle took her to Paris to see the city and attend the Summer Olympics to help her recover from her grief.

While in Paris, Josephine became friends with a woman whose sister had married a Russian Count. During a ball in the spring of 1924, that sister (Zakhar's aunt on his mother's side) introduced him to Elizabeth. Chaperoned by her Aunt Josephine, Zakhar and Elizabeth began a courtship.

One day, Mikhail dispatched a messenger requesting Zakhar meet him at his club. "You're looking well, Uncle," said Zakhar as he settled in front of the fire in a private room. As they enjoyed each other's company, the men savored the fine Russian vodka which the club had secured for its deserving customers. After a while, Mikhail broached the purpose of his invitation. "I am not so isolated and deaf that I am not privy to the latest gossip, Zakhar."

Zakhar attempted to conceal a grin. "I cannot imagine anyone ever thinking that of you, Uncle."

"Huh, uh," grunted the old man. "My mind is not failing either."

Zakhar laughed, "Of course not, Uncle."

Both hid their mirth as they sipped the vodka.

"Now that we are of the same mind, tell me about this American woman—Elizabeth Griffiths."

Zakhar was not surprised his uncle knew the young woman's name. Even though he also thought Mikhail knew more details than he let on, Zakhar explained that both her parents were deceased and she was an only child who was under the protection of her father's sister and her husband.

"It is my understanding her father was very wealthy?" Mikhail asked with sharp eyes.

"Yes. Before her uncle left to return to America, we

discussed the matter. I asked for her hand in marriage. He was pleased that his niece would be titled by marrying into nobility. The vast estate has been placed into a trust, but naturally I will have access."

"That is good. Your father had gold in the vault in Geneva, Switzerland, but it cannot maintain you in the matter to which you have become accustomed. Beyond that, it would be quite risky to access it if you are being watched by the Bolshevik revolutionaries."

"I have thought of that, Uncle, but I am willing to take the risk. Not only do I plan to go to Geneva to get enough gold to get to America, I am going to take the jewelry. The Czar is dead. There is no chance anyone will know of the jewelry."

"You do not know that. Spies are everywhere. Who's to say the jeweler hasn't told the Bolsheviks. Do not take anything for granted. They will view your father's wealth and the jewels as property of Russia. They will not hesitate to kill you to return it to Russia."

Zakhar nodded his acknowledgment.

"Do you plan to remain in America?"

"I have given my assurances to her uncle that we will live in America, but we will travel here. Elizabeth enjoys Paris."

"I am glad to hear this news. It will be safer than remaining here. What is the timing of this arrangement?" asked Mikhail.

"As soon as I return from Switzerland, we will wed."

"You will leave for America soon then?"

"Not so soon. Elizabeth is expecting to see the Olympics here this summer. After that, we will depart."

"The sooner—the better. I am told the Russian secret police are active here and in other European countries— spying on members of our family."

Zakhar sipped his vodka. "Elizabeth's uncle will make the arrangements. When we are ready to leave, I will go to the American embassy, and the papers will be there. They will arrange first class accommodations on the finest ship crossing the Atlantic."

"I see. So, until you are married, she is under the protection of her aunt in Paris?"

Out of love, Zakhar did not let his uncle see the weariness he felt from his uncle's obsession with the GPU and fears of their surveillance. "Yes, but they are staying with friends. I can assure you security is more than adequate. Her aunt is anxious to return to America, so she will depart after our vows are exchanged. The Olympics are not much later, so Elizabeth and I will travel soon after that."

His uncle nodded. "Good. I think you will be safer in America, but do not forget to exercise caution. Watch for the spies."

"I have never noticed anyone suspicious watching me."

Mikhail slammed his hand on the table, splashing the vodka. "They are watching you! You must be aware."

Zakhar did not like seeing his uncle upset. "I will be more careful. I will have a wife. Soon, a son I hope. I will be watchful," he assured Mikhail.

Mikhail's breathing slowed, and he nodded and took another sip.

"What about you, Mikhail? Will you go with us to America?"

Mikhail shook his head. "It is too late for me. I will live out the rest of my life here. I thirst for return to the Motherland, but for what purpose?" His face twisted in anger as he spat, "It is lost to those communists."

Zakhar sat silently sipping his vodka, contemplating his uncle's brooding. Mikhail's eyes cleared, "You marry this woman and go to America. Maybe one day, you can return, but our homeland will not be the same as when you left. You have my blessing, Zakhar."

Chapter 26

Kat had not heard from Jeffrey in recent days and began to worry he was losing interest in their relationship. She rubbed her head with both hands. "Oh, God, I just can't think Mama was right. I am so lonely. I want a man." She threw back her head and slammed her hands down. Even worse was the thought her mother had warned her. "God, she will never let me forget she was right." Her thoughts drifted back to their first conversation.

From the first time Jeffrey visited their house and met her mother, her mother disliked him. Her mother's warning was still as clear as if it had been given yesterday. She had waited up for Kat the first time they went on a date. "Sit. We talk."

"Mama, I'm tired. I've got to be at work early. Now is not a good time."

Her mother's eyes hardened. "There is never a good time. You must hear what I have to say." She nodded her head toward a chair.

Kat plopped down in the chair. "Okay, Mama. What is it?"

Her mother slammed her hand down on her lap. "That is no way to speak to me! I raised you and your brother to respect your parents. I have worked too hard— me and your father both—to have you sit in my house and disrespect me."

Kat had heard this before. "I'm sorry, Mama. I didn't mean it that way. I'm tired, and I've got a lot on my mind at work." That wasn't entirely true, because C.P. was not pressuring her on getting the inventories pulled together. "Please. Tell me what's on your mind."

"That man. He is no good. I do not want you seeing him."

"What do you mean by that? He has a Master's degree. He is well educated. He works for a professor who gives lectures all over the world."

Her mother's arm made a swiping motion. "That means nothing if he cannot be trusted."

Kat's jaw dropped. "What do you mean he can't be trusted? You only met him once, Mama. What is it you don't trust about him?" Kat did not say it, but she was thinking, "You just don't like me dating! I'm going to date! I need a life. I'm too young to hole up here! If I have to take on a second job to find us a place to live, I will."

"I know how they think."

"How who thinks?"

"Russians. He wants something. He is using you."

Kat burrowed her brows. "He is not Russian."

Her mother continued to stare at her like she was a child.

"Mama, I don't understand. He was very nice to you when he came the first time. He brought a bottle of Russian vodka. You won't even open it."

"Trash."

"You threw it away?" Kat nearly screeched. "I don't get it, Mama."

"He is a weasel. He come to our home and asks about when Count Voskoboynikov come here. He asks if we know about this."

"Mama, he is researching the history. It is amazing to think that a member of the Russian royalty once stayed in town. Articles were written in the newspaper back then about it. Cheryl, who owns the newspaper, when she found those articles, she even wrote about it. The professor he works for is interested in it, for god's sake, because they study Russian history. What is wrong with that?"

"If that's all they want to know, they can read old newspapers. They have ways to find about family without coming here. They are after more."

"What on earth could that be? I don't understand. What is wrong with asking people if they remember the Count's visit or if they remember hearing their elders talk about it? That's of interest to people. He thought you might remember hearing about things because your parents and grandparents were Russian. I don't see what is so bad about that. People are curious. Maybe the Count talked to someone about his hobbies—maybe about his plans, maybe about life in Russia before he

left. That's history." Kat's frustration was growing. As long as Kat could remember, her mother had been suspicious of strangers.

Her mother stood. "We both need sleep. You must hear me, Katrina. I cannot stop you from seeing this . . . Your papa's word is 'cheat'. But I warn you to be careful what you say and keep your heart locked away. He will hurt you."

She had built her hopes that Jeffrey and she could be a long-term thing. She had imagined moving in together. She did not care whether it was in Bekbourg or Cincinnati. He was slipping away, and she was determined to hold on. Kat knew he did not like it when she was clingy, but she was desperate. After looking at her phone lying beside her, she grabbed it and punched the number. After several rings, he picked up. "Hello" ground out of his mouth.

"Hey, Honey. I was hoping we could maybe see each other. I haven't heard from you in a few days."

"I've been busy. Maybe later in the week. Right now, I've got a lot of materials to read. I can't talk now."

She sighed. Once before, she dangled having copies of the manifest to entice him to see her. This time, she had another ploy: "Oh, okay. I heard something today at work I thought you might want to know. But I understand if you don't have time."

He couldn't resist the temptation. "Yeah, what's that?"

"Well, I'd rather tell you in person." When he did not say anything, she hoped she sounded convincing. "I think you'll find it interesting."

She heard him huff, "Okay, let's meet at Frau's."

She knew his favorite place was Knucklepin's, a decades old watering hole. "I know you like Knuck's wings and burgers. We could meet there if you want."

"No, let's meet at Frau's."

"Oh, okay. I just thought since we ate there last time, you'd like to go somewhere else."

"I don't want to go to Knuck's," he barked, but then softened his tone. "It's quieter at Frau's—better place to talk."

Kat brushed her hair, sprayed on some perfume, and put on lipstick. They arrived about the same time. Jeffrey told Kat to find a table and he would order them a beer. When he arrived at the table with the beers, she smiled at him. "I've missed you."

He took a sip of beer as his eyes roamed the room. "Like I said, I've been busy. We're on a short time frame to get everything pulled together before Dimitri has to leave right after the first of the year."

"Yeah, I understand. I'd just hoped we could be together more." She smiled as she tilted her head to the side and curled her hair with a finger. Just then, a waitress walked up and asked if they were ready to order. After she left, Jeffrey asked Kat what she had been doing. After a few minutes, he wanted to know what she had overheard at the depot. She told him about Cheryl asking

Andrian if he thought the Count being in Bekbourg and the body that had been found in C.P.'s guest room basement could be connected.

"What did he say?"

"He didn't say much. He didn't think so, and felt like no one would ever know."

"Was that all she said?"

"Yeah."

The waitress interrupted by delivering their food. Kat was pouring ketchup on her fries, when he asked, "Was that it?" as he took a bite of burger.

"There was something else. You know Andrian is supposed to be working with Cheryl on finding information about when the Count was here, but I caught him in a lie today."

"Yeah?"

"He showed her a picture of the Count's wife with Mr. and Mrs. Schriever when she was getting ready to leave Bekbourg." She stopped and pulled out a copy she had made when Andrian stepped out of the room. Jeffrey studied it. "He made it sound like that was the only picture he found, but it wasn't. I was working in the depot the day he found a stack of pictures in one of those boxes, and one of them was this picture he showed Cheryl, but there were others in the box. He didn't tell her anything about them."

Jeffrey looked confused. "Maybe they didn't have anything to do with the Count."

"But they did. When I saw him looking at them,

he studied them real close. He pulled out this picture and put it with some others, but he put the ones he kept looking at in an envelope and put them in the box. I saw him put that box further back in the corner and put two other boxes on top."

"So how do you know they were important?"

"When he left to go to lunch, I went and looked in the box. The pictures were taken the day the train arrived."

"Were there any of the Count in those?"

"No, which surprised me since Andrian seemed upset as he looked through them. But he's moody anyway, so I don't know." She took a bite and thought for a minute. "Maybe he didn't lie. There weren't any pictures of the Count and his wife in those—just other passengers. So, maybe he thought Cheryl would not be interested in them."

"Where's the box now?"

"It's still there in the corner near the door."

They talked for a while about other things while they finished their dinner, and Jeffrey asked for the check. Kat told him her mother was watching Joey if he wanted to do something after dinner. She was disappointed when he told her he had to do more research. She suggested they meet again soon. He told her he would call her. She was disappointed he did not try to kiss her when he walked her to her car.

Chapter 27

Andrian had been meaning to get the pictures out of the box and hide them at his apartment until he could get back to Cincinnati and put them in his safe deposit box. He couldn't believe what he saw in the pictures of the passengers exiting the train. It was two men who were of most interest to Andrian. He was going to go through the few remaining boxes tonight. If there was anything pertinent, he would take it to his apartment along with those pictures he had hidden in the box.

When he read Cheryl's article that had been carried in the Cincinnati paper about the Count stopping in Bekbourg, he knew he had to come here. Then, lucky for him, he came across an article in the Cincinnati newspaper about C.P.'s plans to turn the depot into a railroad museum and the need to hire an archivist. He had driven to Bekbourg the next day and turned in a resume. Because he had worked for the University of Cincinnati in the alumni office, which included finding historical events for publication in the alumni newsletters, C.P. thought he was qualified and hired him. A month after Cheryl's article was published, he started work for C.P.

At first, he had virtually no time to look through the railroad files about the Count. C.P. had a list of topics he wanted located and researched for the museum. Then, Cheryl had asked C.P. for access to the railroad files regarding an old bridge collapse, and C.P. freed up Andrian to help Cheryl with that task. Then, he learned from Kat that a professor's assistant had been in town asking questions about the Count. That spooked him, and he started working nights to locate materials. That's when an idea came to him. He approached Cheryl about them working together on the Count. He knew C.P. would have no problem if he was coordinating with Cheryl on the Count's visit in Bekbourg, particularly since it was a possible exhibit for the museum.

Only, it had backfired spectacularly. Andrian's grandfather had warned him about Dimitri, so when that damn professor showed up in Bekbourg, he knew the playing field had changed. Because she had no background, he had not concerned himself Cheryl would stumble onto the truth. But, with Dimitri sniffing around, the dynamic changed, and whatever he and Cheryl found together would likely find its way into Dimitri's hands. He was still seething that Kat had given them copies of the manifest. Because of Dimitri's presence, and Kat's prying, he had returned to spending more nights sifting through materials at the depot. Time was of the essence, and he was determined.

When Andrian arrived at the depot that night, he did as he always did and kept his flashlight turned toward the floor. He did not want lights flashing across the windows and alert someone to his presence. Once he got to the windowless room where the boxes were stored, he could turn on the light and finish reviewing the boxes.

He only had a few boxes left to review. He went to turn on the light and froze. Why did the floor creak? Someone was here. "Kat, is that you?" he spoke out to the darkness.

His body tensed, and his heart raced. Fear gripped him as he turned slowly and swung his flashlight beam around the room. Not knowing whether to flee or even breathe, he listened, but his breathing interfered with his attempt to decipher if there was an intruder. He suddenly heard another creak behind him, but before he could swing around, someone smashed something to his head. He crumpled to the floor as his flashlight bounced away.

Chapter 28

Paris 1924

Mikhail secured travel arrangements for Zakhar to go to Geneva—where he stayed in a hotel in the countryside. While there, Zakhar enjoyed the company of other European nobles, including a distant Romanov cousin. One day, the cousin, a few years older than Zakhar, suggested they ride horses in the countryside. They came to a small river and dismounted. The cousin asked about Mikhail.

Zakhar was hesitant to share that his uncle had slowed down, although he suspected news had gotten around. Mikhail had also cautioned him about what he said regarding the turmoil in Russia. "You do not know where loyalties lay, Zakhar."

"He is well, but age has slowed him somewhat," responded Zakhar to his cousin.

They tied up the horses and walked along the river. "Does he hear much from Mother Russia?" his cousin inquired.

"Very little, and news is slow."

"I could not help but notice your cigarette case. My suspicions are that the Czar's jeweler made that. The Czar liked to give them as gifts."

Zakhar pulled up. His cousin stopped and looked at Zakhar. "It is no secret, Zakhar, your father was respected by the Czar. You now hold his title of Count. The GPU bastards have infiltrated Europe. I overheard you say at dinner last night you have business here. Trust no one, my friend. Have eyes in the back of your head. Your life is in danger, and should you have any gold or jewels they deem belong to Russia, they will track you wherever you are." His cousin looked around. "They could be watching us now."

Zakhar arched an eyebrow and followed his cousin's eyes. He returned to look at his cousin expecting to see an indication of humor, but there was none. The conversation with his cousin rattled Zakhar. Even while in the hotel, he found himself looking over his shoulder and surveying his surroundings. When he neither spotted a suspicious someone nor felt threatened, he began to feel silly. Four days later, he went to the bank to remove some gold and jewelry from his father's vault. He could not carry all the gold pieces, so he took what he needed for his travels to America. He did not un-wrap the jewelry— opting to leave it in the disguise. There were papers in the vault, but he also left those behind.

Leaving the vault area, he entered the main lobby. A foreboding halted his movements, and he surveyed the expansive area, letting his eyes cross over a man standing off to the side who had eyes on Zakhar. Perhaps it was paranoia, but his cousin's warning slammed his mind. He pulled out his pocket watch as though waiting for someone. He edged toward the main entrance, and then walked out with another man as though an acquaintance. As soon as he exited, luck was with him as a horse-pulled cab was sitting near the entrance. He rushed and demanded the driver move. He peered out the back and saw the man from the bank sprint out and another man dash up to him. They were looking in his direction, but there was no transportation to pursue him.

He studied the driver, but nothing seemed untoward about the older man. He continued to watch as the cab rolled toward the hotel to make sure they were not being followed. When they arrived at the hotel, his eyes easily scanned the grounds. As he exited the coach, he was watchful and maintained that caution when he entered the hotel. Despite being jittery, he pretended nonchalance until he reached his room. Once there, he pulled his pistol and searched throughout to ensure no one was there or had rummaged through his belongings. After being convinced his room was secure, he sloshed vodka into a glass and sank into a chair. He was shaken. He plotted the safest way to return to Paris.

When he arrived in Paris, he cautiously approached his aunt's residence where he was staying. After a couple of days, he began to think he had overreacted at the Geneva bank. Then, one afternoon when he left to visit his uncle, he spied a man, who looked similar to the man in Geneva, leaning against a wall looking at him. As he turned to hail a nearby horse-drawn cab, he noticed the man straighten and quickly hail a cab. When his cab took a turn, Zakhar jumped from the cab and hid as it rolled on. Soon, the cab he had seen came rushing after his cab. From that point, Zakhar monitored his surroundings and avoided patterns of sameness in timing and routes when in public.

Elizabeth and her aunt had planned an elaborate wedding reception, so she was unrelenting as he protested such a large gathering. They retained more security. After the wedding, they left for an estate in southern France, but his wariness was ever present. One day, Elizabeth approached him. "Zakhar, time is growing close to when the Olympics start."

"Yes. I have been thinking that perhaps we should book our passage to America."

Her eyes widened. "Are you suggesting we not stay in Paris for the Olympics?"

"Yes. I do not think it is safe for us. The Bolshevik secret police will certainly be present at such an event."

Elizabeth pouted. "But I have been looking forward to the Olympics. American friends will be attending. They will wonder about our decision not to attend. They would not understand this concern of Russian secret police."

Zakhar understood she was young and naïve, but he had to impress upon her the seriousness. "Elizabeth, I forbid you to say anything to anyone about the GPU." When he saw her recoil, he softened his words. "I know you do not understand the way of things in Russia, but I was followed in Geneva and after I returned to Paris. The sooner we depart for America, the better."

"You did not tell me you were being followed," she replied—putting her hand to her mouth.

"I did not want to concern you."

"That is why you preferred a private wedding reception and were anxious in Paris."

"Yes."

She quieted. "Why are they following you? Is it because of who your father was?"

"Partly that is the reason, but they are following anyone who they believe has treasures belonging to Russia. They believe gold and jewels belonging to the imperial family were smuggled out of Russia. They are ruthless in their quest to follow members of the royal family whom they believe have such. They will kill them to obtain the gold and jewels."

"But why are they following you?"

"When I went to Switzerland, I went to a vault containing my father's belongings that I wanted to take with us to America. They have been following me since. They must think I have something of value that belongs to Russia."

Her eyes were wide. "Do you?"

Zakhar thought Elizabeth too young to tell her the truth about the jewelry. "No, but I have no control over what they think."

"Can you not tell them?"

Zakhar used restraint. "No. I do not want to get near these men who want to see me dead, and even if I told them I do not have anything they seek, they would not believe me."

"I suppose that is true," she said. "Is that why you have not been using your favorite cigarette case?"

"Yes. It was a gift from the Czar, but in the twisted and greedy ways they think, they believe it should be returned to their coffers." When she remained silent, he tried to entice her, "We can go to America and settle in your father's home. You yearn to see your Aunt Josephine. We can leave earlier to see her. You told me she lives in Cincinnati, Ohio?"

"Yes."

"I look forward to visiting Cincinnati and seeing your aunt and uncle again."

She was rethinking the importance of attending the Olympics. "I have started to think of home. Perhaps it is best we leave for America." He told her he would make the arrangements.

They soon departed for Paris. Once there, he visited the American embassy where he found all the papers in order. The staff assured him they would book first class accommodations on the next luxury ship sailing from

London for America. Unbeknown to Zakhar was that the GPU had a spy in the embassy—who learned of his plans for their transit and passed on the information to the Bolshevik revolutionaries located in Paris.

Zakhar requested that Elizabeth tell no one of their exact plans for departing Paris. All the while they made their way to London, he remained vigilant. Seeing no one following them, Zakhar had grown hopeful he had shaken the spies by the time they reached London. On the day their ship was to embark, first class was allowed to board first. Once they were shown to their suite, he slipped out and walked to a railing to watch people boarding. He scrutinized every male passenger. Shortly before the ramps were to be raised, he saw two men walking up the ramp. He stepped back in case one looked his way. He recognized one of the men as the one he had seen outside his Paris residence. "Dammit! How did they know? They are following us to America!" he said to himself. He consoled himself that they could not get near them in the first-class section of the ship. Once they got to America, he would have to find a way to lose, or kill, them.

Zakhar had changed after he began courting Elizabeth. After his father died, he knew his title fell to him, but he was lackadaisical about its formal use. As the nuptials were being planned, he insisted people refer to him using his title—Count. Being married to Elizabeth gave him access to tremendous wealth. He wanted people to recognize his influence and power. In that vein, Zakhar decided to open the package containing the jewels he had retrieved from the Swiss vault. When he opened it, he was awed by the opulence of the necklace. Certainly, he had witnessed the royals wearing breath-taking jewelry, but now, he possessed a piece commissioned by the Czar for the Empress. Unless the jeweler in Paris had given out details of this necklace, no one would know of its history. Out of caution for drawing the attention of Russia's secret police, he decided against allowing Elizabeth to wear it in public, but he saw no harm in her displaying it among their contemporaries—particularly in America. Indeed, in the confines of the ship's first-class accommodations, the Duke and Duchess and other royals and wealthy Americans traveling aboard would be impressed by its magnificence.

Watching the white-capped waves ripple as the luxury liner cruised toward New York, the spies contemplated their predicament. "So, you had no success with the maid?" Yegor Dobynin snapped as he exhaled smoke.

Sascha Krayevshy smirked, "Oh, I had lots of success."

"But not in the way that is important to our success," bit Yegor. "Why would she not give you the key? You claim to be a gift to women."

Sascha watched his cigarette butt float toward the waters below. "I am, but her man boss keeps all the keys and unlocks the room doors. We can't get into first class. It's locked down."

"What do we do? Kill him and get the keys?"

"Give me another cigarette."

"Het," Yegor snorted. "Get your own. You smoked more of mine than me."

"Relax, Yegor. We will think of something."

"Damn! We are stuck on this ship. I am thinking of killing that bastard next to us. He is too nosey."

"Then, we might be found out, and we cannot let that happen. We have no place to escape. Give me a cigarette. It helps me think."

Yegor swore and snarled, "Here, but this is the last one. Your plan better be a good one."

Sascha struck the match and enjoyed a couple of draws. "We will keep trying to find opportunities on the ship, but the Count does not know we are on the ship. When we dock in New York, we will follow them and find the right opportunity to detain him."

"He's in first class. They won't let us off this ship in time to follow him. Also, how do you know he will have any jewels or gold on him?"

"You think too much, Yegor. Even if he doesn't have any of the Czar's treasures or gold on him, he will tell us what he took from the vault and where to get it. It's simple."

Yegor spit over the railing. "You don't even know if he has jewels or gold belonging to the Czar. You convinced them to let us follow him just because you saw him go into the vault area."

Sascha exhaled. "Why else would a Romanov go into a Swiss vault? That is where they hid our country's treasures. He suspected me and ran, did he not? Yes, I know he is hiding something. Our reward will be nice, Yegor. You will be glad you listened to me."

Yegor flicked his cigarette butt over the railing. "I am not so sure. If we fail to find treasures through this Count, we will be killed if we return to Russia empty-handed. We will find ourselves being the hunted." He stomped away leaving Sascha to ponder their next moves.

Chapter 29

Kat had a restless night contemplating her life. She had married when she was eighteen and immediately got pregnant. Joey was now six years old, and she had been a single parent for four years. As soon as the divorce was final, her ex-husband remarried and moved out-of-state. He didn't care about seeing the boy and had told her as much. She was lonely and wanted a life. Her mother was of the old ways and did not understand.

When Andrian first started working at the depot, she tried flirting with him, but he wanted nothing to do with her outside of work, and even then, she felt most times he wished he could work alone. He would not even go out to lunch with her.

Then, a few weeks ago, Jeffrey knocked on the front door. She and her mother were sitting in the living room, and Joey was playing on the floor. He told them he was researching the Count who visited Bekbourg in the early 1900's. Someone at the library had told him of their family's Russian heritage and suggested he might talk with them. Kat had not read Cheryl's article, but her mother had. Kat was embarrassed by her mother that day. She would not speak a word and stared at him like he was a criminal.

He returned a couple of days later, asking about Kat's great-grandmother, whose parents had brought her over from Russia as an infant. He had obviously been researching their family. Her mother left the room and went to her bedroom—mortifying Kat.

Kat wanted to be helpful. She explained that she worked at the railroad and might be able to find something in their files. When he went to leave, she walked him out to the porch, and he asked if she would like to go to dinner sometime.

Kat took that as a sign he was interested. Her mother harped that he was after something—using her—but that seemed ridiculous because what could that be, she asked herself. She dismissed her mother's muttering as not wanting her to have a life.

They started dating and spending evenings in his motel room. When Andrian started work at the depot, she told Jeffrey about the new archivist who would be researching railroad history who might be helpful. He was pleased with the news and encouraged her to learn what she could from him about the Count. As time went on, he assured her that anything she learned from either Andrian or Cheryl and passed along to him would enable him to better assist the professor. Later, when the professor came to Bekbourg, Jeffrey explained that, because he and the professor were very busy, they sometimes found it difficult to find time to talk and update each other. He encouraged her to keep him informed if the professor and Andrian met.

But, the professor never came to the depot, and Andrian did not seem to be learning anything new. Cheryl had stopped coming by the depot, and Kat never heard Andrian talking on the phone with anyone about the Count. Kat came to realize that the less information she had to share with Jeffery, the less he wanted to spend time with her. Indeed, over the last couple of weeks, the only times he had been interested in talking with her was when she contacted him about the manifest and then today about the photos. Kat did not want to admit to her foolishness, but she could not help but think Jeffrey had used her to learn what others were learning about the Count.

How many times has Mama reminded me of her warnings against my low-life ex-husband? Oh, god! Mama already thinks I am foolish. If Jeffrey breaks it off, that will just reinforce her low opinion of me. I am such an idiot!

Kat threw back the covers and sat up and rubbed her face in agitation. Seeing four-fourteen on the clock felt like defeat—no chance she could go back to sleep. Her mother was an early riser, so Kat decided to leave her mother a note and go into the office. Her mother would see Joey off to school.

When she pulled up, Kat was surprised to see Andrian's small Ford Escort sitting in the parking lot next to the depot. She glanced at the building and did not see any lights. *Ha, bet some woman picked him up here, and they are together somewhere. Wonder who she is and where they are?* She was musing about what Andrian was doing as she inserted her key to unlock the door. She flipped on the lights and headed to the kitchen area to put on coffee. She then picked up her bag and headed into the main room where their desks were. As she walked toward her table, she glanced toward the side room and saw something unusual lying on the floor. Flutters started in her heart as a chill ran through her body. Her legs felt heavy, but she managed to inch forward until her worst fears materialized. Her piercing scream bounced around the walls as she fled out the door. She was gasping for breath as she yanked her phone from her jeans pocket and dialed 911. Through her panic, she conveyed to the dispatcher there was a bloody body lying on the floor at the depot. She screeched that no, she did not know if he was alive—she had not gone near the body.

The emergency personnel were quick to arrive. Andrian was unconscious but alive. Darrell Logan, the deputy on night shift, arrived soon after the EMS, and Sean was not far behind. Before they left with Andrian, the tech told Sean Andrian's vitals seemed strong, but they could not evaluate the extent of the head injury or possible internal injuries. Kat explained to Darrell, and then to Sean, about coming to work early and finding Andrian. The last time she had seen him was the previous afternoon when they both left work at the same time. She had no idea what he was doing there, and there were no surveillance cameras on the premises.

Darrell found a broken lock on a back door. Sean brought in a local forensics tech, but in the end, nothing of note was found to suggest the identity of the intruder. Kat was asked to look through the depot to see if anything looked suspicious. Nothing appeared out of the ordinary until she came to the room where Andrian had stored the boxes. She noticed the box in which Andrian had kept the photos was missing. Since Andrian's car was unlocked, Sean checked it, but the box was not in there.

Sean called C.P. and briefed him on the situation. C.P. was baffled why someone would have broken into the depot. "Do you know why Andrian would be here after hours?" Sean asked.

"No. Does it look like a fight, Sean, or do you think he surprised someone?"

"It's hard to say, but Kat said the lights were off when she arrived. There was no evidence that anything in the room was disturbed, so I don't think there was a scuffle or something like that. My guess is that he walked in on someone. Kat says a box is missing."

"What type of box?"

"She said there were photos in the box. They had to do with when the Count was in town. There were other papers, but she did not know what they were. She said Andrian had been particularly interested in the photos."

"I don't know anything about that. Do you think Cheryl might know?"

"That's a good point, C.P. I'll ask her." He turned as he heard a familiar voice. "Speaking of which, the owner of the newspaper just showed up."

C.P. chuckled, "Keep me posted. I'll check on Andrian and let you know what I find out."

Concern showed in Cheryl's eyes. "Andrian's in the hospital? What happened?" Milton arrived the same time as Cheryl and stood chewing gum with a pen and notepad.

Sean explained someone had attacked Andrian. He did not know the extent of his injuries, but Kat had found him when she arrived for work. It appeared whoever entered came through the back door—as its lock had been broken. Kat arrived to find the front door locked as it usually was in the morning. He told them a box containing pictures appeared to be missing. The pictures were taken on the day the train arrived in Bekbourg carrying the Count. "According to Kat, the box was there yesterday. I checked his car, and it's not there. Do you know anything about the pictures?"

Cheryl shook her head. "No."

"Any idea why someone might have taken it—if they did?"

She frowned and shook her head. "No. I didn't even know there were more pictures. The only one he showed me was of Elizabeth standing on the platform with the Schrievers the day the train departed for Cincinnati. I'll ask Kat about that. Is she doing okay?"

"She's calmed down, but she's still pretty jittery. If you find out anything you think I should know . . ."

She smiled. "I'll be sure and tell you."

Milton asked Sean a few more questions for the media report after Cheryl walked away to find Kat. Kat was pale as she sat in the kitchen, her fingers hugging a mug of coffee. "Hi, Kat. You doing okay? Anything I can do to help?" Cheryl asked as she sat down near her.

Kat shook her head. "It was awful walking in and seeing that. I hope he is going to be okay. I panicked." She shook her head. "I didn't even think to see if he was alive. I want to go to the hospital, but the sheriff asked me to hang around here for a while longer in case he has more questions. I guess C.P. will check on him."

"Sean said Andrian came back here sometime during the night. Do you know why?"

Kat frowned. "No, but I know he did that sometimes. When I came in some mornings, I could tell he had been going through those boxes. I might see a box on his table. Sometimes, there were more boxes that had been brought into the room. I would find some sitting on the floor near his table like they were ready to go to storage. I think he worked at night a lot. Maybe he had trouble sleeping. That's why I came in early this morning. I told the sheriff all this."

"The sheriff told me you thought a box was missing."

Kat hoped Cheryl could not read her mind. After she had time to get away from all the turmoil of finding Andrian and talking to the sheriff, after she was able to pour a cup of coffee and sit in the quiet of the kitchen, she began to think about how she had told Jeffrey just last evening about the box. She did not want to say anything about that conversation, because she had no proof that it was him who took the box. In fact, she could not even think of him breaking into the depot to take the box and bashing in Andrian's head. But, who would have done such a thing? *How odd was it that I had just told Jeffrey about it and now this?*

"Kat, are you okay?" Cheryl reached over and touched Kat's arm, bringing her back to the conversation.

"I'm sorry, Cheryl. I'm having a hard time concentrating. I didn't sleep well last night, and now this. I really don't know what's going on. All I can tell you is that the box he was looking through yesterday is missing. It's the box where he found the picture of Elizabeth and the Schrievers on the day the train was leaving. There were other pictures in there. When he was out of the office, I needed to stretch my legs, and I went over and opened it. There were a few other pictures with the one he gave you. I think it was the day the train arrived, because there was a lot of snow on the ground and still falling. It showed some passengers getting off the train and standing around, but the Count and his wife weren't in any of the pictures I saw."

"Okay. I appreciate you talking to me. If there is anything I can do, let me know."

"Thanks, Cheryl. As soon as the sheriff tells me I can go, I'm going to the hospital to check on Andrian. Then, I think I'll go home. I don't think I can get any work done today."

Chapter 30

As Cheryl and Milton walked back to the newspaper's office, she told Milton about the box of missing pictures. "What's interesting, Milton, is that I feel something has been off with Andrian. You remember how much he helped me on the story about the bridge collapse?"

"Yeah, I remember."

"It's different this time around. On this thing about the Count, it's like he is dragging his feet or disinterested. Which is odd given he sought me out for us to work together. I can't put my finger on it. But there's more. Something keeps eating at me. I can't shake the feeling that there is a connection between the man found buried in C.P.'s guest house and the Count staying there."

"Let's assume you're right. You've not really found much to go on. Any ideas about how you can break the logjam?"

"Yes. The trip to Cincinnati the other day didn't prove useful in finding anything about the Count, but hopefully my trip to Connecticut to talk with Elizabeth's granddaughter will yield some information—although she told me she didn't know much about him. She's not a descendant of the Count, because her mother, Elizabeth's daughter, was born four years after the Count died. But, it's a step."

"You know I'm a firm believer in running down rabbit holes. Let me know if I can help."

Chapter 31

Sean stopped by the hospital to talk to Andrian. Other than entering the depot and becoming suspicious after hearing a noise, he did not remember what happened. Andrian told Sean he was at the depot to work. He was a "night owl" and liked going in during the night for a couple of hours. He would then go home and get a few hours of sleep and return to the depot. C.P. had never stipulated the hours he worked as long as he was making progress and would meet the deadline for the museum's opening. Andrian told him he had no idea who would have been there. When Sean asked him about the missing box, at first, Andrian was confused. Once Sean described it, Andrian squinted. "How do you know it's missing?"

"Kat told us."

Sean noticed his frown. When Andrian did not respond, Sean asked, "Do you know why someone would want the box?"

Andrian started to shake his head and winced. "No."

"What was in the box?"

"Pictures and some old papers—things like time sheets, old receipts. I can't see what anyone would want with those—they were decades old."

"Anything about the pictures?"

Andrian was calculating his response. "Some had nothing to do with the Count being in town. There were a few taken the day the train arrived in Bekbourg: pictures of the train sitting there in the station with passengers milling around. Some showed porters helping passengers. There was also one on the day the train left Bekbourg with the Count's wife and the Schrievers."

"Nothing of particular interest about those pictures?" Sean asked.

Andrian paused. "I don't even know how anyone would know about them."

"You know of anyone who would want to harm you?"

"No. I barely know anyone in Bekbourg. I don't know. You think it was a homeless person who broke in, and I just happened to come in at the wrong time?"

Sean considered the question. "I don't know, but why would they take that particular box? Kat told me it was on the bottom of the pile."

Andrian closed his eyes. "I can't think of anything, Sheriff. If I do, I'll tell you."

Chapter 32

Kat went to the hospital, but she was unable to see Andrian. C.P. had been allowed to see him, but only briefly. Andrian had suffered a concussion, but he was going to be okay. Sutures had been necessary to close the wound's gash to his head.

She left the hospital, but the last place she wanted to go was home. She was shaken with what had happened to Andrian. She sat in her car in the hospital parking lot—leaning her head on her hand as her elbow rested on the door window. She could not dislodge the distrust that had bubbled up about Jeffrey. "Why in the hell would he want the box? Why would he be at the depot last night?" She kept running mental circles trying to convince herself that Jeffrey would not have done it, but she was unable to completely assuage her feelings.

Chapter 33

Kat dragged herself into the house. Joey came running and grabbed her legs in a hug. "Mama! You're home!" he squealed.

She leaned forward and hugged him as she fought back tears. "Hi, Buddy." The aroma from Pirozhki hit her. "Mmm. Babushka is baking our favorites."

"Yeah! I'm starving. When can we eat?"

Smiling, she took his hand. "Let's go see what your Babushka says."

"Hi, Mama. It smells good in here."

Her mother had been stoic her entire life and rarely displayed warmth—even though Kat knew she carried compassion. It was not surprising she did not acknowledge Kat's compliment. "Put plates on table. Joey hungry."

Kat's mother had been raised by parents who never conquered the English language, and despite being raised her entire life in Bekbourg, she still spoke broken English. Kat opened the cupboard and took out the place settings. She glanced at her mother and saw a woman who had worked hard her entire life. She had dropped out of high school at sixteen and married Kat's father. Kat's grandmother was widowed, so her parents moved into her grandmother's house—this house. Kat's father, now deceased, worked as a brick layer. In addition to running their household, Kat's mother baked pastries at the local bakery six mornings a week from four o'clock a.m. until nine o'clock a.m. for thirty years. When Kat's marriage fell apart, her mother quit her job to help out with Joey. She was a short, stout woman. Smiles were elusive, saved entirely for Joey, but then rare. It slammed Kat what a rock her mother was—had been. *God. I need her. Oh, Mama, I've made such a mess.* Kat wiped her eyes, which threatened to spill tears.

During dinner, Joey's lively chatter kept Kat distracted. Afterwards, he ran into the living room to watch a video. At Kat's insistence that her mother allow her to clean up, her mother sat and sipped her coffee while Kat tidied up the kitchen. Kat had never been able to hide things from her mother. "What happened?" her mother prompted.

Kat could not bring herself to admit how witless she had been to fall for Jeffrey. Kat finished drying the baking sheet and poured more coffee for her mother and then herself and sat down. "Something terrible happened at work." She proceeded to tell her about the break-in at the depot and what had happened to Andrian, but she avoided any mention of her suspicions about Jeffrey. "Andrian will be back to work soon."

Her mother stared into Kat's eyes. Kat hated when

she did that, because it made her feel her mother could read her mind. Kat sipped her coffee to avoid her mother's eyes. Finally, her mother asked, "The boss. What he do about this?"

Kat felt relief her mother did not pry outside her story. "C.P. has already had a new back door installed with stronger locks. He's also having more lights added in the front and back. He went to the hospital to see Andrian."

"He a good man."

"Yes, Mama, he is. The Pirozhki was delicious. Thank you."

Her mother raised her hand to dismiss the compliment. "Go bath Joey."

Kat stood and rinsed out her coffee cup and left. Her mother's eyes bore concern as they followed Kat from the room.

Chapter 34

Kat waited until her mother had gone to her bedroom and then grabbed her purse and keys and left. Her thoughts were so jumbled she thought her head would explode. She needed to know if Jeffrey was responsible for breaking into the depot. If he did bash Andrian over the head, maybe there was a good explanation. Maybe she was jumping to the wrong conclusions. She needed to give him a chance to explain. She had not lost hope he was innocent. That was her hope beyond hope. What she really wanted was to rekindle their relationship. Best case was that he was innocent. Even if he had done it, if there was a good explanation, she could see their working things out and getting back together. That's what she really wanted.

Little did she realize as she got out of her car to walk to his motel room that it would turn out to be the worse night of her life.

Chapter 35

Kat showed up at the depot the following morning hoping Andrian would come in. Fortunately, having been released yesterday afternoon, he did not have to spend a night in the hospital. Maybe that meant he would come in to work today. She *really* hoped so. Was she being dense to think he would be in today? All she knew was that she *really* needed to talk to him, *today*.

She was too distracted to get anything done, so she sat at her desk drinking coffee, staring into space and listening to the radio. The longer she sat there, the greater her burden felt. She suddenly heard the depot door open and reflexively tried to smooth down her hair where she had been running her hands through it all morning. She took a deep breath. "Oh, God, please let this go okay. Please don't let Andrian be too mad at me," she whispered. Only, she looked up to see an older gentleman enter. He was dressed in dress pants and dress shirt with a bow tie and a nice leather jacket. Shaking herself from this unexpected turn, she managed to speak. "Can I help you?" she asked as she turned down the radio. *He might be looking for C.P.*

He walked into the large room. "I'm sorry to disturb you. I have been meaning to stop by and introduce myself, but I'm afraid my timing is poor. I saw in the morning paper where there was a break-in and a young man was assaulted night before last. How is he doing, if I might ask?"

Kat was able to pull herself together enough to realize who he might be. "Are you the Russian professor?"

He smiled. "I see my reputation precedes me."

Kat had never met a professor, and she was in awe to be in the presence of such a successful person who traveled around the world meeting with important people. She put her hatred for Jeffrey aside to ingratiate herself with him. "It is nice to meet you, Professor. Andrian is not here today, but he should return soon. I was told he is going to be alright."

"I take it you work here?"

"Yes, I'm Kat Clark. I'm working on inventorying everything."

"I see. Are you okay from that terrible ordeal with Mr. Kray? These things can be most upsetting to people who know the victims."

She didn't want to release her emotions on a stranger, so she meekly answered, "Yes, I'm fine."

"Good. Good. Of course his recovery comes first, but when he is up to it, I'll plan to come back and talk with him."

"I'll leave him a message. Can I ask him to call you?"

"Thank you, but due to my schedule, I'll just plan on dropping by in a few days."

"Okay."

"I am glad you are here, though. I talked with a history professor at the local college, and she told me your family is Russian."

Kat nodded. "That's right. My great-great grandparents emigrated here from Russia."

"That's what she told me. When I heard that, I thought you or your mother might know some interesting stories about when the Count was here."

Kat frowned. "I guess Jeffrey didn't think to tell you that my mother didn't know anything."

"Pardon?"

"Oh, he came to our house in early September when he first started researching the Count. Not long after Ms. Seton published the article about the snow storm. Someone at the library told him about our ancestors being Russian. I got to know Jeffrey. When I found the passenger manifest, I gave him the copies."

Kat noticed Dimitri's surprise. "I'm sorry, Ms. Clark. Jeffrey and I have been going in different directions trying to learn what we can about the Count. I'm afraid he hasn't had time to update me. What is this about the manifest?"

At least I am able to focus on something else besides Jeffrey and Andrian, Kat thought as she turned her attention to assisting the professor. "I gave Jeffrey a copy of the manifest to give to you. I made a copy for you and for him. It showed the passengers who were on the train that got stranded here because of the snow storm—the one that the Count and his wife were on."

Dimitri paused. "I see. You are most generous to share your time in helping Jeffrey. Thank you for your assistance. Is there anything else you have found?"

"Not much." She told him about the picture of Elizabeth with the Schrievers but did not mention the box.

"Jeffrey and I have been remiss in keeping each other informed. I must say I am grateful for your efforts, which could prove beneficial in our research about the Count's time here. If it would not be inconvenient, would it be possible for me to get a copy of this passenger manifest and the picture?"

"I don't know what Andrian did with the picture, but I know where the manifest is. It's in another building. It will take a few minutes. I don't want to take your time. I would be glad to drop it off wherever you may be staying."

"That is most gracious. I am staying at the B&B downtown."

"I'll drop it in the mailbox on my way home."

"Thank you, Ms. Clark."

"Oh, I am glad to help."

Dimitri did not see a reason to speak with Andrian. If he needed more information, it seemed Kat was the source. Dimitri's thoughts now turned to his assistant. *Damn you, Jeffrey. You didn't think I would find out. I'm on to you, ole chap.*

After Dimitri left, the reprieve Dimitri's visit had brought Kat evaporated. Her legs felt heavy as she shuffled back to her chair and flopped her head back. "Please, please, please, Andrian. Just show up. I need to tell you what happened."

Chapter 36

Max greeted Sean. "Need a table for lunch or just here for a shot of java?"

"I'm meeting Cheryl for lunch, so a table would be good."

About that same time, C.P. walked in and spoke with Sean and Max, and then Cheryl followed about five minutes later and joined the men. Max pulled the lunch menus to seat Sean and Cheryl. Cheryl asked C.P. if he had lunch plans, and he decided to join them.

After they had placed their orders, Cheryl asked C.P. about Andrian. He told her he was planning to go back in to work this afternoon and was doing fine. "That was the damnedest thing, Sean. I still don't know why someone would have broken in. Anything new on the investigation?"

"No. We've interviewed people who work in your offices there, but they don't know anything. Alex talked to business owners in the area, but they don't have video cameras that show footage around the area. One of the tenants in an apartment over one of those retail stores was up and saw a car pass on the road below but could not give a description. She said it did not have its headlights on. Of course, the street lights would cast enough light to drive in that area."

"Well, I hope you find who did it. Hell, Andrian's just been with me a couple of months. He's a good employee. Don't want him quitting because he thinks it's not safe around here."

"How was it he ended up working for you?" Sean asked.

"He saw one of Cheryl's articles in the Cincinnati paper about my plans to start the scenic railroad and open the museum. He came here and applied."

"C.P., do you know anyone who would be behind these break-ins?"

C.P. looked a long time at Sean. Cheryl's watchful eyes flickered between the two men. Finally, C.P. responded. "You're wondering why my guest house was broken into and now the depot. No, Sean, I don't. I can't imagine what they were after in the guest house or the depot. If I thought this was directed at me, I sure as hell would tell you, but I can't think of a thing."

Sean nodded, but did not comment. C.P. turned to Cheryl, "Mary is plowing through the hotel—deciding what can be restored, preserved, discarded. She said she was going to give you a call. That's another story you might want to feature in your newspaper. It can include its history, its restoration, and—when time comes—its grand opening."

"Of course. It is a beautiful hotel with a colorful past." The three talked and finished their lunch. C.P.

excused himself to catch a flight later that evening. Sean offered to walk Cheryl to her office. "So nice to have my own lawman escort me," she teased.

Sean surveyed the few people who were strolling along the sidewalks in the downtown. "Have to protect the owner of the newspaper."

She laughed but asked the burning question: "You think the two break-ins have something to do with C.P.?"

"I don't know. People can do strange things. For example, if someone has something against him, they could be trying to intimidate him. I'm not sure C.P. had considered the possibility, but he might now that I've asked."

"I never considered C.P. could be the connection, but I'm not the brilliant Bekbourg County Sheriff." He grinned as she looped her arm through his. "I booked a flight this morning. I leave tomorrow to fly to Old Greenwich, Connecticut, to meet with Elizabeth Griffiths' granddaughter."

"That's some nice digs."

"I'm looking forward to seeing the area and also meeting with Libby—that's her name. Unless something comes up, I plan to be back late the next day."

They had reached the front door. They turned to face each other. "Buddy and I will miss you, but we'll hold down the fort."

She smiled. "I love you." She tip-toed and brushed a loving kiss on his lips.

His eyes shone. "I love you too, Honey."

Chapter 37

Kat finally shook out of her stupor and paced aimlessly around the depot—drinking coffee and trying to organize her thoughts for what to tell Andrian. Her nerves were on edge with the possibility he might not come in today. If not, she might call him and ask if she could stop by his apartment. She had to get the guilt off her chest. Her body was clammy, and her head hurt. He had told her time and again to mind her own business. God, she had to be convincing that she had not gone behind his back, that she thought C.P. had given the green light to both of them to share information with the professor and his assistant. Lunch time had passed, and she was beginning to think he was not going to come in this afternoon when she heard the door open.

She sucked in air when she saw the bandage around his head and dark circles around one eye. "God, Andrian, you look terrible. Are you sure you should be here?"

He went to his table and looked at the documents spread around. "Who's been going through my desk?" He looked accusingly at her.

"The police did. I guess they thought a clue might

be there. Maybe the prowler went through your desk."

He swore. "Yeah, I guess." He looked through the piles. "It doesn't look like they took anything."

"The police or the prowler?"

"Either."

"Well, that box that was sitting in the other room," she pointed to the room off their large working room, "is missing. I don't know if anyone has told you."

He walked to the opening and looked in. "Yeah, I remember the sheriff saying something about it." He entered the room and looked around, confirming that the box was missing.

Kat waited until he came back out. "Wonder what was so important in that box?"

He shrugged as he moved back to his table.

"I made some coffee about an hour ago. There's some left. Want me to pour you a cup? I can make another pot if you want fresh coffee."

He looked at her, "If you want to pour me a cup, I'd like one. Don't bother with a new pot."

Kat considered telling him about Dimitri dropping by earlier but decided against it. He obviously did not feel good, and she did not want him to leave before she got off her chest what she needed to tell him. She brought him a cup of coffee and backed up to lean against her desk. "Andrian, I've got something to tell you."

It went worse than she could have imagined. Andrian was livid that Jeffrey had clobbered him and stolen the box. After he stormed out the door, she sank into her chair with tears running down her cheeks. "Oh, God, what have I done? Why can't I ever think things through? Things can't get any worse."

Chapter 38

Kat had never felt so miserable in her entire life. She couldn't fathom the thought of going into work. If Andrian was there, she could not face him. She had moped around the house all day, fearful of what Jeffrey had done to Andrian and what he might do. She was feeling depleted knowing she had set in motion a chain of events that had left Andrian in the hospital, and then the confrontation with Andrian yesterday when she told him about Jeffrey having the box. Being cooped up in the house all day with her mother eyeing her like a caged animal had closed in on her. She couldn't bear being in the house and around her mother another moment, who was already suspicious she had made another bad choice.

She grabbed her purse and sped out, heading to Knucklepin's to get a drink and try and clear her head. She walked to the bar and ordered a beer. As she turned to look toward the room, the waitress whom she had seen leaving Jeffrey's motel room walked by. Kat could not believe that bitch worked here. The waitress clearly remembered seeing her with Jeffrey the couple of times they had been in Knuck's together, because she smirked at Kat as she walked by. Given all the other pressure she was experiencing, this was the final straw. Her balloon had been pricked. Her face reddened, and her chest tightened. Kat snarled loud enough for those around her to hear, "Bitch."

Not realizing Kat's state of mind, the waitress flipped back her hair to display a hickey on her neck. The waitress didn't see that a man sitting beside Kat grabbed her arm to stop her from going after the waitress.

The waitress had moved on by the time Kat jerked her arm free from the man's grip. Kat threw down some money on the bar and stormed out—sobbing in anger by the time she reached her car. What an idiot she had been to get taken by Jeffrey. Why could she not have seen it? Within minutes, her mother had seen through him. Now, Kat was the laughing stock. That bitch waitress had probably already told everyone who would listen. She grew more disgusted at herself and more furious at him for using her. And more fearful, if that was possible. *God, I hate that ass! He has ruined my life!*

She sat in her car for a long time—her mind in a fog of fury and despair. The car lights barely registered as customers continued to arrive at the bar. Suddenly, it dawned on her who stepped out of a car—Jeffrey! She slumped in her seat and waited for him to leave Knuck's—no matter how long it took.

Chapter 39

Jeffrey had not been returning his calls, so Dimitri stopped by his motel, then Frau's and finally Knucklepin's, where he saw him sitting at the bar sipping a beer. When Jeffrey saw the professor, his eyes widened. "I'm surprised to see you here, Dimitri. Are you meeting someone?"

Dimitri looked around the scantly-lit room filled with battered oak tables and chairs, and a bar lined with round bar stools. Dimitri suggested they move to a table sitting along the far wall. A waitress dropped off laminated menus. She took a drink order for Dimitri and offered to refresh Jeffrey's. Once she had moved on, Jeffrey tried to assess Dimitri's mood. "I saw where you called, but I was finishing up looking into Gregory Geisen's life here." Jeffrey did not know why Dimitri had asked him to research Geisen. The only connection he could see was that he had attended several of the events with the Count. Dimitri had explained he was trying to get a fuller picture of the Count's time in Bekbourg and those he hung around with, but Jeffrey wondered if there was another reason.

Dimitri's eyes were dark. "Have you learned anything?"

Jeffrey took a swig from his beer. "Yeah, I guess you wanted to know the source of his wealth. In 1909, he founded the G.E. Geisen Paper Products, which made him a very wealthy man. The library has countless rolls of microfiche on him. I scanned enough to see that he was highly regarded here. The paper company passed out of the Geisen family several years back. While I was at it, I researched Harry Schriever. He started the milk company before the turn of the century. Didn't find anything nefarious about him either, if that's what you were looking for."

The waitress brought the drinks, but neither man was ready to order.

Dimitri narrowed his eyes with the thought Jeffrey was looking into Schriever. "Any other research you're doing, Jeffrey, and haven't told me about?"

Jeffrey set his glass down and looked hard at Dimitri, "What's that supposed to mean?"

"Jeffrey, Jeffrey. You are not as smart as you think you are. Did you think I wouldn't find out that you came here checking into the Count soon after the article was published? You intentionally hid the article from me while you secretly started your own inquiry."

"You're misinterpreting things, Dimitri. When I came across the article, I figured you'd want to know more about it, so I got a head start while you were in Europe. I thought I had put the article where you would find it with a note I was already working on it. I didn't say anything, because I thought you saw it when you got back and had no issues with me researching for you."

"There was no note, Jeffrey."

"I thought I put one on it."

Dimitri did not believe him. "What's your excuse for failing to give me the manifest or the photograph of Elizabeth with the Schrievers?" Dimitri's look hardened when he saw surprise register on Jeffrey's face. "I've figured you out, ole chap, and it's not going to work," Dimitri sneered.

The waitress, who had approached the table to take their order, veered away when Jeffrey jerked closer toward Dimitri—causing his beer to slosh and the plastic salt and pepper shakers to wobble. The dam within Jeffrey finally broke. "I'll tell you what's going to work, *ole chap*. A partnership—fifty/fifty, or I'll see to it that your reputation is *ruined*."

Dimitri looked around. "Keep your voice down, you fool. Had I not picked you up out of the gutter, you'd be there to this day. You try smearing my name, I'll bury you so deep, you'll never see the light of day. You're fired. I want you off my property by the end of this week, and I don't ever want to hear from you again."

Jeffrey snarled, "You're an ass, Dimitri. You don't fool me, and this time, you're going to pay."

Dimitri stood and walked away, leaving Jeffrey to pay for his drink.

Jeffrey was deep in thought when the waitress he

had been seeing walked up. "Sug, you decide on what you want to eat?"

Jeffrey was curt. "I don't want anything."

The waitress looked around. "That's shitty that man left you holding the bill."

Jeffrey seemed to pull out of his haze. "It's okay. He owes a lot more, but he's going to pay up soon."

She pouted her lower lip. "He's not very friendly."

Jeffrey did not respond but started to pull out his wallet.

"I get off at nine. You want me to come by your motel?" she winked. "I'll make you forget all about that creep."

Jeffrey handed her money for the drinks. "Can't tonight. Got some work I've got to do."

"Rain check then?"

"Yeah, rain check."

Chapter 40

Sean returned from taking Buddy for his last walk of the night and settled in his chair with a beer. He picked up a crime novel he was about a third of the way through. Before he focused on the book, he noticed the unwelcomed silence. Cheryl had brought a light into his life—bright with love and joy. From the first time he met her, he admired her energy and curiosity as well as her dedication to her profession and compassion for others. He reached his hand down to rub Buddy. "She'll be home tomorrow night. Tonight, it's just you and me, boy." Sean gave Buddy another pat and opened the book.

About twenty minutes later, his phone rang. It was Dispatch telling him someone had been shot in Highland Heights.

When he arrived at the scene minutes later, Sean was met by his deputy, Darrell. Medics were working with a man Sean did not recognize, who was lying near the sidewalk. It was about eleven-thirty, but a few people from the neighborhood had started gathering. Alex and Creed, another deputy on night-shift, were on their way to the scene. Sean instructed Darrell to push the bystanders back and ask for witness statements.

The medics were working with the man, but he appeared to be in serious condition from bullet wounds to his chest. Sean surveyed his surroundings. The most notable thing was that the man was lying near the iron fence encircling C.P.'s property—toward the back where the guest house was located. All the interior lights in both the main house and guest house were off, but outside lights from the main house and street lamps cast faint light around the area. Typical for the area, cars were parked along the street.

One of the medics spoke up and told Sean they were going to put the man in the ambulance and take him to the hospital. He handed Sean the wallet and whispered to Sean he was not sure the man was going to make it to the hospital. Sean opened the wallet and found a driver's license with a Cincinnati address. Jeffrey Blankenship. Sean pulled out his phone. He did not want to call Cheryl and likely wake her up, because she had a long day tomorrow in Connecticut. He dialed Bri, who was still awake. She confirmed Jeffrey was the professor's assistant.

"What's going on, Sean?" she asked.

"Is the professor there?" he asked.

While Max went to the professor's room to get him, Sean explained what had happened.

"Oh, my gosh!" exclaimed Bri. "What is happening? Andrian was assaulted and now this." Just then, Max told her the professor was not in his room. At Sean's request, he went to see if his car was there. "Bri, do you know where Dimitri might be?"

"No. Wait, Sean. Max said his car is not here either. We don't know where he is."

Sean took down Dimitri's number and told them if he came in, to call him. Fortunately, Bri knew the motel where Jeffrey was staying.

By then, Alex and Creed had arrived, and Creed was roping off the area. Alex went to assist Darrell in questioning bystanders and neighbors.

Under normal circumstances, Sean would have asked the local forensics team to investigate the scene, but his instinct told him something else was going on—*why near the guest house? Why on a night when C.P. is gone?* Sean called for assistance from Ronnie Vin's forensics team. If this turned into a murder, which—based on the preliminary reports from the medics—appeared probable, he wanted a thorough search of the scene.

Alex approached Sean with a middle-aged man. Sean knew the man, who lived two houses up the street. He told Sean he heard three or four gunshots and rushed to look out the window. He could not see anything, so he grabbed on his robe and went downstairs. By the time he got there, he saw a small dark car with no lights speeding away.

About two hours had passed, and Sean was still waiting for Ronnie Vin's team to show up when he got a call that Jeffrey had died. He left Alex in charge of the scene to direct Ronnie's team when it arrived and asked Creed to go with him to the hotel where Jeffrey had been staying.

"Man, I can't believe it," the motel night attendant told Sean as he walked him to unlock Jeffrey's motel room door.

Sean instructed him to wait outside as he and Creed put covers over their boots and slipped on gloves and went into Jeffrey's room. Nothing looked out of the ordinary. The bed was still made, but the cover was rumpled—like someone had been sitting on it after the housekeeper had made the bed earlier in the day. Sean made a note to ask when the maid had last cleaned. Sean saw a box scooted against the wall. On closer inspection, he noticed a similarity to the boxes he had seen in the side room at the depot. He carefully lifted the top and saw an envelope with pictures and other loose photos along with papers. "What is Jeffrey doing with the box?" he wondered. Nothing in the bathroom looked out of order.

After his quick search, Sean asked Creed to seal off the room until the forensics team could analyze everything—particularly the box. He talked to the night manager. He learned that Jeffrey had first checked into the motel around the first of September and then two more times before this last time around the middle of October. He didn't know much about Jeffrey's schedule or visitors, other than he had never had any complaints. The night shift maid had already left, so they would have to wait to talk to her.

Sean walked back to the office with him so he could make copies of all the records of Jeffrey's stays, including names of the maids and other motel employees. In particular, Sean wanted to know which maids had cleaned Jeffrey's room. Sean also told the night manager to keep records of all guests during Jeffrey's stays in case they needed to talk to them.

Chapter 41

After leaving the motel, Sean returned to C.P.'s to find the forensics team was on the scene and Alex was waiting to update him. "Sheriff, forensics discovered a window pane on the back side of the guest house broken out."

"I'll make sure to ask Cole if it was already broken."

"Another thing. Darrell found the victim's car up the street. Want us to impound it?"

"We need forensics to look through it. Coordinate with them to see if they want to take it to Columbus or use our site." Sean looked around. The sun was not ready to rise. "I need to call C.P. and tell him that Cole needs to halt work again. I'll call Cole and tell him myself. You and I both need to get some sleep. I'll leave a message for Kim to tell Syd and Arlo I want to have a meeting at ten o'clock."

"What about talking to the professor? Does he know yet?"

"Yeah, I was able to reach him and told him Jeffrey was dead and that we needed to talk to him. He said he was in Cincinnati and had driven there late last evening, that he had some things that needed handling. He's going to drive back today so we can talk.

"What was his reaction?"

"It sounded like I woke him—as it was the middle of the night. He seemed surprised. Wanted to know what had happened, but I told him I didn't want to go into the details over the phone. I also asked if he knew the next of kin we could notify, and he's going to bring that."

"Was that usual for him to go back to Cincinnati?" asked Alex.

"I have the same question. I'm going to talk with Bri this morning and ask her."

After a couple hours of sleep, Sean touched based with Cole and called C.P. to update him. He also called Lucky. On his way to the station, he stopped by the city building to talk with Bri. Sean confirmed that Dimitri and Jeffrey had checked into their respective lodgings the same day in October. Bri told Sean she had seen Jeffrey once at the B&B but would ask Max and her housekeeper if they had seen him more often.

"Was Dimitri at the B&B a lot?"

"I can't say a lot. He was usually gone throughout the day or either in his room. He walked around town almost every day he said for exercise. Most evenings, he had dinner at the B&B. He just came and went."

In response to Sean's question, Bri told him that a week before, Dimitri had made a quick trip out of town for two nights and did not bother to check out.

"That was the longest time he was away. At the end of the first week, he went back to Cincinnati for a night."

"When he was gone for the two nights, did he say where he was going?"

"No, but he was flying because he was driving to Columbus to catch a flight."

As Sean started to leave, she asked, "Does C.P. know?"

"Yeah, I called him right before I headed here."

"What did he have to say?"

"He said he never believed in poltergeists but maybe should rethink that about the guest house."

Bri laughed and gave Sean a scone from a box she had brought for the employees.

Sean went into the squad room where he found Arlo, Syd and Alex waiting. Alex had already briefed Arlo and Syd on what had happened. Sean began the meeting by telling them that the guest house had been broken into—that Cole said the window was not broken when they left yesterday afternoon.

Arlo spoke up. "That's the second break-in at C.P.'s guest house. Assuming Blankenship broke into the house last night, do you think he broke in the first time?"

Syd added, "Before C.P. bought the place, it sat empty for a few years. We don't have reports of any break-ins there. Within a little over two weeks, there've been two break-ins. What's so special about the guest house?"

"Does the professor know why his assistant might

have been breaking into the guest house?" Arlo asked.

"These are all good questions," said Sean. "I'm going to talk to the professor this afternoon when he gets back from Cincinnati. Syd, I want you to drive over to Cincinnati and check out the professor's alibi. He said he drove over late yesterday evening to stay at his house. Also, Blankenship lived in a garage apartment on the property. Check that out, too. I've already contacted the local police, and they were going to secure the garage area."

She nodded.

"So, we've got one person of interest. Arlo, maybe you ought to take some notes on your magic white board," Alex suggested.

Syd groaned.

Arlo was the showman of the group. "Right-O! Great minds think alike," he saluted as he headed toward the extra large whiteboard. Syd rolled her eyes, and Alex hid a grin.

Alex wrote at the top: "Mystery of the Guest House." Syd, the reserved and serious deputy, shook her head.

"Okey dokey. Syd, you're the brains. Sorry, Chief—I mean except for you." Sean just looked at Arlo, "So, Syd. When did the first break-in occur?"

Arlo wrote the date of each break-in. "Now, what's the connection?"

When no one immediately answered, Alex offered, "What about the body found buried there?"

Sean enjoyed these sessions. His deputies were

intuitive, smart and dedicated. He had found that these discussions helped bring their investigations into clearer focus. While he had already considered that the dead body might be a connection, he was glad to see they were considering that as well.

Arlo made a note. Sean's deputies had asked several of the older people around town who might know something about tales passed down about the Count's visit in town. While some had heard stories, nothing proved useful in identifying the victim found in the guest house's basement. The police files and the *Tribune's* files had not shed light on missing persons during that time that would have fit the description.

"The FBI thought the body might be Russian," said Syd. "Wasn't Jeffrey assisting the professor in learning about the Count, who was Russian?"

Arlo and Alex looked at Syd. It was Arlo who spoke. "Now I know why the Chief keeps you. Good point." He made note of her observation.

Alex's shoulders shook in silent laughter while Syd ignored Arlo.

"What about the break-in at the depot? The box that was stolen was in Blankenship's motel room. How does that fit in—if it does?" asked Alex.

Silence filled the room. Arlo added that question to the board.

"Why did he have the box?" asked Syd.

"I don't know. Once forensics completes their analysis, I'm going to look through it," Sean said.

Arlo wrote on the board and spoke at the same time. "We know there was a small black car seen driving away without lights right after the shots were fired. We need to find out who that car belongs to."

The deputies got quiet when Sean pulled out his phone and placed a call. After he disconnected with Bri, he told them Dimitri drove a two year old black Toyota Corolla.

"That's a small black car," noted Alex.

"You have any reason to suspect the professor killed his assistant?" asked Arlo.

"I'm not ruling anyone out, but, for now, he's the only one who comes to mind. He had an association with Blankenship. Alex, when Dimitri gets back here, I want you and I to talk to him. In the meantime, I want you to canvas the area—knocking on all the doors—and see if anyone knows anything. I know you and Darrell talked to some witnesses, but we need to check with them again and talk to others."

Alex nodded.

"Arlo, I need for you to talk to the motel's day manager—as well as the day and night-shift maids and other employees. Also, check with guests who were there the last time Blankenship checked in."

"Will do, Chief."

"Okay. Everyone, keep me posted on what you learn."

Chapter 42

Dimitri called Sean when he arrived back at the B&B and agreed to come to the station.

Kim had already shown Dimitri to the conference room and brought him a mug of hot water for his tea bag when Sean and Alex came into the room. "What happened to Jeffrey?" Dimitri demanded. "You said he was dead. How?"

"I need to ask you some questions, Dimitri."

He pulled himself together. "Of course. Pardon my behavior. I can't believe he is dead. He's been my research assistant for over twenty-five years."

Dimitri gave Sean contact information for Jeffrey's next of kin.

"Professor Shlykov, what can you tell us about Jeffrey Blankenship?"

Dimitri explained how he had been in the graduate program and worked as a teaching assistant but also assisted Dimitri in his research for extra money. Dimitri had come to rely on Jeffrey's research skills and offered him a job after graduation. He was not sure how long Jeffrey would stay—as he might explore a doctoral program or decide on something else. Time went on; the working arrangement worked for them both; and Jeffrey stayed on.

In answer to Sean's question about how they had become interested in the Count, he explained how the Cincinnati newspaper had published Cheryl's article about the Count and his wife being delayed in Bekbourg. He was in Europe on a consulting engagement and was not aware of the article until he returned. Naturally, he was fascinated to learn of a member of the royal family having been here. He had come across the name of Count Zakhar Voskoboynikov, but only as a member of the Romanov family, so he had never researched him or his linage. Thus, he came to Bekbourg to see what he could learn. "As you can imagine, this was a momentous find. Jeffrey, who has excellent research skills and had already accumulated a vast amount of knowledge through his research for me on other Russian topics, was here to assist in finding out whatever we could."

"Did you know about the break-in at the train depot and the assault on Andrian?"

"Yes. I did hear about that. I understand that Mr. Kray is doing okay?"

"Yes. He is back to work."

"Good. Good to hear."

"Did you know that a box was taken that night from the depot?"

Dimitri looked puzzled. "No, I had not heard that. You think whoever broke in that night also stole a box?"

"Do you know why Jeffrey would have wanted the box?"

"Jeffrey?" Dimitri puckered his lips. "I am lost, Sean."

"We found the box that was reported missing the night of the break-in in his motel room."

Dimitri rubbed his goatee in confusion. "Why on earth would he have that box in his motel room?"

"That's what we were hoping you could help us with?"

Both Dimitri's eyebrows arched. "I can assure you I don't know anything about it. He never said anything to me about a box. What was in it?"

"I've not had a chance to review the contents, but once forensics completes their inspection, I'll look through it." Sean watched Dimitri closely. "There was an assortment of old documents and some photos."

"Photos?" He thought for a moment. "Again, I don't know anything about this, but I would be glad to look at them and see if I notice anything."

"You don't know why someone might have killed him?"

"Of course not. The box that contained these photos was still in his motel room?"

"Yes, so we don't know if there was a connection or not between his death and the documents. Again, we will know more once the lab results come back, but it appears he had broken into the guest house. Any ideas about why he may have been there?"

The professor shook his head. "This does not sound like the Jeffrey I know. I cannot help you on that one either."

"Cheryl's article appeared in the Cincinnati paper the third week of August. You didn't check in the B&B until about two months later. Why so long?" Sean wanted to see if his answer had changed from his response at the GilHaus.

"Well, I didn't get back to the States until the first of October and, as you can imagine, a great deal of correspondence and research and other things were waiting for me that Jeffrey had organized. It was about two weeks later when I came across the article. Naturally, I immediately made arrangements to come meet with Cheryl."

"Did you know that Jeffrey had already been here before that?"

Sean noticed Dimitri's jaw clinch. "He knew I couldn't extricate myself from my commitment, and the story was remarkable. He decided to get the ball rolling on researching the Count's stay here."

"Did Jeffrey tell you he was researching the Count before you returned from Europe?"

"No. I think he knew the whole notion of a Russian royal member being here would distract me from the important work I had going on."

"When did you learn that Jeffrey was working on the project?"

"I can't say exactly, but he had found some useful information about the Count's life leading up to the revolution."

It did not go unnoticed that Dimitri was vague about this. Sean thought it odd Jeffrey did not put the article where Dimitri would see it first thing upon his return from Europe. Even more curious, since Jeffrey had already been to Bekbourg, why did he not tell Dimitri immediately after his return that he had started work on the new project? During the dinner at the GilHaus, Dimitri said that Jeffrey did not start new projects without conferring with him. What did Dimitri think when he discovered Jeffrey had been conducting the research but had failed to tell him? There were more questions to ask about this at a later time.

"But Jeffrey did not mention the box or pictures?"

"No."

"What time did you leave to drive back to Cincinnati?"

"It was late. I don't remember the exact time."

"Why did you go?"

Dimitri smiled. "I needed to do some laundry and change out some clothes, for one thing. I also wanted to pick up some research about a project I have accepted after the first of the year in Denmark. I've been working on it too while I am here."

"When was the last time you saw or spoke with Jeffrey?"

Dimitri tilted his head. "Surely you don't suspect me?"

"We're just trying to get a picture and timeline of things."

"I'm sorry, Sean. I'm upset about all of this. I met Jeffrey for a quick dinner at Knucklepin's last night. I wanted to touch base on where he stood on some research he was doing before I left town. It was already dark outside, but I don't remember the time—not even a ball-park guess. I'm not one of those people who pay much attention to the time."

Sean nodded. "We appreciate you coming in. We know it must be hard. Twenty-five years is a long time to work together."

"Thank you. The grief is hard. It's like my right arm is missing."

Sean and Alex stood. "If you like, I'd be glad to take his things from the motel room and his computer. There likely is research about the Count that would be important to me."

"We need to complete our investigation before we release anything."

"Of course. And, if you want me to look through the photos to see if there is anything of interest, I am volunteering my services."

"I appreciate that, Professor. I may circle back to you on your offer."

"Excellent."

Chapter 43

Cheryl could not help whispering words of aston-
ishment at the enormous homes lining her route to Libby
Ellsworth's home. Even in the grips of November, there
was a majestic beauty in the estates in Old Greenwich.
Located in Connecticut's Gold Coast, these grand homes
bore witness to old money, and new money as well.
Cheryl slowly drove a path winding along the Long
Island Sound until she came to the address she was looking for. She pulled into the circular driveway and admired
the stately two story white brick home. The two-story
portico was centered in the front and supported by round
columns. Off to the right side was an equally tall turret.
Black shutters bordered all the windows. Two chimneys
were in view. Symmetrical medium-height shrubs lined
the house's front, and taller manicured evergreens offset
the house's end opposite the turret. The estate spoke of
understated grandeur.

A drive off the circular driveway led to a garage
around back. She parked her rental and approached the
house. A housekeeper answered the door and politely
invited her in. Gleaming dark wood floors stretched the

length of the foyer and hallway beyond. A round table with a large vase of fresh cut flowers was centered in the foyer. She was escorted into a spacious sitting room that doubled as an office. A timeless elegance surrounded Cheryl. A fire sparked in the fireplace and warmed her from the outside chill and dampness. The long draperies were pulled off the windows to provide clear views of the outside. Framed family portraits were prominent on the walls and bookshelves. Cheryl's attention was directed to a wall holding an ornate gold frame that encased a large canvas painting of a striking couple.

The housekeeper had just offered something to drink when Libby entered the room. She was dressed in black wool slacks, matching blazer and a medium gray turtleneck sweater. She was not quite as tall as Cheryl's five-feet, ten inches. Her straight dark brown hair hung to almost her shoulders and was parted in the middle. She was attractive and did not wear makeup. Cheryl estimated she was in her sixties.

Over the phone, Cheryl had briefly explained she was a reporter who lived in Bekbourg and was working on a story about Libby's grandmother, Elizabeth, and the Count. Cheryl was surprised, but pleased, when Libby had readily agreed to meet her.

They chatted a few minutes, and then Libby turned to the purpose of Cheryl's trip. "After we talked, I looked Bekbourg up on the map. It is a very small city." She paused to sip her coffee. "I have rarely been asked about him until recently. You are the fourth person in the last two months to call me about the Count, so I am curious why the sudden interest. None of the men were very forthcoming about what was going on. That is why I wanted to talk to you—I thought you might be willing to tell me more."

Cheryl's surprise was obvious, because Libby tilted her head. "I take it you are not aware of other people reaching out to me?"

"No. The story was only carried in the Bekbourg and Cincinnati newspapers. Do you mind telling me who contacted you?"

"For starters, an FBI agent."

"The FBI?" Cheryl's brows arched.

"Yes. He was polite but cryptic. What I told him I ended up telling the other two men. I don't know much at all about the Count. My grandmother never discussed him with me, and very little with my mother. What I knew was they married in France, came to the U.S. to live, and were married less than a year when he died of pneumonia. He is buried in our family plot in Newport, Rhode Island. I don't even know how he fit into the Romanov family."

Cheryl found it odd the FBI was interested in the Count. "Surely, the FBI could have looked up his history."

"Well, I think the FBI agent had, because he didn't seem surprised."

"Well then, why call you?"

Libby sipped her coffee. "I think the main purpose of his call was to find out if the Count had given Grandmother anything of value. I didn't know of anything. He specifically asked about jewelry. There isn't any jewelry. I would have known if there was. My mother would have known. There isn't any, and I told him that. I haven't heard back from him. He wouldn't tell me why he was asking."

"That's very interesting."

"I thought so. Then, a couple of weeks later, a man who said he was doing research for a university professor who specialized in Russian history called. I can't remember his name. I was at our home in Sarasota when he called. He asked about the Count, and I told him what I told the FBI. He didn't ask about valuables or jewelry, but then the third caller did. It was a professor. I wrote his name down." She picked up a slip of paper. "Dr. Dimitri Shlykov. He was the only one who told me anything about the Count. He explained the Count was a distant cousin to the Czar, and he got out of Russia before the Revolution and went to France. His mother was part of the French royal family. The Count had two older sisters. One was in London when the Bolsheviks took over, and the other was married to a member of the royal family and did not escape Russia in time."

"Did the professor ask about the jewelry?"

"Yes, and I told him the same thing as I had the FBI. I didn't know what was going on, so I never mentioned to the research assistant or the professor I had talked to the FBI. I was still in Sarasota when the professor called, and had mostly dismissed it from my mind until you called.

I thought it was time to learn what this is all about."

Like Libby, Cheryl was puzzled. "I wonder if anyone checked with the family line of the Count's sister or mother to see if they had anything of value."

Libby smiled. "I'm glad you asked, because I asked the professor that very question. He said if anything was in Europe it would likely have surfaced by now. I don't know if that's true, but I could tell he wasn't interested in talking about that possibility."

She looked at Cheryl. "You must have an idea about what this is about, because you're here to discuss the Count."

"This is baffling to me. I came here to learn about your grandmother and the Count. Like I told you on the phone, I came across some articles written when they visited Bekbourg in 1925, and I published a story based on those five articles. Since then, I have become more interested in them. That's why I'm here. I don't know anything about Russian valuables or jewelry."

"I see." Libby's shoulders slightly slumped in disappointment. She poured them more coffee.

Cheryl stiffened her back. "I wonder if that is why Dimitri and his assistant are in Bekbourg?"

"What do you mean?"

She explained how they had shown up after reading her story. "Dimitri told me he was there to learn about the Count, but I wonder if there is more to his story. I wonder if he thinks he can find out something in Bekbourg about valuables or jewelry. But why Bekbourg?"

"Do you have a copy of your article?"

Cheryl pulled out a copy. "This is it. I brought it for you."

Libby's eyes went straight to the Count's face. "This is the first picture I have ever seen of him."

She stared at it before turning her eyes on her grandmother's picture. "Grandmother looks so young. She never was much for smiling."

She suddenly looked up at Cheryl. "Look at this necklace! The stone is huge. It looks like a sapphire, although it's hard to say since this is in black and white."

Cheryl and Libby found themselves staring at what looked like something in a royal jewelry collection. "Do you think this is what they were asking about?" Libby asked Cheryl.

"She was wearing this in Bekbourg. Oh, my gosh. But why would they think it has anything to do with Bekbourg?" she asked aloud. Both women continued looking at each other as their minds tried to reason though the quagmire.

Libby snapped her eyes back to the picture. "I wonder if this is the jewelry Grandmother was talking about."

Cheryl frowned. "When was this?"

"The last time Grandmother and I were in London, she was quite elderly. There was a special exhibition at the Jewel House, and she wanted to go. As we were touring the collection, she stopped in front of a glass case containing an exquisite sapphire. Grandmother was not the sentimental type, but something about it was mesmerizing. I thought something was wrong, because she stood looking at it so long. I asked her if she was okay, and it was the most she ever said to me about the Count. She told me the Count had let her wear jewelry like that on the ship coming over, but once they were in the U.S., she had only gotten to wear it twice. Once to a small dinner party she hosted at the home in Rhode Island when a U.S. Senator was one of their guests. This must have been the second time," she said pointing to the picture. "She only told me it was at a soiree. She was vague, but she never saw it again and never knew what happened to it."

Cheryl's face pulled tight. "Cheryl, is something wrong?"

Cheryl told her she did not know if there was any connection, and then she told her about the remains found in the guest house.

Libby brought her fingers to her lips. "How on earth could that be connected? There wasn't any jewelry found with the body, was there?"

"No. I don't know if there is a connection, but my husband is the sheriff. When I get back, I'm going to ask him and see what he thinks."

Cheryl pulled out the five articles and handed them to Libby. Libby read all of them while Cheryl sipped her coffee.

She smiled. "This sounds so much like the times. Grandmother was taught her role from her childhood, and that was to be the wife of a man in the upper rungs of the social elite." As they talked, camaraderie grew between the two women. Cheryl asked what her grandmother was like. Libby explained a woman who took her role in society seriously. She was a perfect helpmate to her husband and instilled order and responsibilities in her children. "Grandmother was smart, and Grandfather recognized her business sense. Later in life when he grew ill, he relied on her to oversee his business operations."

Cheryl inclined her head toward the large portrait on the wall. "That is a fabulous painting. Is that of Elizabeth?"

Libby did not need to look. "Yes, those are my grandparents. They were in their forties when it was painted."

Elizabeth was unsmiling and stood with an air of confidence. "She was young when she married the Count." Cheryl reflected, "That took confidence and, given what was happening in Russian at the time, courage. Members of the Romanov family were targets of the Russian secret police."

"She was young," Libby agreed. "I guess marrying into Russian royalty was grandiose among her friends and society, but I'm not so sure she would have chosen it for herself. What little I know about the situation, it was her father who wanted her to marry into a royal title. I supposed the novelty to both them, her being married to a Russian Count and him having an heiress wife, worked for the times, but it wasn't about love."

"Do you know where they met?"

"In Paris. My great-grandfather made his fortune in textiles. He owned a huge estate in Newport, Rhode Island, which is where Grandmother grew up. But, he built this house, and this is where she loved to spend her time. Her father died suddenly, and her mother had died when she was young. His sister became Grandmother's guardian and wanted her to fulfill her dad's wishes. They got married in Europe and came to the states to live. They arrived at the family home in Newport sometime in the summer and spent the summer and fall. Grandmother was very close to her aunt, who lived with her husband in Cincinnati. His health was not good, so Grandmother and the Count decided to travel there to spend time with them after the holidays."

"Did she ever talk to you about their time in Bekbourg?"

Libby thought while she took a sip. "I don't remember her ever mentioning Bekbourg. Except for that about the jewelry, Grandmother never talked to me about her life with the Count at all. She told Mother a few things. One of them was that she and the Count had taken the train to see her aunt and uncle in Cincinnati and that he died after that and was buried in our family plot. The other was the Count wanted to live at the home in Newport because it had more security, although she would have preferred here."

"They must have lived a fairly quiet life. I went to Cincinnati to see what I could find about their time there after they left Bekbourg. I reviewed the microfiche of the two major newspapers at the time and could find nothing. I was surprised to find more written about them in the Bekbourg newspaper than in Cincinnati's papers. There was no mention of their arrival in Cincinnati or even mention of any social engagements. To be honest, there wasn't much about Elizabeth's aunt and uncle either. There were some articles about her serving on Boards for charities and fine arts. His name occasionally appeared in regards to the bank he owned."

"Mmm." Cheryl could tell Libby was thinking about something as she sipped her coffee. She looked at Cheryl. "Do you have time to look at something?"

"Yes."

"There is a box in the attic that, to my knowledge, has never been opened by anyone. Mother showed it to me when we were looking through all the things stored up there. She said Grandmother had packed it up after the Count died and never opened it again. It contained things of their life together. I have no idea what's in it. I don't think Mother was comfortable going through it, because it was like looking into Grandmother's secrets. Because no one ever talked about Grandmother's first marriage, I had no interest in her life then. I don't know if I would have ever opened the box, but with everything we've discussed, I'm curious. If you have time, I'll bring it down, and we can look through it."

Cheryl offered to help her carry it, but she asked the chauffeur to carry down the box. It was a square box, about eighteen inches on all sides.

By the time the box was placed on a table, if Libby had any uncertainty about going through its contents, it was gone. She pulled open the lid and started pulling out papers. She and Cheryl looked at them—odd clippings of her time in Paris, all written in French. "Like I said, she met the Count in Paris. Here's a flyer about the World's Fair. I don't know if she went, but knowing Grandmother, she probably wanted to."

Libby pulled out a couple of other things until she came to something and read it. She handed it to Cheryl. "Look, this is the Count's obituary."

Cheryl started reading and then yanked her head up.

Libby's eyes narrowed in concern. "What's wrong?"

Cheryl reread the obituary and then looked back at Libby, "This says he died in Cincinnati about four weeks after they left Bekbourg."

She handed the clip to Libby for her to read. It stated that Count Zakhar Voskoboynikov, a member of the imperial Russian family, had passed away from complications of pneumonia. It mentioned leaving behind his wife, Elizabeth Griffiths, the daughter of the late Franklin Stanley Griffiths and the late Sarah Rebecca (McDonald) Griffiths. A private burial was planned, and Mrs. Griffiths requested privacy.

"Mmmm. I was wrong. I thought he died here. What do you think happened?"

Cheryl's lips twitched to the side in concentration. "Your grandmother must have waited to bring him back to Rhode Island to bury him. Maybe the bad weather was part of the reason, but not for that long. Maybe, she couldn't bear returning so soon after his passing. With both her parents deceased, perhaps she couldn't face it alone."

Libby nodded. "How could they have waited so long to bury him back then?"

"That's a good question, but I suspect they had a way to embalm the body and kept it refrigerated."

"Yes, I guess. This is interesting. Let's see what else we can find."

Libby proceeded to pull out other things. She found a pair of women's gloves and mementos from establishments in Paris. "Grandmother didn't do a very good job of organizing this box." She then grabbed hold of a folded piece of paper. Her eyes widened when she unfolded it, "Look, Cheryl. It's the death certificate."

It confirmed the Count's death in Cincinnati, but nothing was new from the information contained in the obituary. Libby then pulled out an envelope with a doctor's name and Cincinnati address in the upper left corner and looked at Cheryl. "I wonder what this is?" she said as she opened it. Libby quickly glanced over it and handed it to Cheryl. "You're not going to believe this. It's a doctor's invoice and report."

Cheryl's eyebrows arched as she read the document. "He was shot in Bekbourg!"

It revealed that the doctor had made daily visits to Elizabeth's aunt's home to attend to the Count. The

Count had been shot in Bekbourg and treated by a local physician, who according to the Cincinnati physician, had carefully removed the bullet from his left shoulder and treated the patient against infection. No signs of infection were present in the patient, who seemed to be recovering. However, almost a week after arriving in Cincinnati, the doctor's notes showed the Count developed respiratory problems. The doctor began treating the Count for influenza. Pneumonia set in shortly thereafter. Despite his best efforts, the doctor could not save the Count, who had a history of respiratory illnesses.

"Do you think this somehow relates to the body in the basement?" Libby's look was intense.

"I don't know, Libby, but how can it not be?"

Libby shook her head in understanding. "Let me see if there is anything else in this box," Libby hastily began pulling more things from the box.

She came to a small ornate wood box. When she set it on the table, they both took deep breaths when they recognized the jeweler's name—a world renowned jeweler from Paris. Cheryl whispered. "They made jewelry for the Czar."

The women looked at each other. Libby's eyes were wide. "Do I dare open this?"

"You think that necklace is in there?"

Libby seemed to exhale. "Oh, my god! What do you think?"

Cheryl shook her head indicating uncertainty.

Libby looked at Cheryl. "I guess we have to open

it, but what if the jewels are in here? What will I do? The jewels will be priceless."

The tension was so high Cheryl had to do something to calm both their nerves. "If it's in there, just don't faint or have a heart attack."

They both started laughing. When they finally stopped, Libby said, "The time has come." They both turned their attention to the box. Libby clicked a small lever and paused. Both women were holding their breath. Libby opened the box. It was beautifully lined in velvet, but empty. She picked it up and turned it over, examining it closely. Cheryl watched. Libby then felt around inside. "There isn't a hidden compartment."

They both realized they had been holding their breaths when they exhaled.

They sat down. "You know, I'm not sure this box is large enough for the necklace in the picture."

"That's an excellent point, Cheryl. But, what would it be for? Neither Grandmother nor Mother wore jewelry like this." After a brief pause, Libby held up a finger. "Wait. I just remembered something. The Count had a cigarette case that supposedly had been given to him by the Czar himself. Mother told me Grandmother didn't feel right keeping it, and on her first trip back to Paris, she took it to a museum. It must have been beautiful. After the museum authenticated it, they issued a press release. At Grandmother's request, they honored her request to remain anonymous. Do you think this could be the box to that case?"

"It looks like it could be the right size for a cigarette case."

Libby nodded in satisfaction that the mystery of the box had been solved.

"Is it possible there is something stored in a family safe or safe deposit box?"

Libby assured her she knew that those jewels were not in the family possessions.

Cheryl told her of the picture of Elizabeth on the platform with Harry Schriever when the train was preparing to depart for Cincinnati. "Schriever made his private rail car available for them to travel to Cincinnati. He must have arranged for the doctor and care and then helped your grandmother get him on to Cincinnati. Schriever would have made sure anyone he used to help didn't talk. It's been a secret all these years."

Cheryl picked up the photo and looked at the huge brilliant sapphire circled by a swirling design of four emeralds and rolls of smaller diamonds. "I wonder whatever happened to these jewels."

Libby's lips puckered. "The Count got shot in Bekbourg. Do you think someone stole them? Do you think that is why he was shot, trying to protect the necklace?"

"I don't know, but it's possible. There would have been no reason to have left the jewelry in Bekbourg, but if they had, your Grandmother would have most certainly gone back to get it."

"Unless Mr. Schriever had the jewelry delivered

to her in Cincinnati or Rhode Island. Again, though, I agree with you that there would have been no reason to leave it in Bekbourg."

Before Cheryl left, Libby made copies of the obituary, death certificate and doctor's report. Cheryl also took a picture of the jewelry box.

Cheryl was glad she had booked the last flight out. She had turned off her phone with the intent of checking it before heading toward the airport, but time did not allow for it. She arrived at the gate with a few minutes to spare and turned it on to see that Milton and Patti had been trying to reach her. She knew Patti would be gone for the day, so she called Milton. He didn't even bother with a greeting, "Have you talked to anyone from here?"

"No, why? What's happened?"

"Jeffrey Blankenship was shot overnight near C.P.'s guest house. He died at the hospital."

Cheryl was stunned. "Do they know who shot him?"

"Nope."

Milton gave her the short version. During her flight home, she wondered how things could get weirder.

Chapter 44

Syd drove through the neighborhood where Dimitri and Jeffrey lived. The brick houses had been well-constructed by the builders in the early 1900's. While some homes had been neglected, others were well-maintained. It was a quiet neighborhood with a mixture of young families with children as well as the elderly who had lived there for decades. Autumn flowers and decorations reminded Syd of the approaching holidays.

She pulled in front of Dimitri's house and looked around. She did not see anyone out and about. The local police had been there and cordoned off the garage until it could be inspected. They had already reported back that nothing looked out of the ordinary in the garage apartment.

As Syd surveyed her surroundings, a man in his thirties came out of the house next door and approached. He introduced himself as "Scott" and told her he lived next door with his mother. He told her he had seen the police out there earlier and asked what was going on. She asked if he knew Jeffrey and Dimitri. She learned that Dimitri walked around the neighborhood on a regular basis but that he often traveled. Scott knew Jeffrey lived in the garage apartment and sometimes was seen around the house doing odd jobs, but they had a regular lawn service who attended the small landscaping area. "Dimitri was friendly enough but never went out of his way to be social." Scott had nothing against him, per se, but did not care for Dimitri's arrogance.

Scott talked more with Jeffrey. "He's very smart and keeps up with what's going on in the world. He's kind of interesting to talk with—although he's pretty sarcastic. Sometimes if I'd heard something on the news, I'd ask him about it. Usually, he'd know about it, and we'd talk some. If he wasn't familiar with it, he would research it, and the next time he saw me, he'd have an opinion.

"Did something happen?" he asked.

"Jeffrey's dead."

"What? How?"

"I don't want to go into everything now. Can you tell me if you ever saw anything going on here that seemed suspicious or unusual?"

He thought for a minute, "No, I can't think of anything like that."

"Did you ever hear Dimitri and Jeffrey arguing?"

He shook his head, "No. Jeffrey worked for the professor. He lived in the apartment over the garage. When the professor was out of town, Jeffrey didn't stay in the house as much. I'd see him walking back to the garage and then he'd come back, but if the professor was there, he'd work from about ten o'clock to around four in the house."

"Was there anything to their relationship other than an employer/employee that you know of?"

His eyes got big. "No. I didn't really see them interact much at all. Jeffrey told me he was a research assistant for the professor, and that's all I knew or thought."

"Have you seen anyone over here in the last few days?"

She could tell he was thinking. "Well, not really. It's been pretty quiet. I did see the professor's car come in late last night. I stay up late watching TV and reading. My room is up there," he said pointing to a window on the second floor overlooking Dimitri's house and the side the garage was on. "I saw car lights flash and got up to see what was going on, because I knew they were in Bekbourg." Syd nodded. "I thought someone might be trying to break in. We don't have that happen in this neighborhood, but it happens not far from here sometimes, so I checked. It was Dimitri. I watched him unlock the side door and walk inside."

"About what time was that?"

"I'd say it was about one-thirty or two o'clock." Syd thought to herself, *It's about a two-hour drive from here to there, so he could have been in Bekbourg when Jeffrey was shot.*

"How can you be sure of the time?" she asked.

"The show I was watching goes off at two, and that's what I was watching when I saw the car lights."

"What did you do then?"

"Nothing. I just went back to watching TV."

"When was the last time you saw the professor before that?"

"Oh, I don't know. It's been about three weeks. I knew he had been out of the country for a long time. He wasn't here long before he went to Bekbourg."

"What about Jeffrey, when was the last time you saw him?"

"About the same time—about three weeks ago."

Syd knocked on the other neighbors' doors but did not learn much more about Jeffrey and Dimitri than Scott had shared. He was the only one who knew about them being in Bekbourg, and no one had seen Dimitri in several weeks.

Chapter 45

Dimitri had been waiting for the opportune time to stop by the depot again. The archivist's car was not there, so he went to the depot door and knocked before entering. When he opened the door, he saw Kat standing at her desk, looking his way. "I certainly hope I did not startle you, my dear. With that horrible break-in, your nerves must be on edge."

Kat's shoulders relaxed. "Oh, hi, Professor." She started around her desk toward him. "You didn't scare me. I heard your knock and knew a robber wouldn't knock first."

He chuckled. "I'm glad knocking put your mind at ease."

"If you're looking for Andrian, he's not here, but I can tell him you stopped by."

"No need, my dear. I just wanted to check in to see how he was doing."

"Oh, he's recovering, but he's not coming in as much right now. C.P.'s fine with that. He wants him to take care of himself."

"Naturally. I am glad to hear that. I am certainly

dealing with my own grief. Jeffrey had been with me for twenty-five years."

Kat's mind recoiled at the mention of that SOB's name. Just the thought of him nearly made her nauseous. She somehow managed to keep it together. "I'm sorry, Professor. It must be a hard time for you."

"Indeed. I'm just now coming to grips with him being gone."

Kat nodded.

"Of course, the sheriff talked to me and was seeking my theories on what could have happened. Naturally, I could not assist as much as I wanted to."

Kat nodded, but Dimitri noticed her discomfort. "My dear, please sit down. You are looking pale." He rushed to grab a chair for her. "How insensitive of me to be rattling on about this. I should have known better than to have been talking about such a distasteful topic." Kat sat down. "There, are you feeling better?" he asked.

"Yes. I'm sorry. I don't know what happened to me."

"No worries as long as you are doing better."

She nodded.

"Good. There is one thing I was going to ask Andrian, but perhaps you will know. The sheriff asked for my assistance. He told me that a box from the depot was found in Jeffrey's room. He suggested Jeffrey may have been the one who broke into the depot and took the box. Of course, I knew nothing about that and find it difficult to believe that Jeffrey would have done such a thing. Do you know what was in the box?"

Kat pushed her hair away from her face. "Uh. There were some pictures and papers."

Dimitri firmed his lips in concentration. "Mmm. Do you know if anything pertained to the Count? Why would he want that box?"

This topic was repulsive to her. Kat really wanted the professor to leave, but she did not want to telegraph her feelings. "Well, all I can think of are those pictures, and I don't know why he would have been interested in them. They just showed people standing around who got off the train when it got snowed in here."

"I see. Was the Count or his wife in them?"

"No. Just other people getting off the train."

After Dimitri left, he wondered why Jeffrey had seen the need to steal that box. He would certainly like to see what was in it and look at those pictures.

Chapter 46

Bekbourg, January 1925

Zakhar had not shared the details with his uncle about the financial arrangements he had negotiated with Elizabeth's uncle before the marriage, because he was not at all sure Mikhail would have approved. Mikhail believed what belonged to the wife before marriage fell under the ownership and control of her husband. Elizabeth's father had been more "enlightened" about such matters according to her uncle. While Elizabeth's uncle was generous with the dowry Zakhar had received, the bulk of her father's estate had been placed in trust to prevent it from falling into the hands of a husband who might run through with the fortune. Naturally, Zakhar would enjoy the spoils of Elizabeth's fortune—he just would not control it.

She was attractive with short, bobbed hair and alabaster complexion. Marrying had not been at the top of his priorities, but he recognized he could not live off his aunt the rest of his life. He also needed wealth, which had been denied him when the revolutionaries took over. It was quite fashionable for pauper nobles to marry wealthy heiresses. When introductions were made between him and Elizabeth, the plan gelled in his mind. Although Elizabeth's persistence and inquisitive nature were irritating, her fortune bought a great deal of tolerance.

When they arrived in America, they settled into the grand estate in Newport, Rhode Island, where she had grown up. She had suggested the home in Connecticut, but once she described the two estates, he opted for the Newport home—due to the exterior fencing and security. Despite living the life of luxury, Zakhar could not fully relax for fear the men he had seen on the ship might trace his whereabouts. He had spied them watching him from the ship's deck as the porter was carrying his and Elizabeth's luggage off the ship. Then, one day when the chauffeur was taking him into town, he saw them along the road outside their gated compound. He hired extra security stationed around their estate, but his anxiety increased. The Bolshevik spies knew where he lived. His security men chased them on two separate occasions when they were spotted outside the perimeter, but they were quick in their escape.

Around the holidays, Elizabeth was informed her uncle had fallen ill, and she wanted to travel to Cincinnati to see him and spend time with her Aunt Josephine. Zakhar did not want to leave the security of their home, but he did not want to get on the wrong side of her uncle, who controlled the trust. He devised a scheme to shake the spies. The luxury train going through Cincinnati was the New York Central. He would send decoys to New York to board the train. Meanwhile, he and Elizabeth would take a longer route through Baltimore and Wheeling, West Virginia, to Cincinnati. Shortly into the train trip, the Count's valet fell ill. The physician on the train recommended he be hospitalized, so at the next scheduled stop, the Count made arrangements for his care. This left the Count without an attendant. Elizabeth's attendant would assist where possible until they arrived in Cincinnati—where alternative plans would be made.

Zakhar was watchful while boarding the train in Rhode Island. To his relief, he did not see the spies. Nevertheless, he was observant throughout the train and took extra precautions when securing their train car.

One night, while they dined with the owner of one of the largest steel corporations in the country, Clayton McClellan commented, "Count, I take it you are used to this heavy snowfall and frigid weather."

Zakhar sipped vodka as his eyes roamed the dining car. "Yes. Russian winters are severe, so this is not of concern to me."

"I hope the train will not be delayed. I have a pressing meeting in Chicago." When Zakhar did not respond, McClellan's wife, Beatrice, picked up the conversation with Elizabeth by inquiring about her connections to Cincinnati.

Since the cruise to America, Zakhar had not allowed her to wear the magnificent necklace. He brought it with him to take to Cincinnati for her to wear during private affairs, but tonight, she had asked to wear it to impress their dinner companions. He had refused her request. Consequentially, his being distracted throughout the evening was another aggravation. Elizabeth's exasperation slipped when they entered their sleeping quarters. "Zakhar, must you watch everyone in the dining car? At times, I felt compelled to keep the conversation with Beatrice going simply because you appeared disinterested in conversing with Clayton."

Her nagging irritated him. "It is them who sought us out, Elizabeth. You Americans are fascinated with European nobility. The fact they were seen dining with us was Clayton's objective. He and I have little in common."

"You are still thinking you are being followed by Russian spies," she huffed. "Have you seen any on the train?"

"No, but I must remain vigilant."

This was unwelcomed news to Elizabeth. "For how long? When will you be satisfied you are not being followed?"

"When they are dead," were his thoughts, but instead, he ended the conversation, "When I decide they are no longer a threat. Enough of this conversation."

Chapter 47

It was not until the following evening that Cheryl and Sean had the opportunity to catch up. Cheryl greeted him when he walked in the door with a welcome-home kiss and hug. Buddy was dancing around both of them with his tail wagging at full speed. Sean lovingly embraced her. She pulled back to look closer at her husband. She had seen him limping as he walked toward the front door. The injury sustained during his last investigation in the Marines typically grew more painful when he was fatigued. "Come in the kitchen. I stopped by Bri's and got us a hot dinner. It's in the oven. Sit down and let me pamper you."

Milton had stayed in contact with the sheriff's office and briefed Cheryl earlier in the day about what they knew about Jeffrey's death. Cheryl knew Sean would not reveal any further information.

She put everything out for their dinner. "I've got a lot to tell you. I may even be able to help you in your investigation into the remains found in C.P.'s basement." Excitement always caused her eyes to shine.

He grinned, "Oh yeah?"

"First, the FBI recently called Libby about the Count and was asking about jewelry the Count might have given her grandmother."

Cheryl was a pro at paying close attention to people's reactions, and it was all he could do to mask his. He kept his attention focused on what she had to say. She pulled out her article and showed him the picture of Elizabeth wearing the necklace. She told him about what she had learned about the Count being shot in Bekbourg, which was new information. "The Count was staying in the guest house. Do you think he was shot in an attempted robbery, and that the man who was killed was somehow involved?"

"Good question."

She smiled. "I'm glad you think so. But there's more." She told him about Jeffrey and Dimitri both calling Libby and Dimitri asking about jewelry the Count may have given Elizabeth. His sudden frown signaled to her something she said had hit a nerve.

"So, Dimitri was asking her about jewelry?"

Her eyes grew brighter as she leaned toward him. "Yes. So do you think they came to Bekbourg thinking there might be clues here about what happened to the necklace?"

Given what he had heard in Columbus, Sean did not want to say too much. Cheryl was putting the pieces together, and he thought she might be right. "Okay, let's assume you're right—they saw the photo with the necklace. Why would they think it was here?"

Cheryl pointed to her article. "I had the same question and talked to Milton about it. He pointed to this sentence in my article, which I had picked up from the last article published in the *Tribune* back in 1925. It says that the Count and Elizabeth were planning to stop by here on the way back to Rhode Island. Maybe they needed to stop here to get the necklace?"

Sean thought before responding. "I see your point, but why would the Count leave the necklace here? Isn't it more plausible to think it was stolen? And, if that's the case, who would have stolen it and where would it be?"

Cheryl puckered her lips while she pondered. "That's a good point, but why was Jeffrey shot near the guest house, and why did someone break into it?"

"You know, this all assumes the jewelry is missing. And it may be missing, but perhaps not in the sense it was lost. Maybe the Count sold it to someone."

"Like Schriever? But why do that? He didn't need the money. He and Elizabeth were wealthy."

As he ate, Sean considered her point. "Well, Elizabeth was an heiress, but I wonder how much access the Count had to the funds. If her fortune was tied up in some way, like in a trust, perhaps not as much as you might think. A lot of the Russian royalty who were lucky enough to escape Russia did so without being able to take much of their wealth with them."

Cheryl nodded. "Good point. So, if he sold it, it had to be to someone here, on the train, or in Cincinnati, because he died in Cincinnati. Rich people lived here and in Cincinnati, but also, we know that Clayton McClellan, the steel magnate, was on the train. On the other hand, if it was stolen, I'm thinking that had to have happened here in Bekbourg, because of the dead body found in the guest house."

He smiled. "Reminds me of the saying about finding a needle in a haystack." She was deep in thought, so he continued, "It could be like you said: they were planning to return here to get the necklace. But, from what you told me, they made friends here. Perhaps they simply wanted to stop by here and visit with their new friends."

She considered the possibilities before responding, "You're right, but I've got a feeling there's something else to this story."

Sean smiled. He knew she would not stop looking.

As he helped her put away the dishes, he made a mental note to call Lucky and tell him about Jeffrey and Dimitri each contacting Elizabeth's granddaughter as well as asking him to make sure it was the FBI who actually called her.

Chapter 48

Sean's curiosity about the guest house led him to arrange with C.P. to search it. Cole was already waiting for Sean. Before Alex arrived, Cole helped Sean check out the guest house's attic. Cole examined all the brick to the chimney. There were no loose boards or anything odd about the rafters. Cole explained his crew had only recently completed all their work in the basement and had installed new electrical boxes. They were preparing to strip all the plaster where water pipes and electrical conduits needed replacing and gut the kitchen and powder room on the first floor. Then, they would start work on the second floor

Once Alex arrived, he and Sean started in the basement. "What are we looking for, Boss?"

"Any place where something of value could be stashed—especially jewelry or jewels."

They examined the walls, feeling for loose blocks. Nothing about the rafters stood out. There were a few old items like barrels, iron pots, canning jars and a few tools. They inspected an old table and two ladder-back chairs, but nothing looked out-of-the-ordinary. The coal furnace checked out. They next examined the steps leading to the first floor. Alex felt every brick on the fireplace in the living room, and every spot on the firebox within reach. Sean inspected the kitchen pantry and then moved to the kitchen cabinets. A smaller version of the china cabinet in the main mansion was in the small dining room. After inspecting it, Sean and Alex pulled it away from the wall. "I don't think this has been moved since the house was built. The wallpaper still has bright colors behind here compared to the faded wallpaper in the rest of this room," said Alex. They pushed it back in place after looking at the wall. After conducting a thorough search, they moved upstairs.

There were two bedrooms with a small closet in each and a hall bathroom. In each bedroom was a tall chest. It looked as though the original wallpaper was in both, but unlike the downstairs where the same wallpaper had been used throughout except in the kitchen, the bedrooms had different wallpaper. Sean and Alex repeated their steps looking for unusual seams in the wallpaper, checking places on the walls where pictures had been hung, inspecting the hardwood floor planks and baseboards and crown moldings. They examined the closets and checked the tiles in the bathroom. Alex scooted out the chests, but nothing was atypical about the walls. They inspected the chests. Alex carried around a step ladder and checked the light fixtures.

They had come up empty in their search. "I'm damn glad you and Cole had already checked out the attic before I got here," Alex grumbled as he wiped soot, cobwebs and dust off his uniform. "If the people breaking into the guest house hope to find jewelry, I think they are barking up the wrong tree." Sean grinned as his deputy swiped dust from his hair.

As they headed back to the station, Alex said, "I found out something this morning that might be important in the Blankenship investigation. I talked with a woman who lives a street over from C.P.'s. The night of the murder, she was walking her dog and saw an older, dark colored car parked on the street right up from the guest house. She said it wasn't a real big car. As she walked by, she noticed a light colored streak on the front passenger panel, like a scrape or dent. This was about an hour before Blankenship was killed. She thought she saw someone sitting in the driver's seat, but she couldn't be sure. She thinks she's seen the car around the neighborhood before. She said there's an old woman in town who sells baked goods from her home and delivers them who has a similar car. She couldn't be sure, because she just glanced at it."

"Mmm. The other witness said he saw a smaller sized dark car leaving the area soon after Blankenship was killed. That could be something. If someone was waiting on Blankenship, they had something in mind."

"I walked over to the B&B and checked out the professor's car. It's not damaged, so it wasn't his that was parked," said Alex.

Chapter 49

"Hey, Amigo. You look like something the cat drug in."

"Yeah, well, you try climbing up chimneys and scrounging around in basements and see what you look like." Alex was sitting at his desk in the deputies' work area doing paperwork.

Arlo grinned. "What kind of crime were you trying to solve?"

"I don't know how you would categorize a treasure hunt." Alex liked to pull Arlo's chain.

Arlo's grin faded. "Come again?" When Alex kept working on his report Arlo pushed further. "Does this have something to do with the break-ins at that guest house?"

Alex laid down his pen and leaned back in the chair. "So, for another story she's working on, Cheryl went to interview the granddaughter of the Count's wife. While the wife was here in Bekbourg, she was wearing some jewelry priced in the stratosphere. The picture in Cheryl's newspaper article shows her wearing a necklace. According to the granddaughter, no one has seen the necklace since."

Arlo whistled and put a toothpick in his mouth. "So, they think the Count left some priceless jewelry in a guest house all these years, and now people are treasure hunting here?"

Alex shrugged. "There is some reason it's been broken into twice since Cheryl's article ran. Blankenship was helping research the Count for a professor who's an expert on Russian history."

"You're still here, so I take it you didn't find the jewels?"

"Nada. But, keep this to yourself. The sheriff doesn't want this to get out."

"Yeah, I get that. We'd be overrun with fortune seekers from all over the world."

Alex nodded. "So, what's up with you?"

"I found out some things that might put a lift in our investigation into Blankenship's murder."

"Yeah, what's that?"

"The night maid told me she had seen a woman visiting Blankenship's room starting the second time he checked in. She noticed her coming out of his room one night and getting in a small dark car. She didn't pay much attention to the car. Blankenship only stayed about three or four nights each time he checked in until this last time. Well, the third time he was here, she saw that same car almost every night. This last time, she hasn't seen the car so much. Figured whatever was going on had fizzled, because another woman started showing up. She drove a light-colored SUV. I told the Chief this after I talked to the maid. But, now there's a second act."

About that time, Sean walked in and looked at Arlo. "Kim said you were looking for me."

"Yeah, Chief. I was just getting ready to tell Alex the latest. Perfect timing."

Sean sat and leaned back to put his feet on a desk.

"So, there was a guest who checked out of the motel the morning Blankenship was killed. He and his wife are older, and they were in town because her sister's health is not good. They live in Pittsburgh and come down every so often. Anyway, he doesn't particularly care to hang around at his sister-in-law's house. Her husband is dead, so no one to talk to, and he can't hear the TV with all their gabbing. He'd drop the wife off in the afternoon and go pick her up at night because the sister slept late. Anyway, he smokes, and his wife doesn't like him smoking in the motel room, so he'd smoke outside—sometimes pull the chair from his room and sit out if it wasn't too cold. Late in the afternoon the day before Blankenship was killed, he saw a man walk up to Blankenship's door and bang on the door. The man had a bandage around his head. The guest said he knew Blankenship wasn't there, because his car wasn't in the parking lot. After the man banged on the door a couple more times, he got in his car and drove off. The man said he was positive it was a Ford Escort, because his wife used to have one. It was a black car."

Alex spoke up. "That sounds like Andrian."

"Yep, but there's more. Remember what I told you about the maid seeing a new woman coming to see

Jeffrey since he checked in this last time?"

Sean nodded.

"Well, that's not all this man saw. He had seen the woman who drives the white SUV visit Blankenship's room a couple of times. I'll call her Woman Number Two, since she was his second squeeze play. So, he was out smoking. Knew Woman Number Two was in there, because her car was in the parking lot. He notices a small, dark car pull in, and a woman eventually gets out and starts walking toward Blankenship's motel room. He's never seen her, but he'd only been checked-in a few days. As Number One gets close to Blankenship's door, Number Two comes out, and it is clear some hanky-panky has been going on. The woman is laughing loud, and Blankenship is standing in the doorway with no shirt with just his jeans on. He is laughing, too. Number One just stands there until Two starts to walk away. He said One is so close that Two has to have seen her, but Two walks on by but keeps laughing as she heads to her car. Woman One rushes toward Blankenship's door yelling and calling him every name in the book. He grabs her and yanks her into the room and slams the door. The guest said he lit another cigarette to see if anything else happened. After about five or ten minutes, the door swung open and Blankenship pushed her outside. She didn't fall, but the man said it was a rough push.

"It was dark, so he couldn't see her face or whether Blankenship had roughed her up. The woman walked to her car and sat there for a few minutes before driving off."

"When did this happen?" asked Sean.

"Two nights before Blankenship's murder."

"Do we have any ideas who either woman is?"

"Number One drove a small black car. He wasn't sure of the model except it looked older and like American-made. He said he thought it looked like something was on the front passenger panel—like mud or paint—but he wasn't paying much attention to the car, because he was trying to see her, but couldn't. But, this might be helpful. He sometimes goes to Knuck's to grab something to eat and have a beer during the evenings. He said just about every time he was there, he saw a white SUV that looked similar to the one Woman Number Two drove, because it had a bunch of things hanging from the rearview mirror."

"Well, that's something," suggested Alex.

"Yeah. So, I thought I'd run by Knuck's around dinner time and see if I can find the SUV or ask around."

"Good idea, Arlo. If she's there, call me, and we'll go in together to talk with her."

Chapter 50

Cheryl studied the train's manifest, willing it to reveal a clue. After talking with Libby, she was convinced someone was after the jewels and there was a connection to the body found in the basement. It seemed unlikely anyone in Bekbourg would have tried robbing the Count. After all, even though the *Tribune* had published articles, no pictures of the couple were published and she doubted anyone other than the immediate circle of people in close contact with the Countess would have even known about the necklace. The city was also still covered with almost two feet of snow with bone-chilling temperatures. *If I'm right and someone was after the jewels, they must have been on the train.*

She zeroed in on trying to identify the nationalities by surnames. Most of the surnames were of English origin. She noticed a couple of Italian surnames and even more French, Irish and German. A few surnames stumped her. She guessed some to be Norwegian and Eastern European, but she did not know which countries. A thought came to her to call a professor she knew at the local college, Hillsrock Community College, who taught world history.

Cheryl explained to Dr. Rolton what she needed. The professor was glad to help, and Cheryl dropped off a copy of the manifest. The following day, Dr. Rolton called and set a time to discuss the manifest.

By the time they finished their conversation, Cheryl was grateful for Dr. Rolton's help. She identified four passengers she thought had a Russian surname. One was the Count. The other men who had Russian last names were Yegor Dobrynin, Sascha Krayevshy, and Boris Solyanka.

Cheryl smiled at the professor. "This has been helpful. I appreciate you reviewing the manifest as quickly as you did,"

"Call on me any time. You know Bekbourg has a mix of Europeans who live here. Some of the families go way back. We even have some who are of Russian descent."

"Mmm. Now that you mention it, I did know there are people here who are from Eastern Europe." Cheryl was especially interested in the people with a Russian heritage. "Do you know who has the Russian background?"

"I do." She walked to a bookcase and pulled out a folder. "There was a family with the last name 'Nikoleav' who escaped Russia to come here in the early 1900's. They came to Bekbourg because the man had an uncle who lived here. When they immigrated here, they had an infant daughter, Katia. Starting with Katia, there are five generations who have grown up here—well, the newest generation is still very young. Until the most recent, the women kept their last name, Nikoleav, and all of them passed down old Russian pastry recipes. Klara Nikoleav still bakes for a few of the families around town but mostly for special occasions."

Cheryl recognized the name, Klara Nikoleav. Cheryl had heard Bri talk about how, when Bri and Max first opened the B&B, Klara made pastries for them. She had slowed down in her baking, but for special occasions, Klara sometimes would make them for Bri. Cheryl did not know her ancestry was Russian. *It would be interesting to talk with her and see if she knows anything about the Count. I would like to know more about Klara before I talk with her. Bri may be able to help.*

Cheryl dropped by to ask Bri what she knew about her, but Bri had never gotten to know Klara personally. Since Klara's children had likely attended high school in Bekbourg, Cheryl next turned to Kye, who taught for nearly forty years at Schriever High.

After they were settled in Kye's living room, Cheryl asked Kye if she knew Klara Nikoleav.

"Of course. She used to work at the bakery down town. Her Pirozhki was especially delicious. She retired when her daughter got divorced. Her son was two-years-old at the time, and her daughter needed help with childcare. I think Klara was ready to retire anyway. She's in her sixties—maybe pushing seventy."

"I learned today that she has ancestors who emigrated

from Russia. I thought she might know something about the Count's stay here, or at least some folklore about it. I plan to talk with her."

Kye nodded. "I should have thought to mention her. She has a daughter who lives in town. She was in my class."

"What's her name?"

"Kat. That's her nickname. Her birth name is Katrina." Kye sipped her coffee. "I remember Klara from the bakery, but she never talked much. Her daughter was just the opposite. She was a chatterbox in high school. I got the impression there was a generational gap between Kat and her mother. Kat's mother, Klara, believed in the old ways, according to Kat. I remember hearing her complain at school about how her mother never moved out of the old fashion Russian thinking and traditions. She was determined not to be like that. And, she isn't."

"Why, what happened?"

"First, early on in school, she insisted on being called 'Kat' instead of by her real name, 'Katrina.' Until word got around among the teachers, there was some confusion at the elementary school during parent/teacher conferences. It was hard to understand Kat's mother because of her heavy accent, and she didn't know who they were talking about when the teachers wanted to talk about 'Kat.'" Cheryl laughed. "Later on, I remember talking to some of the workers at the bakery. Klara was upset when Kat decided to marry an English man. Not that there are a lot of eastern Europeans around here to choose from, but she did not approve of this young man. That was on top of Kat having no interest in baking, which is a real shame. All the women in that family were famous around here for their pastries. But, a big blow to Klara was when Kat decided to change her last name when she married." Kye shook her head. "I've seen it before. The old ways butting heads with modern times."

"What's Kat's last name?"

"Clark."

Cheryl sat forward, "Kat Clark?"

Kye was curious, "Yes, dear. Do you know her?"

"I've met her. She works for C.P. Kye, it's crazy, but it seems this entire story I've been working on keeps coming up Russian." They both laughed. "I talked to a history professor at the local college, and three names, in addition to the Count's, on the train manifest are Russian. No one had the last name, 'Nikoleav,' but I wonder if there is a family relation to any of the three."

"They were on the train coming into Bekbourg with the Count?"

"Yes."

"Then, unless they stayed here, it seems likely they were just passing through, doesn't it?"

"I need to see if I can find a list of who took the train on into Cincinnati."

"Are you still planning to talk to Klara?"

"Yes, but now that I know Kat is her daughter, I'm not sure how much she will know. Kat knows I have been working with C.P.'s archivist to find out as much as possible about the Count and his wife, but she never said anything about any stories her mother knew. Surely, if her mother knew something, she would have told us. Don't you think?"

"I would think so."

Chapter 51

Sean hung up the phone and leaned back to stretch his legs to consider what Ronnie had just told him about her lab results. Jeffrey had been shot twice in the chest with a twenty-two caliber. He had a Glock in his coat pocket, so he never thought, or had a chance, to pull it when approached by the assailant. Soil samples taken from his shoes matched the dirt in the guest house's basement. She also found minute dirt particles from the basement on the stairs leading up to the kitchen, on a step going to the second floor, and in front of the window on the first floor where the window pane had been broken out. As she pointed out, the dirt particles could have come from workers' shoes, but the evidence clearly pointed to Blankenship being in the house.

A flashlight was found in another coat pocket, and he was wearing gloves when he was shot. He was looking for something—could it be the jewels? Had he been in the guest house before, or was the first break-in by someone else, and if so, who and for what reason? What was so important for him to break into the depot and steal the box? Apparently, that was the only thing stolen—nothing else from the depot was found when Ronnie's team searched his motel room. According to Kat, the box was along a wall under some other boxes—why did he take that particular one? If that was the box he was after, how did he know it was there? Someone must have told him about it, but why? As far as Sean knew, Kat and Andrian were the only two people who worked in there. He needed to follow-up on that point. Maybe Jeffrey had been working with them in the depot, but according to Andrian, he had not been working with Jeffrey. And, if he could be believed, the professor did not know anything about the box. In fact, Andrian told Sean he had never seen Dimitri in the depot. Now, from what the witness told Arlo, it appears Andrian was at Jeffrey's motel the night before he was killed. Why? Had Andrian somehow found out he had the box, but how was that possible? He needed to talk with Andrian again.

Chapter 52

Sean and Arlo went to Knucklepin's and learned that the waitress who drove the white SUV was off this evening, so they drove to an older apartment building on the west side of downtown. They heard a TV playing when they knocked. A woman, not the waitress, opened the door. Sean asked if the waitress was home. The woman's eyes were large as she eyed the two lawmen. "Sure, she's here. Hold on. I'll get her."

They waited for a couple of minutes before the waitress came to the door. Sean asked if they could talk with her. Glancing to the side toward her roommate, the woman picked up her purse and announced she needed to run to the store. The waitress offered them a seat.

She turned down the TV and eased into a chair across from them. She pulled a pack of cigarettes from her jeans pocket. "You all smoke?" Sean remembered he'd seen her at Knucklepin's dressed much like she was now, wearing jeans and a pullover sweater. Her streaked hair was bunched on top of her head. She was thin except for a full bosom.

Sean shook his head, and Arlo told her "no." Sean

noticed her hand slightly trembled when she clicked the lighter.

"We have some questions about Jeffery Blankenship."

She inhaled enough to suck in her cheeks and then blew smoke upward. "Okay."

"Did you know Mr. Blankenship?"

"He came into Knuck's sometimes."

"Is that where you met him?"

She nodded her head yes.

"Do you know he was shot?"

"Yeah. One of the workers called and told me. I saw in the paper where he died."

"Why did they call you?"

"Well, he was a customer. We all tell each other things like that."

"You didn't know before you got the call?"

She shook her head no.

"Did you ever see him outside of Knucklepin's?"

She took another drag on the cigarette and nodded her head yes.

"How did you know him?"

She paused as she took a smoke. "We saw each other some. No biggy."

Under Sean's questioning, she confirmed what the maid had told Arlo, that she had only started seeing him recently.

"You see him anywhere else other than Knucklepin's or the motel?"

She shook her head no.

"Tell us about the last time you saw him." Sean was expecting it to be at the motel, but it turned out to be at the bar.

She described seeing Jeffrey sitting at a table with a man whose description fit Dimitri. "I thought they might be going to order, so I kinda hung close by when I didn't have to help out another customer. They were talking low, but neither one looked very happy, so I started to think it was something serious. I couldn't help but hear Jeffrey call him an 'ass.' Jeffrey said something like, 'I know too much,' but it was hard to hear, and I didn't want them to think I was eavesdropping."

"What happened?"

"Well, he got up and left, and I went over to Jeffrey to see if everything was okay. I could tell he had a lot on his mind. I told him I thought the guy was creepy and tried to see if he wanted to talk. He didn't. Only thing he said was that the man owed him money and was going to pay up soon. That's about it."

"What happened next?"

She stretched back her head as if to relieve tension. "I asked him if he wanted me to stop by later that evening, but he said he had something he had to do. Then he left."

"When was this?"

She took her time in exhaling the smoke. "It was the evening he was killed."

"What time?"

"I don't know for sure, but probably around nine o'clock, give-or-take."

"What time did you get off?"

She shrugged her shoulders. "At one o'clock."

"Let's step back. When was the last time you went to Mr. Blankenship's motel room?"

"Two nights before that."

"Tell us about that night."

She thought for a minute as she smoked. "If it's not busy, the boss will let one of us girls leave. I got off about nine o'clock and called Jeffrey. He told me to come on by, and I did. I didn't stay too long."

"How did he seem? Anything odd?"

"No, he was about as he always was. Look, it was just for kicks. I never stayed long, and that suited us both."

"Did you notice anything new in his room, like a box or something?"

She thought for a minute. "No, but I wasn't paying that close attention to the room."

She ground out the cigarette and got up and offered them something to drink. They declined, but she got herself a diet soda.

"You don't remember anything else about your time there?"

She popped the soda top and thought while she took a sip. She suddenly strangled and jerked forward to stop coughing. She banged her chest a couple of times and calmed down. "Sorry about that. It went down the wrong way. There was something else. That woman he was trying to dump was walking toward his room when I was leaving. Man, I saw fire in her eyes when she saw us. I thought maybe that was enough for her to get the message, but I guess not."

"Why do you say that?"

"That bitch was in Knucklepin's earlier that last time Jeffrey was there—the night he was killed. I know she was looking for him. She was standing at the bar looking around. A customer I know was standing at the bar when she was there. He told me he stopped her from coming after me. Anyway, she finally left before he arrived, but I saw her sitting in her car. She was still sitting there when I went out for a cigarette. I didn't go near her. I thought about telling the boss, but what the hell, she wasn't doing anything. After Jeffrey left, I took a cigarette break, and her car was gone."

"Why did she want to come after you?"

"I guess she was jealous from seeing me coming out of his motel room."

"Did Mr. Blankenship ever say anything about her?"

"No, not really—just that he wasn't seeing her anymore. I didn't want to get involved if they were still an item. I had seen them in Knuck's a few times a few weeks or months ago—I don't remember how long, but it had been a while. I asked, and he said they were history. I guess she couldn't let go."

"What happened when she saw you at the motel?"

"I could tell she was shocked, and then she got mad as hell." She lit another cigarette. "I wanted to be gone from there because I knew a hissy fit was coming."

"What happened then?" Sean prodded after she

stopped talking.

"I heard her yelling something, but I didn't stop to watch the show. By the time I got to my car, I looked back, but neither was there. I guess she went into his room. Anyway, I left and don't know what happened. I didn't say anything to Jeffrey about her when I saw him at Knuck's that last time. It was his business, not mine."

"What was the other woman's name?" Sean asked.

"I asked some of the girls. One of them said it was 'Kate' or 'Kat'—something like that. I don't know for sure."

"What kind of car did she have?"

"A small dark car."

Chapter 53

As she had done to research matters pertaining to the railroad for prior articles, Cheryl again turned to Jules Leroux for assistance.

"My dear, Mrs. Seton, I was delighted when you called." Even though they were in Frau's, a decades old casual diner, he helped her into her chair. She could not help but smile at his formality. "I hope you don't mind, but I took the liberty of ordering your fruit cup and poached egg just like you like it. And, here is your coffee—right on time."

The waitress smiled as she poured Cheryl's coffee and refreshed his. "Jules here gave me an order for you—fruit and poached egg. All good?"

Cheryl smiled. "Just what I was planning to order."

The waitress nodded and moved along.

All the railroaders wore heavy boots, but—while many wore jeans and flannel shirts during cold weather—Jules wore khaki-colored work pants and button-up shirts, most times with a bow tie. After exchanging pleasantries, Jules was eager to assist.

"Now, Mrs. Seton, please tell me how I can assist

you." Cheryl had given up on asking Jules to call her by her first name. It was just who he was.

She handed him the two lists—one the official manifest and the second being the hand-written list of all the people on the train. On the first list showing first-class passengers, the name, "Boris Solyanka" was circled. Beside it was "Eloise Dorgan," which had a "PC" notation. A small dash appeared in front of the Count's name and his wife. There was also a dash in front of "Mr. and Mrs. Clayton McClellan." Clayton McClellan was the wealthy owner of the steel company. She also noticed the initials "PC" in front of other first-class names, including the Count and the McClellan's.

Jules looked at the list. "Ah, yes. Your husband showed me this list. As I told him, I found it odd there was a list of passengers." He explained that many times, passengers paid the conductor as he walked through the aisle after the train was moving. "It looks like the railroad prepared this official manifest of the first-class passengers. This hand-written list is on railroad letterhead, but I can't explain it."

She told him that Andrian thought it was compiled so the railroad had a list of passengers disembarking to eventually compare with those who left Bekbourg when the train was cleared to resume on to Cincinnati. He accepted that explanation as plausible. He told Cheryl that "PC" meant those particular passengers were in the pull cars. "The pull cars had the sleeper compartments. They were called 'pull cars' because the beds were pulled out for sleeping and folded up for comfortable sitting accommodations during the day."

He was not certain what the dashes in front of the Count's and the McClellan's names indicated but suspected it was to show they were VIPs. "The train personnel would know if someone important was on the train. They would want to give people like that special treatment. That's my best guess as to why the dashes are there."

"Why do you think the name, 'Boris Solyanka,' is circled?"

"Unfortunately, my dear, I cannot offer an opinion to that question. Your husband showed me the list and asked about that, too. I asked our conductors, and they did not know either. I'm sorry I cannot be more helpful on that."

Cheryl next showed him the train schedule, which he had not seen. Jules whistled after reading it.

"My first question, Ms. Seton, is why an important person like the Count would have taken this train. If his destination was Cincinnati, the New York Central would have been a much quicker and more luxurious train to have taken. His journey started in Rhode Island and had an overnight stop in New York City. He could have easily transferred to the NY Central. After departing New York City, this shows he went to Philadelphia, and then on in to Baltimore. Hell, it was stopped there for eleven hours. From there, the train made it to Wheeling, West Virginia, where he got on the WVB&C that came through Bekbourg."

"Why all the long layovers in New York and Baltimore?" Cheryl asked.

"It probably had to do with changing cars and changing engines. Again, they probably had to switch the Pullman cars that were heading toward Cincinnati. There are notes about the weather. It was already getting bad, and—keep in mind—they had to go through the mountains as they made their way toward Cincinnati. It was a slow-go as the storm blew in from the west. The blizzard hit about the time the train made it to Bekbourg—at about four o'clock."

Cheryl agreed with Jules that it was baffling they would have chosen this particular train route. Even if the Count was not familiar with the train system, Elizabeth would have known.

Chapter 54

Coming out of the conversation with the waitress from Knucklepin's, Sean wanted to interview Dimitri and Andrian. He suspected the woman described by the waitress was Kat Clark, so they also needed to question her. He decided to start with the professor.

Dimitri was in his room at the B&B, and the housekeeper called and asked if he could come down and talk with Sean and Alex. After about fifteen minutes, Dimitri walked into the parlor. "Sorry, gentlemen, for keeping you waiting. I had to respond to a colleague about a joint paper we are preparing for a presentation in Denmark. Now, how can I be of assistance?"

Sean asked him how his work with Andrian was going.

"Well, now that Jeffrey is deceased, it's not going."

"I thought you and Andrian were working together on research about the Count?"

"Well, I was not personally working with the archivist. I was relying on Jeffrey to coordinate with him."

"How did that turn out?"

"How do you mean, Sean?"

"Did they trade a lot of information? Did Jeffrey learn a lot from Andrian?"

Dimitri rose and walked to the bar. "Would either of you gentlemen like something to drink?" When they declined, he poured a scotch and returned to his seat. "Max and Bri are most generous with their guests." He saluted with the glass and took a sip. "Getting back to your question, I can't say one way or the other. Jeffrey never told me what specific information he got from the archivist. He just informed me about the information he was gathering."

"Had he gathered a lot since being here?"

"I must say, I was rather disappointed there wasn't more about the Count's time here, but I guess the newspaper was really the only source. Jeffrey continued to work on research from his sources to gather information about the Count himself, which is useful. I have relied on my contacts at universities as well."

"You have been here about three weeks. Is there more here to learn?"

Dimitri smiled as he cleared his throat. "Well, I probably have nearly exhausted what there is here to learn, but, until Jeffrey's unfortunate demise, my stay here had been most pleasant. I plan to wrap things up within a few days." Despite his attempt to sound engaging, Dimitri had turned frosty.

"When was the last time you saw him?"

Dimitri tilted his head, "We've been over this, Sean."

"It's normal procedure. We have to verify things."

Dimitri was not entirely appeased, but he responded, "It was on the night I drove back to Cincinnati. I wanted to meet with him to tell him I was going back for a couple of days and touch base to get a status report from him."

"What time did you see him at Knucklepin's?"

"I don't remember. I don't keep up with time much anymore." The waitress said he was at the bar with Jeffrey around nine o'clock, but according to Syd, he did not arrive at his house in Cincinnati until about two o'clock that night. It took approximately two hours to drive between the two locations, so if he had left soon after leaving the bar, there was some time unaccounted for.

"After you left the bar, what did you do?"

"I went to Cincinnati."

"Did you go straight there after leaving Jeffrey?"

"Really, Sheriff, I don't remember. Those types of details I don't burden my mind with. I have much more important things to think about."

"Jeffrey didn't mention to you about having a box that had been stolen from the depot?"

"No, Sean, not a word. Like I told you before, I knew nothing about that box."

"Were you and Jeffrey arguing?"

Dimitri watched the liquid swirl in his glass. "I wouldn't say we were arguing. Anytime you have worked with someone as long as we did, you have your differences—those things happen. I don't remember our conversation. I had other things on my mind."

"Did you owe Jeffrey money?"

Dimitri's eyebrows shot up, "Not that I know of. I paid him at the beginning of the month by bank transfer. He never said anything about his paycheck being late. If he had, I would have looked into it."

Sean had some more questions for the professor, but he wanted to talk with Andrian and Kat.

Sean asked Dimitri to let him know if he decided to leave town. "Of course, Sean, but, I must say, your tedious questioning has soured my stay here."

"You worked with Jeffrey a long time. I'm sure you want his murder solved, too."

"Of course, but I don't see how what I have to say helps. But I am happy to work with you if that means solving his murder."

Sean and Alex thanked him for his time and left.

"I don't understand. He comes here to learn about the Count, but I'm not sure what he's been doing here. He said he's not talked to the archivist. If he's making calls and working through the internet, why not do that from his office in Cincinnati? Do you know if he's been working with Cheryl?"

"You raise a good point, Alex. I don't think he's been working with Cheryl, beyond their first meeting, but I'll ask her. Arlo talked with the librarian. She remembers talking with Dimitri. He told her he was investigating the Count, but most of his questions were about Schriever. She said Jeffrey spent a lot of time trying to find information about the Count, but he also researched Geisen and even spent some time on Schriever."

"Isn't that odd? Why them?"

"Perhaps they were interested in who the Count hung out with. It's possible they wanted to learn more about our influential leaders during the time, but I'm not convinced of that. Other than the library, the newspaper, and the railroad, I don't know where else he or Blankenship would be looking for information about the Count's time in Bekbourg."

"If Blankenship came here without telling him, I find it hard to believe he did that to get brownie points. I mean, they have been working together twenty-five years. Both are mature men. Why not tell the professor as soon as he got back to the states?"

"You have a theory?" Sean asked.

"Well, one possibility could be Blankenship might have been doing an end run around the professor."

"That's a good observation. What would he have to gain?"

"I don't know much about the way the academic world works, but if Blankenship came up with information that no one else had, wouldn't there at least be notoriety he could get for publishing that information? Money would possibly follow if he was asked to speak at conferences. But, if there is something to your wife's theory that the Count left some jewels here, or at least there is a clue here about where they might be, well, the finder would be worth millions. Maybe Blankenship was trying to find the jewels."

"We know Jeffrey broke into the guest house, so

he could have been after the jewels or a clue. If Dimitri isn't after the jewels, then maybe that's not a motive. If Dimitri is after the jewels and he believed Jeffrey was too, then that's a motive. If he was doing an end run around the professor on publishing an article on the Count, and the professor found out, that would also be a motive."

Chapter 55

Bekbourg, January 1925

Katia Nikolaev's parents had escaped Russia when she was an infant and immigrated to the United States. Her father had distant relatives living in Bekbourg, which brought the family to the town. Katia's father was a black-smith and her mother supplemented the family income with her baking. When Katia was sixteen, she married a man fifteen years her senior. They had a daughter and son, and then he died in a lumbering accident. By then, Katia's father was deceased, so they moved in with her mother so she could to help raise Katia's young children while she worked as a cook in the Grand Hotel.

Without his valet, the Count needed someone to assist in translation with the day-to-day activities. Elizabeth was not always available, and McClellan was only around when he was spending time with the men. Since Katia knew Russian, the hotel owner informed Schriever of her skill. With the Count's consent, Schriever requested the hotel loan her out to be Count's full time translator.

The Count was not the only Russian who came into Katia's orbit when the train was stranded in Bekbourg. Because it was widely known Katia and her mother spoke Russian, they were asked by the local authorities to take in two men who were on the train who spoke Russian, some French, but no English. Katia moved her children into her room and gave the strangers their bedroom. From the beginning, Katia could tell her mother was suspicious and said very little around the men. Katia and her mother fed the men in the kitchen while they ate with the children in the living room—giving the men privacy. The men, at first, tried to learn what they could about the town and Katia's family, but following her mother's lead, Katia was circumspect in what she said. The one named Sascha tried to flirt with Katia, which warmed the lonely woman, but her mother's harsh words rebuffed the man. She would shoo the children away from Sascha when he did things to make them laugh. Katia did not know the reason for her mother's hostilities toward the men and was somewhat put off she would discourage the man showing interest in her, but she was guided by her mother's suspicions.

Katia knew from their plain cut, worn wool suits they were not wealthy. They were not much above five-feet-eight-inches tall, but they were wiry and strong. Sascha was the friendlier one, offering to carry out the trash and ingratiate himself into the family. Yegor made Katia uneasy with his beady eyes and an ugly red scar along his jaw.

When Katia returned on the second day from work, Yegor was waiting on the porch. "A Russian Count was traveling on the train. Is he staying at the hotel?"

Katia was distrustful. "I heard that a noble from Europe and his wife are in town, but I know nothing more." She did not want to disclose where the royal couple was staying.

His icy eyes bore into hers. "You know the language and have not been asked to assist?"

Katia stuttered, "It is my understanding his wife is American. If he is Russian as you say, maybe they do not require my services. I have not worked there long. I am merely a cook."

He was studying her—watching for any indication she was lying. Katia started to walk into the house, and he grabbed hold of her arm hard enough to leave a bruise. "Perhaps you can find a way to be of assistance to the Count."

Katia heard her son approaching the door. Yegor squeezed her arm and the coldness in his eyes made her shiver. Just as quickly, he released her as her son swung open the door. She stumbled as she grabbed her son in a shaken hug and pushed them both into the house. He asked her what was wrong, and she claimed she needed to rush to the bathroom, making her son laugh. She urged him to find her mother to help get supper ready. She dashed into the bathroom and splashed cold water on her face. Her pale face shrouded with fear stared back from the mirror. She had heard her parents speak of the

Russian mobsters and the like and knew they were capable of great cruelty and ruthlessness. Oh, my god. Those monsters could kill my children—all of us. Whatever they wanted had something to do with the Count.

That evening when she was certain the two men had left, careful not to raise alarm, she asked her mother about the royal family.

Her mother explained about the Czar, the revolution by the "Bolshevik bastards" and the Czar's abdication. News had spread that he and his family had been killed at the hands of the revolutionaries. "Every day, I am thankful your papa got us out. I am glad your papa is no longer with us to see what has become of our birth country." She scowled, "Those communists have taken over and are butchering those they do not trust." She shook her head. "It is a shame."

"I understand a Russian Count was on the train. Would he be in danger here?"

Her mother's eyes widened in alarm. She looked around as if thinking someone was listening and whispered. "Is that true? Do you know?"

Katia did not want to upset her mother. "I think it may be true, but he and his wife are not staying at the hotel."

Her mother shook her head. "I don't like those men, Katia. There is something I feel. If it is true a Russian Count was on the train, then they could be spies. We must be careful, Katia. Say nothing around those two men. Stay away from them and keep the children away.

That one, Sascha, he is trying to win you and the children over. Do not be taken in."

Her mother's hand trembled. Katia reached over and patted her mother's hand. "Do not worry. There is nothing to worry about."

"One more thing: don't forget. We are of Russian descent. Don't let your guard down. If those men bring harm to the Count, they may try to make us look guilty."

When the hotel told Katia she was being assigned to the Count and would be staying at the guest house, Katia went home and packed a suitcase. She told her mother she had a special assignment and would be working out of a guest house and would not return until the train was running again.

"This has something to do with that Russian Count?" her mother whispered for fear of being overheard by the Russian guests.

Katia yanked her head in both directions to see if they were near. She furrowed her eyebrows in disapproval of her mother's question and put her finger to her lips. "Do not discuss this with anyone." Her words barely reaching her mother's ears, Katia finished throwing her things into the small suitcase and slipped out the back door.

Chapter 56

Sean and Arlo drove by the depot, but learned from C.P.'s administrative assistant that Kat had not been to work since Jeffrey's murder—although she had been in and out to get work to take home. Kat lived in a house three streets away from the depot, down about five blocks in an older part of the downtown where most of the homes had been built in the late 1800's and early 1900's. The small, one-story brick house had a porch extending across the front with two old metal chairs. The paint was peeling along the window frames and on the overhang, and the roof's shingles needed replacing. A few toys were haphazardly laying in the scant front yard.

Sitting on the road in front of the house was an older model black Dodge Shadow. As they walked around it, Sean noticed a white scuff on the passenger-side front panel.

Sean knocked on the door.

Kat opened the door. A young boy was standing beside her. "Mom, it's policemen!"

"Hello," she uttered. Her appearance from a week ago was changed. Her face was pinched and pale, and her hair was limp around her face. She even looked to have lost weight. Sean introduced Arlo, re-introduced himself and asked if he and Arlo could speak with her.

"Mom, are they going to give you another speeding ticket?"

"Sshh, Joey. Go see Mama."

"But I want to stay," he howled.

Sean heard a woman's sharp voice from somewhere in the back beckoning the boy. He put his head down and stomped back down the hall, "Oh, all right."

"I'm sorry, Sheriff. Joey gets excited when someone visits. Please have a seat."

"We want to talk to you about Jeffrey Blankenship."

She absently reached for a plastic toy car that was on the table beside her. She started fiddling with its wheels. She acknowledged she knew him.

"How did you meet him?"

"I met him several weeks ago. He came here, because he was looking into Ms. Seton's story about the Count visiting here. He wanted to know if Mama knew anything about it."

"Why did he think she might know about the Count?"

"I don't really know. Mama's grandmother was brought here by her parents when she was a baby. They were from Russia. He thought since our family had some Russian connection, we might know something. Joey and I live here with my mother."

"Did you or your mother know anything?"

"No."

"So, you met him when he came here to your house?"

She nodded her head. "Yeah."

"Then what happened?"

"I started going out with him some. When he came from Cincinnati to do his research, I would see him then."

"Did you ever go to Cincinnati to see him?"

"No." She continued to glance at the toy as she spoke. She turned it in her hands and then would go back to slowly turning a wheel.

"Was Mr. Blankenship ever in the depot?"

"Yeah, he came there once or twice for us to go to lunch."

"Did he and Andrian work together?"

"No. Andrian barely knew him. He just met him when he stopped by the depot to see me."

"What about Dr. Dimitri Shlykov? Did Andrian work with him?"

"No. The professor dropped by to meet him, but it was right after the break-in, and Andrian was not there. Then, he came back a second time, but Andrian wasn't there then either."

This got Sean's attention. "Did he say why he had stopped by?"

"Well, the first time was to meet Andrian. I guess he wanted to start working together. I was able to help him some. I told him about the picture Andrian found of the Count's wife and the Schrievers. I didn't have a copy of that, but I did drop off a copy of the manifest at the B&B. I was surprised Jeffrey had not given him a copy.

I think the professor was surprised about there being a passenger list, but I gave him a copy."

"What about the second time? What did he want?"

"He said you were asking for his assistance on finding out about the box and wanted to know if I knew what was in it. I told him what I knew, which wasn't much." She paused. "I think it's just as well that Andrian wasn't there. I don't know if they knew each other, but I remember Ms. Seton calling and telling him about the professor being interested in the Count. He was sure in a bad mood after he hung up."

"Andrian never mentioned knowing Jeffrey or the Count?"

"No."

"Do you know if Andrian knew that Jeffrey had the box?"

Her eyes got big. "Yeah, I mean, I thought you told him the box was found in Jeffrey's motel room."

"I mean before Jeffrey's murder. Did he know Jeffrey had the box?"

She didn't say anything.

"Did you know Jeffrey had the box?"

She started back fiddling with the toy again. "How would I?"

"Did you see it in his motel room?"

When she did not answer, he probed, "Did you tell Andrian you had seen the box in Jeffrey's motel room before Jeffrey was killed?"

Her silence told him she had. That must have been

the reason Andrian went to see Jeffrey.

"When was the last time you saw Mr. Blankenship?"

Her face tightened. "The last time I talked to him?"

"What happened?"

She hesitated.

"Ms. Clark, what happened the last time you saw him?"

Just then, an older woman stepped into the room. She did not acknowledge Sean or Arlo. Her Russian words cut through the room as she spoke to Kat. Sean did not understand what she was saying. Kat spoke Russian in return in a pleading voice. Her mother's admonishment brought a snap plea from Kat. Her mother abruptly turned and went back down the hall.

Kat started rubbing her arms in agitation. "I'm sorry about that. My mother grew up here, but Mama is still of the old ways. She is afraid of the police—afraid you will make us disappear—or something like that." Kat suddenly stood. "I'm sorry, Sheriff, but I can't talk anymore."

Sean and Arlo stood. Sean asked, "Whose car is that out front—the Dodge?"

Her eyes widened. "Mama's, but we share it."

Sean and Arlo closed the door behind them. She was already walking back down the small hall.

Arlo commented as they walked to the cruiser, "I was in the military, but her mother—can't imagine going into battle against her." Sean hid a grin.

"What do you think, Boss, about what she told us?"

"If Andrian knew Jeffrey broke in and stole the box, that's a motive for killing him. If the professor thought Jeffrey was hiding research from him to somehow undercut him, that's a motive. Kat obviously is not telling us everything, and his seeing another woman is a motive. I think we need more information on Andrian before we talk to him. I'm going to ask Syd to go back to Cincinnati and see what she can learn about him."

Chapter 57

Mary Zimmstein had called Cheryl the previous day and asked if she would stop by the Grand Hotel. She was trying to clear things out so C.P. could get the renovations underway, and she had come across some things that might interest Cheryl.

The Grand Hotel had been a source of pride for Bekbourg when it opened its doors in 1912 in the downtown near the stately courthouse. Clientele were greeted with elegance and opulence by its detailed crown-moldings, crystal chandeliers, hardwood floors and lavish furnishings. It was right up there with the other grand hotels of its day. Unfortunately, its heyday was short-lived. Its decline started with the Great Depression, and it closed its doors in the late 1930's. One of C.P.'s goals when he returned to Bekbourg was to renovate the Grand Hotel to offer travelers upscale hotel accommodations in the downtown.

Cheryl pushed open the door to enter what once had been the lobby to the Grand Hotel. It now served as a lounge and hostess area for the GilHaus, which was off to the other side. Cheryl walked past the huge desk and knocked on the door leading to what once was the hotel owner's office space. Because she was expected, Cheryl walked on in. She had never seen Mary in jeans, but here she was—dressed in designer jeans, flannel shirt, leather athletic shoes, and her hair pulled back in a low ponytail. Cheryl laughed, "Mary, what a shock. How cute you look."

Mary had a soft laugh. "Well, what else am I going to wear with all this dust and moving things around? C.P. offered to have someone here to move boxes and help with anything else I might need, but I wanted to get organized first. Then, maybe I'll ask for help, but for now, I am fine."

Cheryl nodded. "When I am going through the archived boxes at the newspaper, I work best by myself. I can get through things quickly and organize as I go."

"I have some bottled water if you want some. Or, we can ask the restaurant hostess here to bring coffee."

Cheryl smiled. "Thank you, but I am fine."

"When C.P. and I were dining with you and Sean the other evening, you were talking about trying to find information about when the Russian Count and his wife visited Bekbourg. I came across a box in one of the storage rooms that had the year 1925 written on it. In it was a file labeled, 'Passenger Train Lodging.' It appears the conductor prepared a list of the train's passengers when he realized the train could not make it to Cincinnati. The railroad needed someone with experience to help with finding lodging for all the passengers, and they reached out to this hotel's owner, Hugo Marschall."

Mary took a file from a table and brought it to a small antique coffee table placed in front of two upholstered chairs that looked to go back to the '30's. "These have been cleaned. I wanted a place to sit and have coffee and found these upstairs. C.P. had someone carry them down for me."

Cheryl smiled to herself. *Of course Mary would assure me the chairs were clean.* "Perfect."

They settled where Mary could open the file on the small table. "See what you think, but I believe that Hugo took control of the situation and found places for all of the passengers to stay while the train was stranded here. There are written notes of house addresses near here. For example, see this house address? It's on Main Street. Here are four passengers with the same last name—likely four family members. It looks like they stayed at the house there. Here is another example where it looks like the single passengers were assigned to the boarding house."

Cheryl slowly turned the pages, looking at the hand-written entries. "I believe you are right, Mary. This is exactly the type of information I have been hoping to find. Andrian ran up against a wall in finding much in the railroad files, and I exhausted all the places to look in my archives and those in the library. This is an amazing find. I never thought about the hotel's records."

"Well, who would? I am glad I came across this. I did not make copies, so if you could please return it when you are finished, I would appreciate it. C.P. probably will not want to keep it, but I will discuss it with him at some point once I have things better organized."

"Of course, Mary. I am so grateful you found this and called me."

"I am happy I was able to contribute."

They talked briefly about the upcoming holidays and how Rachel was doing. Even though Mary concealed her emotions, she seemed distracted. Cheryl finally asked, "Mary, I don't mean to pry, but if something is on your mind, I hope you know I can take off my reporter's hat and be a friend."

Mary smiled. "Of course I know that. I have come to count you and Bri and Dilly as close friends."

Frankly, given how private a person Mary was, she expected Mary to claim she was fine and change the subject. But Mary surprised her. "Maybe a good friend is what I need just now." She told Cheryl she cared deeply for C.P. and felt the feelings were mutual and that Rachel loved C.P. and they had a great relationship. "I have been reticent to bring the subject up to C.P., because maybe he is happy with things the way they are. I am hesitant to risk what we have now by making things awkward by telling him how I feel."

Cheryl was silent. She was not sure what to say. She thought she knew how C.P. felt about Mary, but what if she was wrong?

Mary shook her head. "I'm sorry. I should not trouble you with my problems. Please forgive me."

Cheryl put her hand on Mary's. "No, it's not that at all. I am thinking about what you just told me. My personal feeling is that C.P. adores you. When he looks at you, I see pride and love. You both seem so right for each other. Is there a reason he might be holding back?"

Mary shook her head. "I do not know. It could be the age difference, but Cheryl, that does not matter at all to me. We enjoy each other's company and, frankly, have fun together. Every time the phone rings, I hope it is him, and I always look forward to seeing him."

"Mary, what if you both are feeling the same way, but neither takes the risk to broach the subject? You and he have known each other for two years now."

"I know. I don't know what to do."

Cheryl looked into Mary's eyes. "It will come to you. You will know what you should do when the time comes. My advice in the meantime is to keep having fun."

Mary's laugh was genuine. "Thank you, Cheryl."

Chapter 58

"Hi, Lucky," Sean propped the phone against his shoulder and leaned back in his chair to hear what his friend had to say. "Life treating you okay?"

"Can't complain. I hope I don't shoot a hole in your bucket."

"Oh, yeah. What's going on?"

"We've been digging into Jeffrey Blankenship and Dimitri Shlykov and came up with something interesting. Remember we told you about the businessman and a dealer who were murdered in Dallas about ten years ago?"

"Yeah, he dealt on the black market."

"That's right. Well, we think there may be a connection to something that happened four years ago in Houston."

"Okay," said Sean.

"There is a very wealthy collector who lives in the Woodlands, about thirty miles north of Houston, who has an impressive collection of Russian artifacts. This guy is perfectly legitimate, so no underground deals. His father started a drilling company, which is a global giant. Even though he's in his eighties, he inherited it and still runs it. His son and daughter will take over at some point, but I'm getting off target. There is a large museum in Houston that this man was going to loan his Russian collection to for a six-month exhibit. He's done this before with other museums around the country. To do this, the museum hired a security company to transport the items from his house, which is like Fort Knox, to the museum. And, Sean, we're talking about a lot of pieces, from jewelry to china and glassware and silver to jeweled eggs—even a scepter and tiara. When the items arrived, the museum's curator cross-checked the lists and found that a jeweled egg was missing. I don't know the exact worth, but it was in the millions.

"To make a long story short, one of the security guards swiped it out from under everyone's noses and had a planned rendezvous about ninety miles away in Beaumont, Texas, with the black-market dealer who hired him to steal it. Only, the security guard—the thief—stopped at a gas station, and when he got back in the car, someone surprised him with a gun and forced him to drive to a secluded area. This carjacker stole the egg and tied the man up. There was enough circumstantial evidence to convict him, and he's in prison there in Texas. Elias and I took pictures of the professor and Jeffrey and met with him two days ago, but he couldn't identify either. He never met the black-market dealer who hired him, so he couldn't tie the dealer to either. It was dark, and the carjacker had a hood on, so he couldn't get a good description. He said he's glad he wasn't killed by his carjacker.

"He didn't think the person who hired him originally to steal the egg was the same person who carjacked him. He told us the original mastermind didn't care what he stole—just as long as it was of significant value. He thinks the carjacker knew about the plans and double-crossed the mastermind. He got the feeling the mastermind was working solo. A car passing by saw the security guard tied up and called the police. An APB was already out, and the police took him into custody. He never heard from the mastermind or what happened to the egg."

"That's interesting, but how does that fit with what's going on around here?" asked Sean.

"We did some checking, and Dimitri was in Houston at the time. He was staying in a hotel downtown. The records show he was checked-in for four nights before the egg was stolen. He checked out the day the Russian artifacts were being transferred."

"So you think Dimitri is the international jewel thief Interpol is after?"

"I wish it was that simple, Sean. Jeffrey Blankenship had checked into a hotel outside the 610 loop two days before this all went down. He also checked out the same day as Dimitri. They each must have had cash for gas and lodging, because we can't trace their movements from Houston until they got back to Maryland."

"Did the egg ever show up?"

"No. But here's a kicker, Sean. Talk about a coincidence—a few days before Elias and I saw him, Dimitri showed up at the prison to talk to this man. Dimitri gave him his spiel about being an expert on Russian history and had heard about the missing egg. He wanted to know what the man could tell him about the egg. He also asked him about what happened that night he was carjacked and if he could describe the man. The man told him what he told us—the carjacker was tall and skinny and that's all he knew because he was dressed in all black with a hood and dark gloves."

Sean sipped his cold coffee before responding. "Blankenship was tall and skinny. Why would Dimitri be talking to this man?"

"Damn good question, Sean. He told him he consulted with museums and gave lectures about Russian history and his specialty is the Czar's lineage and their estates and jewels—all of which is true. Elias does not want to question Dimitri just yet since it might spook him. Also, we're tracking his whereabouts over the past twenty years to see what patterns we can put together. But, we might finally have a lead."

"It doesn't sound like the man thinks Blankenship was an accomplice, but Blankenship and Dimitri could have been working together and planned it this way in case someone got suspicious of Dimitri."

"And now, Blankenship is dead."

Sean thought for a moment. "If Blankenship did double-cross Dimitri and stole the egg, and Dimitri suspected that, he would have a motive to kill him. But, if Dimitri and Blankenship were accomplices in an international theft ring, why would Dimitri kill his partner? If it's them, they have worked together off the authorities' radar for years."

"Yeah, but we don't even know if they have anything to do with Interpol's investigation. I don't know how any of this helps your investigation into Blankenship's murder. If Dimitri didn't kill him, that means someone else did it," offered Lucky. "You got any suspects yet?"

"I'm looking into a couple of people, but it's too early to call them suspects."

Sean asked Lucky about the date Dimitri visited the man in prison, and it corresponded with the dates Bri had told him Dimitri had left town.

Chapter 59

Bekbourg, January 1925

Patrick O'Doherty, an employee of the hotel, had been assigned as the Count's butler during his stay at the Schrievers. Since Patrick did not speak Russian, Katia translated between the two men. Patty, as he was called by his friends, was an enterprising and charismatic young man who had started in the carriage facility for the hotel when he was fourteen years old and had worked his way through luggage handler and bellhop, to assistant concierge.

Katia had slept little the night before as she considered her mother's warnings. Those warnings swirled in her mind as she translated between Patty and the Count about the Count's requirements for the remainder of his stay in Bekbourg. She was convinced the two Russians intended harm to the Count. She was concerned she might be framed since she was in close contact with him. She needed to warn him. She figured he would know how to handle the situation. She saw her chance when Patrick asked the Count about the attire he wished to wear at the evening's ball.

"What did he say?" demanded the Count.

"Sir, he is asking what you would like to wear to this evening's dinner and dance, but Sir, I fear your life is in danger."

Zakhar looked hard at Katia, "Speak!" he snapped—causing Patrick to look like he had offended the Count.

Before Patrick could say anything, Katia rushed her words. "Two men from the train are staying with us. They were assigned. We had no choice. They are Russian." She then told him about Yegor asking about the Count. "My mother is afraid. She hates the communists and fears they may be spies following you."

Patrick was wondering why there were so many words to a simple question about what the Count wanted to wear to the ball this evening, but seeing the Count's severe expression, he did not interrupt.

The Count asked what the men looked like, and her description, including the scar on the one, sounded like the two men who had been following him since Paris. The Count thought he had lost them. How did they end up on the train? They must have seen through the decoys and circled back. "Damnation!" he roared.

Patrick's eyes went wide. "What are you saying? I just wanted to know what he wants to wear tonight," he murmured to Katia.

The Count's angry attention turned to him, and

Katia quickly assured the Count he merely was asking about the wardrobe selection for tonight. The Count barked the instructions, and Katia quickly translated. Patrick went to work, but while he was sorting through the Count's clothing, he came to a jewelry case. He peeked inside thinking it was perhaps cufflinks or a watch or something the Count might like to wear with his formal suit. Instead, he saw a glimpse of a necklace and thought it belonged to Elizabeth. While the Count and Katia were engaged in their conversation, he slipped it in Elizabeth's bedroom and laid it on the night table where he knew her maid would be assisting her when she returned from tea.

The ball was held at the Grand Hotel. The Count and Elizabeth were the guests of honor. Elizabeth was dressed and waiting for the Count, along with Harry and Kathleen Schriever, in the carriage house. When the two couples arrived at the hotel, Harry Schriever as well as the hotel owner had photographers waiting inside. Both women wore furs, but Elizabeth brought gasps when her fur was lifted. She wore a short blue velvet jacket draped over a sleeveless Grecian styled silk evening dress with the drop waist and silver metallic beading. Zakhar's mouth went dry when the fur coat was slipped from her shoulders to reveal the necklace.

Until near daybreak, the attendees were entertained by string musicians, feasted on delicacies, relished the finest of wine and liquor, and delighted in waltzes and ballroom dancing. Elizabeth was giddy when they arrived back at the guest house, only to face Zakhar's wrath when they entered the bed chamber. "How dare you go into my room and get the necklace."

She stepped back. Her face was flush. "What do you mean?" She had never seen him this angry.

"Where did you get that?" he demanded pointing at her neck.

Her hand followed to the necklace. "I found it on my night table when I returned this afternoon. I thought you left it for me to wear this evening. What have I done to anger you so?"

"I did not leave it there!"

"Well, that is where I found it. Why are you so angry, Zakhar? Everyone tonight was admiring it. I told them it was a gift from you."

His lips firmed. "It is not a gift, Elizabeth. I let you wear it, but only when I give my permission. I do not know how you got it, but in the future, you are not to wear it unless I tell you. Now, return the piece so I can retire for the night."

Katia and Patrick could not help but hear the Count's words carrying through the guest house. Patrick asked Katia what he was yelling about, but she feigned limited understanding and shrugged her shoulders. She wondered why the Count would be so upset with his wife wearing such stunning jewelry, unless it had something to do with the spies.

Patrick interrupted her thoughts. "Do you think I should see if he needs my assistance?" he asked somberly.

"I would wait to see if he rings."

He nodded at her sage advice.

The following day, the Bekbourg Tribune ran an article about the ball.

Chapter 60

Syd spent a full day in Cincinnati, starting with the apartment complex where Andrian had lived before moving to Bekbourg. The apartment manager told her he lived a fairly quiet life and provided her Andrian's previous address. He had lived in the apartment about six years. He was timely on his monthly rent payment, and the few times maintenance had entered his apartment for routine jobs, nothing looked unusual.

Syd knocked on a door beside what had been Andrian's apartment. A young man answered and invited her in once she told him her purpose. He said Andrian was a nice guy. He shared that Andrian sometimes had women friends in but no one steady. His brother sometimes came in for a weekend. He visited his brother, who lived in Houston, a couple of times and went to Florida to see his parents around the holidays. Other than that, he did not know of him traveling much. They got to be friends somewhat. They both were single and sometimes would grab a beer. Andrian had lived with his parents all during college and for a couple of years after graduating college to pay off college loans. After that, he moved into the apartment. His parents subsequently sold their house and moved to Florida.

"I was shocked when I saw him at the mailboxes, and he told me he was moving to Bekbourg. Hell, I had never heard of the town. He told me he saw where the owner of a local railroad was looking for an archivist to get a train museum up and running. I asked him how long he was going to be there. It didn't seem like a long-term project. I asked if he thought he might end up running the museum. Andrian didn't know but didn't seem all that worried about his future."

Syd had made an appointment with his supervisor in the afternoon. She was pleased to find a parking space along one of the streets on the University of Cincinnati campus. As she walked through campus, she observed students hurrying between classes. The campus was a combination of older and newer buildings. Construction was ongoing in rehabbing existing structures. The campus was larger than she had imagined, and she liked that the football stadium was at the heart of the campus. She would like to have seen where the women played basketball, but she had just enough time to grab a snack before her meeting.

Andrian's ex-supervisor was waiting for her when she arrived. He had praise for Andrian's job performance. Andrian was friendly with his co-workers, and there were no complaints there. The supervisor was not aware of Andrian socializing with his co-workers outside of work, except for an occasional planned group event.

They were about to wrap-up when Syd asked, "Is there anything else you can think of I should know?"

He hesitated, but then replied, "Well, I don't know if this is important, but I did get a call from the university's events coordinator. Of course, being a university, we are always bringing in guest speakers. When she called me, she was put out that one of my employees was 'antagonistic' to one of the speakers." He put his fingers in quote. "A retired professor who now lives in Cincinnati and who is an expert on Russian history was asked to speak here. It appears that Andrian asked provocative questions during a Q&A period after the professor's speech. He and the professor exchanged sharp words before the host intervened and asked her own question to get the topic back on course. She told me it wasn't the first time Andrian had been confrontational with that same professor. I have his name around here somewhere." The supervisor pulled out a drawer and leafed through some files. "Ah, here it is. I kept his name just in case I got called again. It's Dr. Dimitri Shlykov."

"What happened the other time?"

"I'm afraid I don't know. All she told me was that the history department asked Dr. Shlykov to come speak, and during his presentation, Andrian asked some questions that Dr. Shlykov took exception with."

Syd got the name of the events coordinator from the supervisor, but she was off campus at meetings. Syd asked her assistant to have the events coordinator call her. She was curious as to the rift between the two men.

Next, Syd drove to the address where Andrian had lived before he moved into the apartment. It was a middle-income neighborhood with houses built around the 30's and 40's. Some were better maintained than others—mostly three bedroom homes, but some with four. Some had garages converted into a room. Small walk-up porches with white wrought-iron railings were the norm. No one was home at the house where Andrian had previously lived. Syd knocked on the doors to the houses on either side, but no one was there. From a street view, she saw that a TV was on in the next house over, so she knocked on that door. A woman in her seventies answered the door. When Syd identified herself and told the nature of her investigation, the woman invited her in. Her husband had a walker beside the chair where he was sitting.

His wife told her husband that Syd was asking about Andrian's family. She muted the TV and asked if Syd wanted coffee or water. Syd declined, but thanked her. The woman answered most of Syd's questions, but her husband sometimes interjected his own view. They told her that Andrian's parents had lived there a long time. They were good neighbors. Andrian's father worked the assembly line at the Ford plant, and his mother started work when the boys were in school. Andrian was the younger of the two boys by about eight years. The elderly couple never knew of any trouble with the boys. The man's father, Andrian's grandfather, moved in with them after his wife died. Andrian's mother had told the woman that he had been sickly as long as she knew. He had worked for several years at the Ford plant as a custodian until he had to quit. He then took on different jobs as he was able to work. After he retired, he worked around the yard, and had a way with flowers. "They had the most beautiful flowers around here," she told Syd. "The only time they did not have blooming flowers was in the dead of winter. We miss them living here. Andrian's grandfather moved with them when they moved to Florida a few years ago. They wanted to be where the weather was warmer year-round."

Her husband said, "My wife is right. They were good people. The only thing is that I had a hard time talking with the men."

"What do you mean?" asked Syd.

"Well, the old man, it was nearly impossible to understand him. His accent was so thick. His son, Andrian's father, was a little better. I'm pretty good at talking with people who speak Spanish, but they spoke Russian, and I sure didn't know that language."

On the drive back, the events coordinator called Syd. She remembered both presentations by Dr. Dimitri Shlykov. They were well-attended, and the professor's talk about the lead-up to the Bolshevik revolution was interesting. "He went into more detail about some of the personalities than most history books." She remembered some of the attendees were uncomfortable with Andrian's "combative" questioning. "I was only at Dr. Shlykov's second talk, and I finally interrupted and moved the questioning away from Andrian. I wasn't at the one when Dr. Shlykov talked to the history department, but I heard a similar thing happened. The Department Head stepped in there."

"What was their sharp exchange about?" asked Syd.

"The professor was suggesting the Bolshevik revolutionaries were short-sighted in what they wanted to accomplish and brought more ruin to Russia long-term than the Czar's continued rule would have. Andrian didn't agree and was asking pointed questions about the heavy-handed rule and the hardships on the peasants. I decided to intercede when it got personal. Andrian said something like it was people like him, meaning Dr. Shlykov, who would rob the country blind and didn't give a shit about the Russian people."

"Do you think they knew each other?"

"I don't think so. I think each man just had strong opinions."

Chapter 61

Usually by this time of the day, Cheryl would have popped into his office at least once. Milton decided to stop by her office to see what had her preoccupied. When he walked to her door, he found her studying papers spread across her desk. "Have time to catch up?" he asked as she looked up.

She leaned back in her chair. "Always for you."

He sat and popped gum in his mouth. "What are you so hard at work on?"

She explained that Mary had given her a list of the passengers who had disembarked the train. "It shows where the hotel arranged for them to stay. The Grand Hotel did not have room for everyone. Some people opened up their houses. The railroad paid them to let the passengers stay with them. The conductor must have written two lists—one for the railroad's records, which Kat found, and one for the hotel owner, which Mary had. They're almost identical in the names that appear on both."

"What has you puzzled?"

She told him about the three other Russians on the

train. She held up a piece of paper. "I have the passenger list found in the hotel's records. It doesn't show a first-class passenger named Boris Solyanka. However, on the manifest found in the railroad's files showing first-class passengers, his name is circled."

"Mmmm. What about the other two Russians. Where did they end up staying?"

"This report," she waved the hotel's list, "shows they stayed with the Nikoleav family. Interestingly, that was Kat Clark's great-grandmother."

He scratched his neck. "Huh. Have you talked to her yet?"

"No, but I'm going to. I learned from the history professor at Hillsrock Community College that Kat's family is Russian. At least her mother's side is. According to the professor, her great-grandmother was brought here as an infant by her parents who emigrated from Russia."

"Learn something every day. If you want, I'll look over those two lists and see if anything jumps out at me about Solyanka. Sometimes, another set of eyes can't hurt."

Cheryl smiled. "I would appreciate it. I know I'm overlooking something. I just can't figure out what it is."

Chapter 62

Bekbourg, January 1925

News came that repairs to the track were nearing completion, and the train would resume service in two days.

At the Count's suggestion, he and Elizabeth were spending a quiet evening at the Schriever's, just the two couples, after the gala the night before. Katia used the quiet time to call her mother to check on her and the children. When her mother answered, Katia was alerted to her strained words. Katia asked, "How are the children?"

Her mother's blunt response: "Fine," raised further suspicion.

Katia's words were slow in coming. "And you? How are you?"

"Fine."

Katia suspected something about the two Russian men, but she did not want to specifically mention them if they were listening. "I saw the two neighbors earlier today," she broached by slowly saying each word. Hopefully, her mother picked up on the clue. An elderly man lived on one side and never ventured out, and the two sisters who lived on the other side were in Florida for several weeks. *"They said you called them the other day."*

Her mother was quiet and then replied, *"Ah, yes. You know how they like to read murder mysteries?"*

"Yes," Katia deliberately replied with a fictitious name, *"especially Gerty."*

"Yes, Gerty. She was telling me about one book where two women plotted the death of a rich woman who everyone hated in the small town in Ireland. They waited until the last minute to surprise her before she was to set sail for a trip. One stayed behind to see that the other was successful when she snuck into the rich woman's home. Quite a mystery according to Gerty. Oh, I must go now, Katia. The tea is brewing. Take care." With those last words, her mother disconnected.

Katia took that strange message to mean that one of the Russians was at their house and the other planned to kill the Count. In the afternoon, the Count had told Patrick he would not be needed during the rest of the evening, so he was working at the hotel. Katia did not know what to do, but she needed to warn the Count. What if the Russians planned an ambush at the Schrievers tonight or tomorrow during the hunt outing?

She went upstairs and readied the Count's bedchamber for the night, all the while thinking of a plan. She finally decided she would go to the hotel and find Patrick and tell him of the plot, but she also had to think how *she could protect her mother and children. Would they be harmed by the Russian who was staying put at their house? If she could get word to the Count, surely he and the other men would know how to solve the problem.*

Chapter 63

The two night deputies had just gone off-duty, and the three day-shift deputies were preparing for the assignments. Sean entered, sat in a chair near his deputies and stretched his long legs in front of him. Alex, Arlo and Syd took that as a sign Sean wanted to talk about the investigation. Alex sat down on a desk, and Syd leaned back in a chair behind a desk. Should it become necessary to scribble notes, Arlo sat near the white board.

"Let's start with you, Arlo. Tell everyone about our conversation with the waitress from Knucklepin's and our interview with Kat."

After Arlo finished, Syd asked, "What are their alibis?"

"I confirmed with the owner at Knucklepin's that the waitress was there until her shift ended at one o'clock." Arlo told them a witness had seen a car parked in the area where Jeffrey was shot that very much fit the description of the car Kat and her mother shared.

Sean spoke up, "We need to talk to Kat again and pin her down on that, but I wanted more information before we do that."

"So, maybe you should add both of them as persons of interest," Syd offered.

Arlo turned to write. "Good suggestion. I'll footnote that the waitress has an alibi. By the way, her car is a white SUV, so it doesn't match any car we've heard about that night."

"Syd, what have you been able to learn about Andrian?" asked Sean.

Everyone listened intently as she reviewed her notes. "Sheriff, I know you don't believe in coincidences. Andrian's family is Russian."

"Come again?" Arlo perked up.

"Yeah. The neighbor told me Andrian's grandfather spoke very little English, and Andrian father's English was broken. He said they were of Russian descent."

Arlo pivoted to the board. "You found out a lot, Syd. I'm putting that Andrian is Russian in a parenthesis next to his name."

Alex grinned at Arlo's theatrics. "I'm sure glad you like writing on the board, Arlo."

True to form, Syd sat stoic.

Alex sat forward. "Him being of Russian descent has to be relevant. And, he and the professor had some familiarity, and it doesn't sound like they were on friendly terms."

Arlo looked at Sean. "Maybe that's why Kat never saw them working together." He explained to the other deputies that Kat said Andrian had not worked with the professor or his assistant.

Alex noted, "I don't think Andrian has been in Bekbourg all that long. When did he move here?"

She checked her notes. "It was the third week in September."

"That's about a month after Cheryl's article was published," Sean highlighted for the group.

Alex flipped through his note pad. "The first time Blankenship came to town was about two weeks after her article was published, so he got here first. He came two more times before he and Dimitri arrived together."

Arlo looked at Sean. "Chief, you think Andrian came here thinking there might be some missing jewelry here?"

"I don't know, but that missing depot box is a connection between Andrian and Blankenship. If Blankenship was the one who broke into the depot and stole the box, he was the one who assaulted Andrian. I guess it could have been Dimitri who did it and took the box to Jeffrey's to store, but Dimitri acted like he didn't know anything about the box."

"What's in the box?"

"I looked through everything. I can't see how the papers relate to anything. I looked closely at the pictures. Everyone getting off the train was bundled up in their overcoats and hats, so nothing looked unusual there. There wasn't anything that jumped out at me when I looked at the faces. I didn't see anything revealing about any luggage or anything. Bottom line, we need someone to tell us more about the box, and with Blankenship dead, that leaves Andrian."

"How does the stolen box have anything to do with missing jewelry?" asked Syd.

"That's a good question, Syd. I'm not sure it does. We need to talk to Andrian again."

Alex asked, "What if Blankenship found the jewels the night he broke into the guest house? If Andrian or the professor shot him, maybe they stole the jewels."

"If either of them did that, why would they still be hanging around here?"

Arlo piped up. "I agree with her, Amigo. I'd be long gone if I had jewels worth millions of dollars and just shot someone."

"Good point," admitted Alex. "So, if they are after some jewels, they haven't found them yet, because they're still here."

"We can't lose sight of Kat. We need to talk to her again. She's got a motive," Sean reminded them.

Alex pointed out, "It's odd that a research assistant would have a gun in his coat pocket."

Arlo looked at his board. "I've got three names, well four if you count the waitress who drives the white SUV, as persons of interests—Kat Clark, Andrian Kray and Dimitri Shlykov. That's better than a blank slate."

Alex mumbled, "Hopefully, we can solve this before the list gets longer."

"They all three drive small, dark cars. The witness saw a small dark car leaving without lights on right after the victim was killed," Syd reminded everyone. "And, according to the witness Alex spoke to, there was a small dark car with something on the front side panel parked near the guest house that night. But we don't know if it's the same car or two separate cars."

"Good point." Arlo added the car information after each suspect's name.

"Syd, check to see if any of these persons of interest own a gun that is the same make as the one that killed Blankenship. Alex, give me thirty minutes and then ride over and tell Andrian we want to talk to him at the station. Arlo, check out Kat's neighbors and see what they can tell you. Also, check with the employees around Frau's and see if they remember anything about Blankenship. He had some receipts in his car from there."

Syd's written report about her trip to Cincinnati raised Sean's interest when he saw that Andrian had spent some time in Houston. He called Lucky to see what the FBI could learn about Andrian.

Chapter 64

Sean walked into the interrogation room. He moved to shake Andrian's hand, "Hi, Andrian. Thanks for coming in. We're trying to run down some information pertaining to Jeffrey Blankenship's death."

"Okay, Sheriff. I don't know how much I can help, but I'll try."

Sean tried to pinpoint a relationship between Jeffrey and Andrian, but there was nothing beyond the brief meeting in the depot.

Sean then questioned him about his relationship with Dimitri. Andrian's surprise showed when Sean asked about the two lectures. Andrian told him he did not know the professor—had never met him beforehand. He attended out of his interest of Russian history and took exception with parts of the professor's lecture.

"Does your interest have anything to do with your family having Russian ancestry?" asked Sean.

Andrian blinked and then recovered. He realized Sean had been investigating him. "Both times, the professor's lecture seemed one-sided. I thought he owed it to the audience to present the other side. I never saw him after that second lecture."

"Did you read the article in the Cincinnati newspaper about the Count and his wife being in Bekbourg before you took the job with C.P.?"

Andrian was growing more measured in answering Sean's questions. "I think I read it. I saw C.P. was seeking an archivist. I was ready for a change and thought the opportunity sounded interesting. When I came here and met with C.P., I decided to take it."

"You gave up a good job working for UC."

Andrian shrugged his shoulders.

Sean was skeptical. Andrian was a young man. Not only did he give up a good job for a university and take a job for a railroad which may not offer a long-term position, he moved from a large, dynamic city with sports teams and other attractions and opportunities to a much smaller town.

"There wasn't something in Cheryl's article that prompted you to reach out to C.P.?"

Andrian rubbed his head, "Like what?"

"You tell me."

Andrian drank water and did not respond.

Sean opened a folder and pulled out pictures from the box found in Jeffrey's motel room. Andrian rubbed his short hair again. "You recognize these?"

Andrian quickly glanced at them. "They look like the ones in the box that was stolen."

Sean took each one and showed it to Andrian. He did not lean forward or show an interest in viewing them.

"Andrian, we have witnesses who remember seeing you walking near C.P.'s house. Any reason you made a habit of walking there?"

"I walk lots of places around town."

"From your apartment, you have to drive there. So why walk there?"

He shifted in the chair. "Just a nice place to walk."

"Ever been in the guest house at C.P.'s?"

He drank some more water. "Yeah, once. After the story came out that the body had been there since the early 1900's, I was curious. I like history, and that was interesting to me. So, I asked C.P. if I could see the house. He asked the contractor to take me inside."

"You go into the basement?"

"Yeah. There and the rest of the house."

"Let's talk about the box. Did you know it was in Jeffrey's motel room?"

Andrian looked hard at Sean. "Look. I don't know what you're getting at, but I don't think I should talk to you anymore without a lawyer. I can assure you though that I didn't kill that man."

Because it appeared he was clamming up, Sean did not want to push him too hard just yet. He decided to drop it for now and see what else might turn up in their investigation.

"Okay, Mr. Kray. We appreciate you coming in."

After Andrian left, Sean and Alex talked, and both agreed Andrian was hiding something. "We only know of two things that happened in Cincinnati that could have even put Bekbourg on his radar," Alex said. "One was Cheryl's article, and the other was C.P.'s job description. Bekbourg doesn't come close to the size of Cincinnati, and he took a job where he works in a train depot all day. Best we've discovered, he doesn't even have any friends here to hang out with. Why do that unless it was something in Cheryl's story that drew him here?" Alex shook his head. "When I walked into that depot to find Andrian, it seemed like a dungeon. It must be boring as hell with no one to talk to all day."

"Well, I think Kat is usually there, too. That desk back in the corner is her space."

"That's good then. At least he has someone else who is usually there, but it's still gloomy as hell in there. I'd go crazy. Although, sometimes I wonder if that might be better than having Arlo around."

Sean laughed. He knew Alex was kidding. Arlo was the jokester around the department, but he was a damn good deputy.

Chapter 65

Cheryl was on her way out of the office for the day and stopped by Milton's office. "You should go home. Martha will be looking for you."

He grinned. "Yeah. Now that the boss is leaving, I guess I can slip out."

Cheryl's laugh was hearty. "Let's walk out together."

"Sure, but do you have a minute?"

"Yes." She took a chair, which miraculously was clear of paper stacks.

"I may have something for you. I compared the list Mary gave you with the railroad list and manifest. On the manifest, I think the Count reserved two sleeper compartments in first class. One was for him and his wife and the other for Boris Solyanka and Eloise Dorgan. We don't know who they were, but they shared this sleeper. Boris, though, was not on the list Mary gave you, and his name is circled on the manifest. So, for some reason, he did not need lodging, which says to me, he was not on the train when it pulled into Bekbourg. Why? That's a mystery. Now, for the other two men you think are Russian, they were not in first class, and they ended up staying with Kat Clark's ancestors. So, you need to find out who Boris was and why he *wasn't* on the train when it stopped here."

"Mmmm. If he wasn't on the train, then I don't see how he had anything to do with the body found in C.P.'s basement."

"You've been focused on the train and the body found in C.P.'s basement, but let me throw out something to consider. What if the Russian found in C.P.'s basement has nothing to do with the train? You mentioned that Kat's family was Russian. Maybe it's a relation to them that was buried. Or, it could have been some other Russian who lived here or stopped in. With the train passing through here from cities east and west, we don't know who could have stopped off here. Hell, the body could have been buried there a few years before or after the Count was in town. The ME couldn't nail down the exact year of death. I guess my point is that we're so focused on tying it to the Count's train, but that might not be the case at all. You also told me that neither the police archives nor ours shows any missing persons records that were relevant to the remains found."

"But, doesn't that support the notion it was someone from the train?"

"Well, only if it happened that week, but we don't know that."

She paused, and Milton pulled out a piece of gum from a desk drawer and put it in his mouth. Milton had been a chain-smoker for years, but after his heart attack, gum had replaced cigarettes. She pushed forward in her chair. "Let's go home to our better-halves."

They both stood and prepared to leave. He said, "I can tell you're not entirely on board with what I said."

"It's not that. You are one-hundred percent right that there is nothing that ties the two events together."

He chuckled. "I sense a 'but.'"

She laughed and put her arm affectionately through his, "But, it's that gut feeling I have."

He knowingly nodded. "You can't do anything about that except plot your next course of action."

"Exactly, but for now, I'm going to think about getting home and seeing Sean and Buddy."

"Great idea."

Chapter 66

Cheryl popped wide awake in the early morning hours and laid there thinking about her next move. Frustrated that she could not get back to sleep, she got up and took Buddy for a run. After spending time in the office, she went to the depot, but neither Kat nor Andrian was there. Cheryl stopped by the main office, and C.P.'s assistant told her Kat was working from home. Cheryl decided to go see if she would talk with her.

Kat answered the door and was surprised to see Cheryl. "Please come in. Don't mind the mess. My son is not good at picking up his toys."

Cheryl laughed. "I feel right at home. We don't have children, but our dog has toys and chew bones spread throughout the house."

"I just made some coffee. Would you like some?" Kat asked.

"If it's not too much trouble, I take it black."

While Kat went into the kitchen, Cheryl noticed papers spread across the coffee table and a laptop on the sofa beside where she had been sitting. Cheryl heard Kat talking to a woman, and when Kat brought in the coffees,

Cheryl said, "I'm sorry. I don't mean to disturb you."

Kat shook her head. "You're not disturbing me. Joey's at school. We live here with my mother. I was talking to her in the kitchen."

Cheryl told Kat about the two Russians—Sascha Krayevshy and Yegor Dobrynin—who were on the train and who stayed with Kat's great-grandmother's family. "Do you know anything about that?"

Kat's eyes were big. "No, I've never heard anything about that. So, you think the Grand Hotel manager put them up here?"

"Well, from what I have gathered, the railroad paid people to host people who got off the train, and the hotel manager kept a ledger of who stayed where."

"Like I said, this is the first time I've ever heard of this."

"Do you think your mother might know something?"

Kat frowned. "She hasn't ever said anything about it. I will ask her, and if she knows something, I'll let you know." Cheryl could tell Kat did not want to involve her mother in the conversation. Kat must have realized how she came across, because she leaned toward Cheryl and whispered, "Mama likes to stay to herself."

Cheryl nodded. "Okay, well I better go. I see you're busy."

"Yeah, I brought all this home, but I'll probably go back into the office next week."

Cheryl stood, and Kat moved to walk her to the door. "Thanks, again," Cheryl said as she left.

After Cheryl left, Kat's mother came into the living room. Kat knew her mother had been listening from the kitchen. "I'm surprised you didn't come in and meet Cheryl. She owns the newspaper. You really like reading it."

"She's good newspaper lady."

"Yes, she is. Did you hear what she asked me about the two Russian men who stayed with our family back then?"

Her mother's eyes hardened. "Why these people not let sleeping dogs lie? Past is past. I need wash Joey's clothes." She turned to leave.

"Mama, do you know anything about that?" Kat raised her voice to be heard as her mother walked down the hall. Ever since Jeffrey had first come to their house, her mother had acted odd when he came around or at the mention of his name. Of course, her mother had been a better judge of character than she, but still, there was something else going on. Dealing with her mother was frustrating, and her being as secretive as she was made Kat's aggravation grow.

"That wasn't productive," Cheryl thought as she walked to her car, but she had come up with another idea when she couldn't get back to sleep, and that was to call Libby with a question she had.

Libby's voice was friendly. "I have been going through my grandmother's things during her time with the Count. I'm glad I talked to you about everything. This has opened my eyes to a side of Grandmother I never knew."

"I'm glad to hear that. Have you come across anything that pertains to their trip to Bekbourg?"

"No, but if I do, I will let you know. Is there something I can help you with?"

Cheryl described the two mystery passengers who were assigned to the sleep compartment next to the Count and his wife—Boris Solyanka and Eloise Dorgan. "Does either of those names sound familiar?"

"Actually, they both do," Libby's voice brightened. "Eloise was my grandmother's maid for many years. She started work for her when she was just sixteen and stayed by her side for nearly forty years. Grandmother cared a great deal about her, and when Eloise started having health problems, Grandmother bought her a place in Florida.

"Boris was the Count's valet. He came over to the U.S. with him after he and Grandmother married. Boris did not speak English—only French and Russian. Eloise knew a little French. The Count wanted Boris close by, and Grandmother wanted Eloise near her, so the Count booked them joint sleeping quarters on the train. They weren't going to contradict the Count, but Boris was not going to travel under those conditions with Eloise even though there was an attraction between them. He slept in a seat in the car near the door. Unfortunately, there was a cold breeze, and he fell ill. A doctor on the train told the Count Boris needed to get off at the next stop and go to a hospital where he could receive the care he needed, and that's what happened. He recovered and took a train back to the house in Rhode Island. Because of his attraction to Eloise, he wanted to stay in Grandmother's employ, and she needed a driver. Eloise and Boris got married and worked for Grandmother until they moved to Florida."

"Okay, that solves that mystery. There were two other Russians on the train who got off here. Sascha Krayevshy and Yegor Dobrynin. Have you ever heard of them?"

Cheryl could tell Libby was thinking. "No, I never heard Grandmother talk about either one of those men."

They talked a few more minutes. After Cheryl hung up, she thought, *At least I know something more than I did before I called her.*

Chapter 67

"Sean, it's Lucky. I've got some information for you."

"I could use some."

"I have a friend who works for the Smithsonian. I emailed that photo of the necklace to her. I hope you're sitting down."

Sean rotated his head to lessen neck tension. "Why do I get the feeling I'm getting ready to get hit by an eighteen-wheeler?"

"More like a M1 Abrams tank. My friend said she is not familiar with this necklace, but the design looks very similar to the royal pieces made by the Czar's jeweler. She wanted to know more, but I kept everything quiet. But Sean, she said if this is what she thinks it could be, it's worth millions to dealers and would be considered priceless by museums. Russia would claim ownership, museums would be falling over each other to get it, dealers would stop at nothing to get it, and black market dealers would kill for it."

"Okay, well if that's all I'm dealing with," Sean deadpanned.

Lucky laughed. "Okay, that's all I've got. I'm still working on Andrian Kray and also the professor and the assistant. I'll be in touch."

How was it he and Cheryl could have become involved with Russian jewels belonging to the Czar here in their small town? "Maybe we haven't." At least he hoped like hell they hadn't.

Chapter 68

After dinner, Sean and Cheryl put on their jackets and took Buddy for a walk to the park. The slow pace of the walk was to be expected—given Buddy's frequent stops. Sean, however, held tight to the leash in case action picked up if the Lab spied a squirrel racing in his path. "How's your research coming?" he asked.

She told him about learning of the two Russian men staying at Kat grandmother's house and her visit with Kat. "Kat didn't know anything about it. Her mother must not have known anything either, because she had never mentioned it to Kat, but Kat was going to ask her."

"Did you know Andrian visited the guest house where the Count stayed?"

Cheryl turned to him in surprise. "The one C.P. is having restored?"

"Yes."

"No, he never mentioned that. When did this happen?"

"It was after the remains were found there."

He asked Cheryl what type of information he had given her from the railroad files. She told him, but expressed her disappointment that he had not found more. "I guess the railroad just didn't have a lot. It was Kat who found the manifest."

"Did you know Andrian's family was Russian?"

"What? No, he never mentioned that either."

He told her about what he had learned about Andrian's family being Russian. Cheryl furrowed her brows. "I wonder why he never said anything to me about that." They took a few more steps before Buddy stopped to sniff at a tree. She looked at Sean. "You're suspicious of something, aren't you? What is going on with Andrian?"

"I'm not sure anything is, but your suspicions that perhaps a treasure hunt is going on here for missing Russian jewels has me thinking about possible connections."

"And learning Andrian is Russian seems relevant?"

He shrugged.

They strolled a few more steps. "And a professor of Russian history coming here—you're suspicious of that too, aren't you?"

"Let's just say that I'm not ruling anything in or out. Someone killed Jeffrey, and I need to find out who and why."

Chapter 69

There was something she was overlooking, but she could not put her fingers on it. She had the papers Mary had given her and the railroad's passenger list spread in front of her. She was also thinking about Andrian and the professor and Sean's suspicions. Why were two Russian men traveling on the train? As she stared at the two names, Sascha Krayevshy and Yegor Dobrynin, a light came on. *Oh, my gosh! Andrian's last name is Kray! Many immigrants with long names shortened their names. Sean doesn't believe in coincidences. Could Andrian somehow be related to Sascha Krayevshy?* She called Sean to tell him.

Chapter 70

Alex came rushing into Sean's office. "Sheriff, I've got something that might be important."

"What's that?"

"You know how old man Brown, who lives in Highland Heights, is always complaining about everything?"

Sean nodded. He was well aware of Brown's numerous complaints—kids riding bikes, dogs peeing on the hydrant and shitting near the sidewalk, garbage flying away from the garbage truck. The City Council had received its fair share of his complaints as well. Brown was an elderly man who lived alone, and his neighbors avoided him like the plague.

"Kim handed me a complaint that Mr. Brown dropped off today. He was fussing about a black Ford that has been parking in front of his house. I wasn't real happy about going to talk to him, but I'm glad I did. Most of the houses on his street only have driveways big enough for a single car—and many of the home owners have two cars. Parking gets tight along the street. Well, over the past few weeks, this car would occasionally park in front of his house at night, and he hates that. Finally, he left a note on the windshield to 'Stay off my damn property.' Of course, it's not his property, but he doesn't care what he says. He thought he had solved the problem because the car didn't park there again until the night Blankenship was murdered. Brown was fuzzy on the time, but he saw it before he went to bed so he guessed it was around ten o'clock. When he saw it, he got so mad, he took a picture of the license plate and wrote a note and told the owner he was going to report him to the police. He made a copy of the note to show to us. Here's a copy of the note. See, the date's the same as Blankenship's death."

Sean studied the paper. "Did he put the note on the car that very night as this date?"

"That's what he said. About ten o'clock. He doesn't know what time the car left, because he went back inside and went to bed. He saw the car was gone the next morning."

"Do you have the picture he took of the car license?"

"Yes." He handed it to Sean. "I ran the tags. It's registered to Andrian Kray."

Sean reflected on that news. "How come Brown filed this complaint today?"

"I asked him that. He said he thought he had. He laid it on a table where he keeps his mail and things, and it got mixed up with them. He came across it yesterday evening and brought it in today. That's what he told me. He's an old man, but his mind seems pretty sharp."

"Did he hear or see anything suspicious that night?"

"No. I don't think he believed the car was suspicious. He just didn't want it parking in front of his house."

"Has it parked there since that night?"

"He said 'no,' but he wants us to tell the driver not to park there again. I told him the city ordinance allowed parking along the street. He didn't want to hear that." Alex shook his head. "I cautioned him about bothering other people's cars parked along the street. The neighbors avoid parking there to keep from riling him. Maybe this driver won't be back."

Sean thought to himself, *especially not if the driver had something to do with Blankenship's death.*

Chapter 71

Andrian was not at the depot, so Syd and Alex went to Andrian's apartment over the retail store, which was not far from the depot. He lived in an efficiency apartment. The kitchen was in front and contained an apartment-sized refrigerator, stove and sink. There was a single cabinet under the sink and one above the sink and the stove. A small bedroom and bath were at the back. Papers were scattered on the small dinette table. Boxes Alex recognized as ones similar to those he had seen at the depot were stacked in the corner. The sink contained dirty dishes, and clothes were scattered on the chairs. Andrian's hair was standing on end, and he had not shaved. He wore a flannel shirt and jeans and was barefoot. A coffee cup was on the dinette table.

"Alex?" Andrian spoke as he looked between Syd and Alex.

Alex introduced Syd. "Mr. Kray, the sheriff wants to talk to you at the station."

Andrian seemed uncertain what to do. Alex saw a discarded pair of socks and shoes. "You might want to put those on."

"What's this about?"

"Can't say, Sir. Please get your shoes on so we can leave."

When Sean walked into the interrogation room, Andrian was agitated.

"Sheriff, why am I here?"

The new information was what Sean had been looking for. He wanted to focus the interrogation on Andrian's potential involvement in the murder. He did not want to confuse things with the jewels and the possibility that Sascha Krayevshy was somehow related to Andrian. "Mr. Kray, we have a witness who can put your car near the guest house the night Blankenship was murdered. I am close to charging you with his murder. What were you doing there that night?"

Andrian bent his head and rubbed both hands back and forth a couple of times over it—before jerking up his head. "It's not against the law to park somewhere and walk around. I'm a night-owl. I like that neighborhood. It's quiet. I had no idea Blankenship was even in the area. I never heard anything. I walked and went home. It had to have been before the shooting, because I did not hear the sirens or anything."

Sean leaned forward. He stared hard into Andrian's eyes. "That's not good enough, Kray. I'll tell you what happened. You knew Blankenship had that box in his motel room. Hell, you went there the evening before he was killed, banging on his door. When he didn't answer, you decided to follow him the next night. You confronted him and killed him." Sean's voice had risen. "What pissed you off so much that you killed him? Was it him stealing the box, or assaulting you, or both?" Sean's voice was steel.

"None of that," Andrian yelled back.

"Don't lie to me! You knew he had the box, Kray!"

"I didn't kill the bastard! Shit!" Andrian took a couple of deep breaths. "Look, I didn't do it. What about Kat? Have you talked to her?"

Sean looked a long time at Andrian. "Kat Clark?"

Andrian suddenly looked contrite but nodded.

"What has she got to do with Blankenship's death?"

When Andrian faltered, Sean pushed. Andrian reluctantly opened up about the day she told him of Jeffrey having the box and suspecting him of breaking into the depot.

Kat was sitting at her desk doodling when he came into the depot. She jumped up. "Oh, god, Andrian. I am so sorry." His head was still bandaged, and his eye was black. He had returned to work the next afternoon after the assault.

He slowly moved to his desk and looked down. He looked accusingly at her. "Who moved my things?"

Her eyes were large. "It was the police. They were trying to find who did this to you."

He nodded and cringed at the sharp pain racking his head.

"Here, Andrian. Sit down. I'll get you a cup of coffee. It's not that old, but I can make some more if you want it."

"Just pour me what you've got."

She rushed into the kitchen and poured him a cup.

"Did the police tell you the box is missing?"

"Yeah," he muttered.

She was rubbing her arms. "Look, Kat. This has you all strung-out. Why don't you go home? I need to work."

She started rubbing her arms faster. He looked at her. He was feeling bad enough and could not handle her stress. "I just stopped by, Kat. I'm going back home. Maybe you should, too."

She blurted out, "I think I know who took the box."

His head snapped up, causing him to grimace. "Who?"

"The professor's assistant."

Andrian rubbed his forehead like he had a headache but kept his eyes focused on her. "He's the one who broke in here and clubbed me and stole the box?"

She nodded.

"Did you tell the sheriff?"

Kat looked at her hands. "No, I didn't know what to do."

"How do you know he did it?"

"I saw the box in his motel room."

He nudged his head back and stared at her a long time. She couldn't bear the sense of betrayal she saw on his face.

Andrian lowered his voice. "Why would he have the box? How would he even know about it?"

She plopped down in a chair and started rubbing her head. "Kat, what the hell is going on?"

She threw her head back and took a deep breath. "I thought I was helping. I knew you were working with Cheryl and that Jeffrey was the professor's assistant. I knew you found those pictures. I was having dinner with Jeffrey, and I told him about the pictures in the box. I swear I never thought he'd do what he did. Anyway, after I found you and the police came, I realized the box was missing. That was all that seemed to be missing. I knew I had told him, and I figured it was him." She paused.

Andrian moved to pick up his phone. "I'm going to call the sheriff."

She lunged for the phone. "No! You can't!" she screamed. She had not considered he would do that.

He pulled the phone close to his chest. "Why not? Why the hell not, Kat?"

"He'll kill Joey! He said he would. He told me he'd burn our house down if I told anyone."

Andrian frowned. "What?" he nearly shouted. His head was starting to pound.

She started crying. "He's going to kill Joey and Mama if I tell anyone, but I had to tell you. I feel so bad. He almost killed you." Andrian put his phone down. Her sobbing started to quiet. "I don't understand what is going on!" she wailed. "You've been secretive. I know you come in at night and go through boxes. You weren't *even going to tell Cheryl about the pictures. Then, you get pissed at me when I told you I gave Jeffrey the passenger manifest. Then, I tell him about the box, and he breaks in here, nearly kills you and steals the box." She dropped her head into her hands.*

He swiped his hand across his mouth. "Look, Kat. None of this is any of your business. You had no right to be telling him anything. C.P. told me, not you, to work with the professor." He swore.

She looked up. "You're not going to tell anyone are you? If Jeffrey finds out I told you, he will do something terrible to Joey."

"I won't tell anyone. Look, I'm leaving."

"I'm sorry," she yelled as he moved to leave. "He was using me, and I was too stupid to see it. I hate him! I wish he was dead!"

Andrian was beyond frustrated. He swore as he dashed out the door.

"So you think she shot Blankenship?"

"Well, she had a reason. She said she hated him and wished he was dead. I just know it wasn't me!"

Sean instructed Andrian that he was not to leave Bekbourg without notifying him. Alex drove Andrian back to his apartment.

Chapter 72

Kat was trying to work at home, but she needed a break. Too much was on her mind. She gathered up a box she was finished with and drove to the depot. She stopped by the main office to assure C.P.'s assistant she was working from home and was there to pick up some more records to review. She asked if Andrian had been in. The assistant told her that he, too, was working from home, but that the police had come by to see him. When she told them he was working from home, they were going to run by his apartment.

Kat barely remembered leaving her office. She broke out in a sweat, and her heart was racing. She knew if they were questioning Andrian, he might tell them about Jeffrey threatening Joey. They would be coming for her. She got in the car and drove home. She stumbled in the house. Her mother was sewing a button on Joey's shirt and knew something was wrong.

"Katrina, what is wrong?"

Kat knelt down at her mother's feet and laid her head on her mother's lap, sobbing. "Oh Mama, I have made a terrible mistake."

Her mother pulled back and took Kat's face between her hands in a firm grip. "Tell me!"

Kat's emotions were raw as the words spilled out from her memory.

Kat looked in the rearview mirror and brushed her hair and applied lipstick. She walked toward his door. Suddenly, the door swung open and a woman she recognized as a waitress at Knucklepin's stepped out giggling. Jeffrey moved to the door frame wearing only a pair of jeans with his belt unbuckled. She turned and kissed his lips. He did not move to hold her, but he smiled when she pulled back. "Bye bye, Jeff. Call me."

She stumbled past Kat, who stood with her mouth open. As Jeffrey moved to look as the woman moved away, he saw Kat. Shock and temper collided. "What the hell, you SOB?" she yelled. Her face was red, and her eyes were flaring. She ran toward him wanting to scratch his eyes.

He grabbed hold of her arms in such a painful grip, she screamed out. "What the hell are you doing here anyway?" he hissed. "Leave before you embarrass yourself," he growled as he shook her. When she wouldn't stop struggling, he glanced around and yanked her into his room. He threw her onto the bed. "Shut up, you idiot!"

Despite the fury in his face and stance, anger overcame any sense of fear. "You SOB! You used me!" She glimpsed the box along the wall behind him. "Oh, my god, it was you! You stole the box and almost killed

Andrian." She started to get off the bed. "I'm going to tell the police!"

He stomped forward and yanked her hard to a standing position. The searing pain caused her to scream out. He growled through clinched teeth. "Listen, Bitch, before you start running your mouth to anyone, you better think about that brat of yours."

Her eyes popped wide open and she stilled from fear. "What the hell is that supposed to mean?" she stuttered.

His eyes narrowed, "You screw with me, and your son will wish you had never met me. I'll burn your damn house down." With her quiet and pale, he squeezed her arms tighter, but the fright she felt negated the pain. "If you know what's good for that boy of yours, you'll keep your damn mouth shut. You understand me, Bitch?" He shook her.

She numbly nodded.

He grabbed her arm and dragged her toward the door. He gritted through his teeth, "Stay out of my sight and keep your damn mouth shut or else." He twisted the door knob and swung open the door and pushed her out. She stumbled but kept her balance.

She did not remember walking to her car. She was trembling. A fool! My mother was right! That damn SOB used me! Her fists balled so tight the veins in her arms bulged. No way in hell will I let him get anywhere near my family. I will stop that monster! That SOB will regret this! He has no idea what he has stirred!

"Mama, I was there that night. I followed him from Knucklepin's. I saw him get out of his car and walk toward the guest house belonging to C.P."

Kat's mother stared out the window. *The police will take my daughter away.*

Chapter 73

As Alex was leaving with Andrian, Arlo passed them in the parking lot. He went to Sean's office and caught Sean as he was grabbing a coat. Before Arlo could ask what was happening with Andrian, Sean told him to grab a coat, that they were heading to Kat Clark's house and he would explain on the way.

The small black car was out front, so they knew someone was home. Arlo knocked a third time hard enough to rattle the window in the door. Finally, Kat opened the door, and it was obvious she had been crying. "Ms. Clark, we would like for you to come with us to the station."

Just then, Kat's mother yanked the door back where she could see them. "Where you take my daughter?"

"Ma'am, we need for your daughter to come with us to the police station."

Her eyes were dark and bore hard into Sean's. "Why?"

"We need to ask her some questions." Sean was polite, but firm.

"It's okay, Mama. I'll get my coat."

Her mother continued to glare at the two policemen.

Kat appeared with her purse and slipped out the door. "Tell Joey I'll be home as soon as I can. His friend's mother is bringing him home after supper." She looked at her mother, "Bye, Mama."

Her mother said something in Russian, and best Sean could tell, she was telling her not to talk to them.

Kat chattered nervously to Arlo about different things as they waited for Sean to join them in the inter-rogation room. Sean brought her a bottle of water. "I've never been in a police station, Sheriff. I haven't done anything wrong, have I?" She was ringing her left wrist with her hand. Her green eyes shone more vivid than the first time they talked.

"I'm sorry about my mother. I guess stories passed down from her mother and grandmother about the old ways in Russia impacted her. She doesn't trust the police. I've tried telling her, but she won't listen."

"It's understandable, Ms. Clark. We have some follow-up questions." Sean went back over some of the territory they had covered before.

Through the questioning, she told how she had met Jeffrey when he came to their house. He had learned from the librarian her family had long roots in Bekbourg going back to the early 1900's and that her ancestors were Russian. She explained that they started dating and she thought they had a future, but then he started to withdraw. She admitted she told him about the box of pictures—thinking that might show how she cared for him and hoped it would rekindle their romance. Seeing him with the other woman broke something in her, and she sobbed as she relived him yanking her into his motel room and threatening the lives of Joey and her mother. She answered questions about telling Andrian and begging him not to tell the police. Kat described her feeling of scorn toward Jeffrey when the waitress rubbed their relationship in her face.

"So, Ms. Clark, you sat in your car at Knucklepin's?"

"Yes."

"You saw Jeffrey drive up and park?"

"Yes, and I just sat there. I couldn't bear going in and seeing him with that bitch."

"Then what?"

"I waited, and then I saw him come out and get in his car. He pulled out, and after he was far enough away so he wouldn't notice me, I pulled out and followed him."

"Where did he go?"

"He drove to Highland Heights and parked. I pulled in a parking place about four spaces away. He sat in the car for a few minutes. Then he got out and started walking toward C.P.'s house. The iron fence that goes around it isn't that high—about three feet. He jumped over it and headed to the small house out back. I sat there for about thirty minutes, and he didn't come back. It then hit me that I had something on him—I was going to call in an anonymous call and tell you that Jeffrey was snooping around at C.P.'s. I hoped you would arrest him, and then I'd be free of his threats."

"So then what?"

"I drove home."

"Did you ever see him come out?"

"No, the last I saw of him was when he jumped over the fence."

"Did you see anyone else walking or driving by during this time?"

"I saw a woman walking her dog. I also saw a couple walking. That's all. It was cold that night, so not many people probably wanted to be outside. That's another reason I left. I was cold, and I didn't want to turn on the engine and let the car run, because it might draw attention."

Sean had a few more questions and then asked Arlo to drive her home. As he stood to return to his office, Kim came rushing up. Sean glanced through the window to see that it was starting to get dark. She handed him a note. "Boss, Alex and Syd are at this address. I didn't want to interrupt your meeting, but a man has barricaded himself in his house and is threatening to kill himself. He and his wife had been fighting, and he thinks she's seeing another man." Sean was already moving to grab his coat and hat.

Chapter 74

Patti walked to Cheryl's office and knocked on the door. "Sorry to interrupt. I know you're trying to put the finishing touches on the morning's edition, but a woman is insisting on talking to you. She says it's important. It's hard to understand her."

Cheryl looked at her watch and frowned, "Who is it?"

"Kat Clark's mother."

Chapter 75

Bekbourg, January 1925

Just then, Katia heard a glass break downstairs. She froze, listening as she might. More glass broke and then a click of some sort. Someone was breaking into the guest house, and she was alone. Panicked, she glanced around—either she could slide under the bed, hide in the closet, or slip behind the heavy drapery. Someone was walking around downstairs and now was at the foot of the steps. She had to hide quickly, so she tiptoed behind the drapery and pushed herself flat against the wall— turning her feet sideways so they wouldn't be seen under the drape—a trick she had learned growing up playing hide-and-seek.

She heard him enter the room. She could not see who it was, but she suspected the Russian. He started throwing open drawers and doors and searching the room. Finally, he poured something from the decanter and sat in a chair.

Katia was barely breathing and her legs felt numb from standing. Suddenly, she heard the front door open.

Who is that? she pondered. The Count and his wife would not return this early. The man in the room stood and quietly slipped behind the door. Oh no. Please don't let it be Patty. Katia had developed a crush on Patrick. She could not see anything and was too afraid to move the curtain and peek. Someone walked in and stopped, obviously seeing the state of the room. The Russian behind the door jumped out and yelled. The Count jumped back but did not run, because the Russian had a gun pointed at him.

"Those jewels your wife was wearing in the hotel last night—they belong to the Russian people. I will start shooting—first your knees and then move from there if you do not give them to me now!"

Katia recognized Yegor's voice.

"There were two men following me. Where is the other one?"

"In case one failed, there is still one to take the jewels to Russia. But I am not going to fail."

"How do I know you won't kill me after I give you the necklace?" the Count sounded calm to Katia's ears."

"You don't, but you will certainly die a more painful death if you don't," Yegor sneered.

"If you kill me, you will never find them," reasoned the Count.

"Perhaps your wife will know where they are."

The Count was quiet and then responded, "She does not know, and I do not want her hurt. If you give me assurances you will not harm her, I will give you the jewels."

The Russian considered the proposition. "I just want the jewels. I will not harm her if you give them to me now."

The Count slowly moved into the room and walked to a chest that had already been searched. He tugged on the heavy piece and struggled as he slid it out. He then moved to kneel behind the piece, but when he did, he snatched a hidden pistol and fired at the Russian. The Russian fired back as he fell, hitting the Count in the shoulder, but the Russian was on the floor after having been shot, and the Count rushed over and shot him in the head.

Katia jerked aside the curtain. When she saw the Count was struggling, she helped him to the bed and immediately tried to stop the bleeding. He implored her to help him drag the Russian to the basement. They wrapped him in a blanket to prevent blood from dripping, dragged him down the stairs and then rolled his body into the cellar below. She then helped the Count to the parlor and raced to the house to summon Schriever. The Count had instructed her to tell Schriever it was an attempted robbery and that the robber had escaped with the necklace.

Schriever rushed in with his personal valet. He took the Count to his house and summoned a physician with strict instructions that nothing was to ever be said about the Count being injured or the robbery incident. Katia ran to the hotel and got Patrick. When they arrived back at the guest house, she told him what had happened.

She said that the Count wanted them to bury the body in the basement and not to ever tell anyone, not even Schriever. Patrick and Katia then quickly buried the body in the basement.

In the early morning hours, Patrick took Katia home. The Russian known as Sascha was not there. Her mother did not know where he had gone—only that he was feeling ill. Later, when Katia was alone with her mother, Katia told her about Yegor trying to kill the Count. She confided that the Count had shot Yegor in self-defense and—at the Count's direction—she and Patrick had buried the body in the cellar. "You were right. They were after the jewels."

"I see," said her mother. "What happened to the jewelry?"

"I don't know," said Katia. In all that had happened, she had forgotten about it. "Yegor seemed to know the Count wasn't at the guest house. He broke in. I heard him and hid."

Her mother's eyes widened. "You were there? I thought you were at the hotel."

"No. How did Yegor know to go to the guest house?"

"A messenger brought something here," her mother explained. "That is when they plotted that one would go to the guest house, and the other would wait here."

"A message—someone wrote in Russian?" Her mother remained silent.

"Why did Sascha fall ill?" asked Katia.

"He drank my tea," her mother calmly replied.

"When he started feeling the effects, I locked me and the children in the back room and listened. He staggered out the door."

Katia paused. "What about Yegor. Did he drink the tea?"

"No. I made him a cup, but he wanted to go to the guest house."

Katia looked at her mother, who looked serene. "Do you know where Sascha went?"

"No. He will either live or not."

"You were not concerned he would come back or Yegor would come?"

She shrugged. "If he lives, he does not want to be anywhere around here now that people think someone tried to rob the Count—rumors get around. We know Yegor won't be back."

"You don't know who the message was from?"

"The mean one, Yegor, acted like it was someone from the hotel who gave him a tip. That's when they made the plans. I couldn't hear what they were saying, but I could tell it was a scheme."

Katia thought it was all odd. Had the Count sent a message to draw them out? Why had he left the dinner and come back to the guest house? If he set a trap, how did he know both wouldn't come? She figured she would never know the answers.

Harry Schriever brought the doctor to his home and treated the Count for two days while waiting on the train to depart. The staff was told the Count had taken ill.

Harry Schriever arranged for the Count to be taken early to his private rail car, along with the doctor who would accompany him on into Cincinnati, so no one would see that he was being helped on the train. He and his wife made a point of being seen with Elizabeth at the depot to keep rumors from swirling.

Katia and Patrick got married that spring. As far as Katia knew, Patty never told a soul. As she grew older, she told her daughter, Kat's grandmother. She never wanted the story told outside the women of the family, who had passed it down through each generation. Klara was waiting until Kat was older, but now, fate had changed things.

Cheryl walked Kat's mother to the door and watched her get in the older model black car. It was starting to get dark, and Patti had already left for the evening. She was anxious to tell Sean what Kat's mother had told her. Cheryl tried to call Sean, but he did not answer. She called the main office number, but Kim had gone home for the evening. It was not urgent enough to call Dispatch. Cheryl then called C.P., hoping he was in town. When he answered, she breathed a sigh of relief. She told him she had something important to tell him and asked if he could meet her at his house. He was already home, so she drove over.

Chapter 76

Cheryl arrived at C.P.'s and started up the walk. He opened the door before she stepped on the porch. "Come inside. You've got my curiosity up."

After she finished telling him Klara's story, he set down his drink. "Does this mean what I think it means?"

"C.P., I think the jewels must be hidden in the upstairs bedroom. That's where the shooting happened."

"The electricity is turned on in the guest cottage. You want us to go to the guest house and see if we can find anything?" he asked.

"I was hoping you would suggest that." Her eyes were bright with excitement.

He grinned. "I'll grab my coat. Mary is in Columbus tonight, so I'm a bachelor. This beats watching TV."

Cheryl laughed.

He explained as they walked over that there were two bedrooms in the upstairs with a bath in between. "It sounds like from what Kat's mother said, we should be looking in those bedrooms for a hidden place for the necklace."

"Yes. I know that stories get changed as they are handed down in families, but that's a good starting point. Is there one more likely that the Count would have used?"

"One is slightly larger."

C.P. unlocked the front door and turned on the lights. He briefly showed her around the main floor before heading upstairs. The house smelled like sawdust, and particles floated in the air under the light beams. Construction horses held up a large sheet of plywood in the dining area, which was used as a work bench to hold tools, cans, small boxes and pencils and paper. Large plastic drums were sitting around. Cheryl saw boxes of nails and hammers lying around. Tool belts lay on the floor and on cabinet frames in the kitchen. "The contractor made sure the foundation was structurally sound. That's when they discovered the body. Fortunately, both the house and this guest cottage are built like a fortress, and we haven't run into any structural issues. They are getting all the wiring and plumbing done. They won't work on the walls, ceiling or woodwork upstairs until they get it done on the first floor. The contractor told me they wanted to get everything done, and then they would paint the whole house."

Cheryl and C.P. climbed the steps to the second floor, which led to a landing. C.P. turned on the hall light and walked to the larger of the bedrooms to turn on the light. "See what I mean. They haven't even started up here. If we don't find anything in here, we'll check the other bedroom."

The bedroom had a small closet and a tall chest standing near the closet.

C.P. pointed to the chest. "There were a few furniture pieces in both houses, which Mary liked. She thought I should keep this and the one in the other bedroom. The men will remove them when they get ready to work up here. The couple who owns the antique store is going to refurbish them."

"It's a beautiful piece, C.P. One of us could check it and see if there is any hiding place."

"That's a plan. I'll carry one of the ladders up here. If we need to check anything high, we'll be ready."

C.P. started with the door and began working his way around the room, meticulously rubbing his hand over the walls—inspecting as he went. He checked the molding around the ceiling as well as the baseboard. Cheryl started with the chest, pulling out every drawer, putting her hands inside and feeling and pressing every point of contact.

As they worked, C.P. mentioned that Sean and Alex had inspected the house. "I doubt they spent this much time feeling every corner."

Cheryl responded, "Well, they didn't have the information we have. If what Kat's mother told me is accurate, we know something happened in one of these bedrooms. I'm sure Sean and Alex closely inspected everything where they thought something could be hidden, but they didn't even know for certain anything had happened here."

"I agree. For all they knew, they were spinning their wheels in this house."

They worked for a while longer, and then C.P. said, "Here, Cheryl. Look at this. It feels like a soft spot under this wallpaper."

Cheryl happened to have a water bottle in her coat pocket, and he found a rag. She watched as he scraped the wallpaper off the wall with a screwdriver he found downstairs. Under it was an indentation. C.P. used the screwdriver to poke away at the plaster. "Look, Cheryl. Hell, I think that's a bullet imbedded in here."

Cheryl looked in the hole. "I think you're right." She looked around the room. "Well, if our information is right, that must be where the Russian agent was standing." She pointed toward the opposite wall near the door—"because the Count was near a chest."

"Yes, but we don't know if the chest is in the same place as it was then."

"Good point. I finished going over every part of the chest except the back. Can you help me scoot it out so I can check the back?"

They heard a loud creak. "What was that?" Cheryl asked, momentarily distracted.

"These old houses are always creaking. Here, let me help you move it. I'll check the wall behind it when I finish up the rest over here."

"C.P., the wallpaper behind here isn't faded like the rest of the paper. I suspect it's always been here close to the closet."

"Makes sense."

Cheryl checked the back of the chest. "I don't find any hidden compartments in the chest, so I'll start in the closet," she said.

She began running her hands over the walls the way C.P. had done. Because there was not an overhead light in the closet, she had difficulty seeing. "C.P., you might consider having them put an overhead light in the closet. There isn't much light that gets in here from the room."

"I'll tell them about that tomorrow."

She finished up with the parts of the walls she could reach and slid the ladder into the closet. She was grateful it was one of those light-weight aluminum ladders. It was a tight fit, but she climbed the rungs and ducked her head to be able to get past the door frame. She turned to the wall above the door and started feeling her way. Suddenly, she came to something that felt like a hairline crack in the plaster. She moved her fingers over it and realized it led to a cavity behind the horizontal board of the doorframe. She needed to take one more step up the ladder, but—given the angle she needed to stand—it would make the ladder wobbly. "Hey, C.P., I may have found something. Would you mind holding my legs while I reach up and see if I can get my hand in this?"

C.P. grasped her legs to steady her while she took another step. She extended her arm and was able to put her hand down the slot. She felt something soft. Her fingers gently slid the velvet fabric up to the edge, where, with the help of her other hand, she was able to secure it. "Got it!"

She slowly lowered her hand to give him the pouch. He laid it in an open drawer in the chest and helped her off the ladder. They looked at the pouch. Cheryl's heart was pounding. "Oh my gosh, C.P. Do you think this could be the necklace?"

He laughed. "Well, there's no time like the present to open it and find out. Now, we wouldn't be here without your sleuthing. You do the honors."

Nervous energy ran through Cheryl. She could not fathom opening the velvet bag and seeing Russian royal jewels worth more than her imagination could register. She gently picked up the pouch and pulled the top. She looked into the bag and saw something shiny. She took a breath and pulled out the necklace that Elizabeth had once worn. "Oh, my god! C.P., look at this."

They both were mesmerized by the jewels before them.

"I'll take that!" ripped through the room. C.P. whirled around, and Cheryl gasped. By instinct, she jerked the necklace and pouch to her chest.

C.P. had grown up in the railroad business, and he had scraped and clawed his way to being an executive by being ruthless and fearless. Many union representatives hated going up against him. He intended command with his calm, authoritarian words. "What the hell are you doing here, Shlykov?" C.P. had seen the gun pointed at them before he even noticed it was the professor.

Cheryl's mind was working on options as she watched Dimitri. She had always thought his eyes seemed cold, but tonight, she saw something deadly. "What are you going to do?" she asked, hoping her voice did not quiver.

"First, I want the jewels." He motioned with the gun for C.P. to step aside so Cheryl could hand them to him.

C.P. moved over, but only by a step. "Dimitri, we need to work this out. Those don't belong to any of us."

Dimitri sneered, "There's nothing to work out. I've got a buyer lined up. Then, I'm going to disappear."

"Then, you don't need to hurt Cheryl or me."

He shook his head. "I wish it was that simple, but I've got to have time to leave the country."

"Sean will figure out you did this," Cheryl said.

"Oh, he will figure out all right, only he'll have the wrong person. See, he already suspects that damn Bolshevik. All I have to do is plant this gun in the right spot, and he'll go down for killing you both. Meanwhile, I collect my fortune and enjoy the rest of my life."

"Was Andrian trying to find the jewels, too?" C.P. asked, trying to buy some time to get a plan.

"I don't know. I met his grandfather. His family carried loyalty to those blasted revolutionaries."

"Was Jeffrey after the jewels, too?" asked Cheryl.

"Ah, Jeffrey! Somehow he found out I had contacts in the black market. That SOB had stolen a painting before I got a chance to claim it. I suspected it was him, but I never got word from the underground. A similar thing happened with a valuable Russian imperial egg. When I learned he had come here before he told me about the Count and then had not given me the manifest, I knew he was double-crossing me. Sean will likely conclude Andrian killed Jeffrey too, because it's the same gun. Regardless, I will be out of Sean's reach.

"Now, Cheryl, if you don't hand over the jewelry right now, I'm going to shoot C.P. in the face."

"Okay." Her hands were trembling. She couldn't think of a way out of this. "I'll put the necklace in the pouch and hand it to you."

She glanced at C.P. as she dropped the necklace into the pouch. She saw his eyes motion to the floor behind the chest. He wanted her to fall to the floor. What did they have to lose? Dimitri was going to shoot them anyway.

She threw herself on the floor, and C.P. jumped behind the chest on top of her. He shoved the chest toward Dimitri, hoping it would fall on him. Dimitri was too fast and jumped out of the way. Several shots rang out as C.P. fell backwards against the wall. Cheryl was screaming as excruciating pain overtook her senses—a second before things went black.

Chapter 77

The sudden, blaring siren stirred Cheryl. Flashing blue and red lights triggered her eyelids to flutter as she became aware of voices. "Ms. Seton."

She heard someone yell to "Get the Sheriff."

She felt the strong hand take hers and knew it was Sean. She rolled her head toward him and saw his smile. "Hello, Beautiful."

She rubbed her thumb along his hand and gradually became aware of her surroundings. A medic told Sean they were ready to leave, and she tried to raise her head. Sean gently put his hand on her forehead to stop her from moving. "Honey, you're going to be okay, but they need to take you to the hospital to check you out. Kye will be there along with Mom and Dad."

"What happened?" she mumbled. Fuzzy images were floating in her memory. She suddenly jerked, "C.P.! What happened to C.P.?"

Sean tried to calm her, "He's on the way to the hospital. We'll know more once they get there. Right now, the medics are ready to take you. I'll be there as soon as I can." He bent over and lightly kissed her lips.

She felt him move back as the gurney started to move. Unconsciousness prevailed as she struggled to remember what had happened.

By the time the medics got her to the hospital, she was waking up. The doctor examined her and wanted to admit her overnight for observation, but Cheryl would have no part of that. Jim and Helen were already at the hospital and—against her protestations—insisted she sit in a wheelchair so they could move her into the waiting room. It was then Cheryl saw her shirt was covered in blood. Kye was already in the waiting room and rushed over to do her own inspection of Cheryl.

Cheryl asked them about C.P., but all they knew was that he had been shot and was in surgery. Jim said, "No one has told us much. Sean called and gave me a thumbnail sketch. Told us you and C.P. were being transported to the hospital, that you were going to be okay, but that C.P. had been shot. What happened?"

Cheryl gave them the abbreviated version, jumping right to her and C.P. searching for the jewels, finding them, and then Dimitri showing up with a gun. She remembered C.P. slamming the chest over in hopes of knocking Dimitri off balance, but he dodged and started shooting. "I was on the ground and saw C.P. get shot. I heard several shots. He fell against the wall and then on top of me. I remember a lot of pain when he fell on me, and the next thing I knew, I was waking up as they were ready to take me to the hospital." She looked at the blood. "That's C.P.'s. It's not mine." She flinched, "Mary.

Someone needs to tell Mary."

Helen, Sean's mother, rubbed her hand. "Bri is driving to Columbus to tell her. She didn't want to call her and then have Mary drive here, at night, in an emotional state."

Cheryl was still confused about what had transpired. "Dimitri was going to kill us. What happened? What stopped him?"

Despite Jim's grim look, she heard pride in his voice. "Sean did. I don't know the details, but he got an urgent call that you and C.P. might be in danger. He got to the bedroom where you all were just as that SOB opened fire. Sean took him out—he's dead."

They had been told by the nurse that C.P. would be in surgery for hours. Since Cheryl did not want to have C.P.'s blood on her when Mary arrived, Jim went to their duplex and got her a change of clothes.

A couple of hours later, Bri and Mary walked into the waiting room and saw Cheryl with a large adhesive bandage on her arm. Mary was stoic as she sat down beside Cheryl and put her hand over hers. "What is the latest on C.P.?" Cheryl had talked to Bri a couple of times over the past two hours. He was still in surgery. "We still don't know anything."

She then asked about Cheryl, who assured her she was fine. Cheryl and Jim took turns telling her what had happened. A silence fell over the room as they waited for the doctor.

Finally, the doctor walked into the waiting room.

Jim was the only one to stand. Jim looked at Mary, who was sitting there with her hands folded in her lap. Her face was pinched, but she had complete control over her emotions. "Doctor, this is Mary Zimmstein. She and C.P. are very close friends."

The doctor nodded. "Ms. Zimmstein, Mr. Traylor suffered two gunshot wounds. One was to his shoulder. We've repaired the damage there. He will need physical therapy, but I expect a full recovery there. The second wound was to his chest. We were able to remove the bullet. There is nothing I can see that would prevent him from fully recovering from that injury, but we are going to monitor him closely for infection and to see how he responds." Mary's shoulders sagged in relief. "He will be hospitalized for several days, and his activities will be curtailed for a while."

"When can I see him?" Mary asked.

"He'll be in the ICU for at least twenty-four hours. We'll monitor him for the next three or four hours, and if everything looks good, you can go in then." The doctor looked around the room. "Just one person at a time. He is going to be in and out of consciousness for the next several hours. C.P. is in good health, which makes me optimistic on his recovery."

After the doctor left, Kye eased out to go home and see to Buddy and get some sleep. Max arrived with snacks, pastries and two large insulated coffee containers. Around dawn, Sean walked in looking haggard. Sean went over and sat on the other side of Mary and asked how she was doing. "Thank you, Sean, for asking. I know your father told you what the doctor said. I take that is good news. I want to see him." She looked at Cheryl. "I think you and Cheryl should go home and get some rest." Cheryl started to protest, but Mary held up her hand. "Mom and Dad are taking Rachel to school and then coming here. Mom's sister and her husband will look after Rachel."

Bri added, "I will stay with Mary until they arrive." Jim and Helen offered to stay, but Mary assured them she was fine.

Mary looked at Sean. "Sean, I hate to delay you, but what can you tell me about how you happened to be there to stop the professor?"

"I had been here at the hospital on another matter, and as I was driving home, Dispatch called me. It's highly unusual for them to put calls from the outside through to me, but they told me that a man was insisting on talking directly to me—that your life," he looked at Cheryl, "might be in danger. I had to think whether to take the call." His lips quirked in a grin, and everyone broke out laughing. "I told them to put him through. It was Andrian, and he told me that you and C.P. were in the guest house, and he had seen Dimitri sneak in. He thought Shlykov might harm you. I had my reasons for thinking he was right. That's how I got there in time. It was Andrian sounding the alarm."

As Sean drove Cheryl home, she said, "I tried to call you before I went to C.P.'s but you were on a call."

"Yes, that's how I ended up here earlier in the evening. We had a standoff, but fortunately, we were able to talk him down. I brought him here to be examined and evaluated in the psychiatric ward."

She said she had several things to tell him. "But, right now, I just want to get home and get in bed and curl up beside you."

He smiled. "You need to rest. You must be sore from C.P. falling on you. Maybe you can use a massage."

Cheryl was almost too tired to laugh, but managed. "That sounds like just what the doctor would order. By the way, where is the necklace?"

"Safe for now in our department vault. That's one of the things I've got to deal with later today."

Cheryl's voice was drowsy. "Dimitri admitted to killing Jeffrey. He was going to plant the gun he shot us with on Andrian—to frame Andrian for killing us and Jeffrey." He thought she had more to say, but when she remained silent, Sean glanced over. Cheryl was asleep.

Chapter 78

Sean left Cheryl sleeping with Buddy lying beside the bed and went into the office. He needed to talk with Andrian. He and Alex drove over to Andrian's apartment.

"I thought you might be coming by." He stepped aside so Sean and Alex could enter. "I talked to C.P.'s assistant, who brought me up to speed on his condition. It sounds like he's going to be okay."

"That's the latest news I got," said Sean. "It was your quick thinking, Andrian, that saved them both."

Andrian pulled out a small chair from the bedroom and one from the tiny kitchen table. "You and Alex sit on these. I'll sit on this box."

"I've got some questions," said Sean.

Andrian shook his head. "It might be helpful if I start at the beginning." Sean pulled out a tape recorder, and Andrian told his story.

"My great-grandfather was a member of the Bolshevik secret police, and he and his partner had been keeping tabs on the Count and his uncle. They followed him to Geneva where they saw him go into a bank's vault area. He seemed suspicious and spotted them and ran. From that time on, they spied on him, because whatever jewelry or money he had belonged to Mother Russia, and they wanted it returned.

"They were able to stay on his trail until Bekbourg. Yegor was able to sneak into the hotel the night of the gala and dressed as a server. When he saw the necklace worn by the Count's wife, he knew it belonged back in Russia and started making plans to retrieve it. On the evening they planned to go to the guest house where the Count had been staying, my great-grandfather fell deathly ill and could not go. He never knew what happened, but he suspected the old woman poisoned him. Fearing she might kill him, he made it to the livery stables and collapsed. They took him to the small hospital run by the nuns. He couldn't speak English, so they didn't know much about him, but he got well enough and caught a train several days later. He got off in Cincinnati, because that was where the Count was supposed to have gone. He thought he might find his partner there, but never did. He later heard that the Count had died of pneumonia. By then, he was still sickly and tiring of what he was doing. He was always sickly after that, but he found a job laying bricks. He shortened his last name to Kray.

"This was the story he passed down to my grand-father who passed it down to my father and me and my brother. Because my grandfather was sickly, we questioned if great-grandfather had actually been poisoned or just had a malady that my grandfather inherited. Anyway, great-grandfather never pursued the jewels and never heard what happened to them.

"Over his lifetime, Granddad had a lot of health problems. During his younger years, he was able to work a steady job, but later in life, he'd work a while and have to quit. When he was doing better, he'd start a new job. One of his jobs was a groundskeeper at the big museum in Cincinnati. One day while he was there, a man claiming to be a professor from a large university in Maryland approached Granddad. He told him he was an expert on Russian history and heard that a headline exhibit of jewels and artifacts once belonging to the Romanovs was coming. They talked a little while about Russia, but Granddad had to get back to work. A couple of days later, the same professor came back. Granddad was suspicious of most people, but there was something about the professor that really made him distrust him. The professor tried to ingratiate himself by bringing Granddad coffee and even a sandwich from the deli there. Then, one day, the professor eased around asking Granddad if he ever had access to displays in the museum and about the security. Granddad did not have a good feeling, and he sure as hell didn't want to be implicated in anything. He told him he didn't know anything and didn't know anyone in the museum. That he just did his grounds job and kept to himself, and he didn't know anybody. He never saw him after that, but it was Dimitri Shlykov.

"Dad and Granddad knew Shlykov had grown up in Cincinnati, but they didn't try to find out anything about him. They didn't want anything to do with him because they thought he was corrupt and—according to Granddad—would cut someone's throat if they weren't careful. They were suspicious he might check into our family, and for a long time, they were cautious about locking doors.

"So, that brings me to why I came to Bekbourg. I knew of my great-grandfather's story here in Bekbourg, and I happened to read Cheryl's article. I saw the picture and read where the Count and his wife were planning to stop in Bekbourg on their return to Rhode Island. I wondered if the jewels were here—or at least if there might be a clue here about what happened to them. I got lucky and saw that C.P. was looking for an archivist and applied.

"Then, when the body turned up in C.P.'s basement, and I read the authorities thought the death occurred around the mid 1920's, I was fairly certain it must have been Yegor. So, I was doing as much research as I could to see what I could piece together.

"In the meantime, Shlykov came to town, and I figured he could only be here for one reason—trying to find what he could about the jewels. Because of what I knew from Granddad and Dad, I didn't trust him, but there was another reason. Like myself, my older brother had heard the family stories about Shlykov. He works as an accountant for a large drilling company in Houston. He knew of course why I moved to Bekbourg but didn't support it. He thought I was tossing in the wind. When we were talking one night, I told him about Shlykov being here and looking into the Count and that I thought he might be looking for the jewels. He warned me to be careful.

"The owner of the drilling company was in his eighties and had amassed a collection of European jewels, which he was going to loan to a museum there. Here's the thing. A couple of nights before his collection was going to be transferred to the museum, he hosted a party at his house. My brother knew about it because some of the top officers in the company were invited. My brother was down on the food chain, but he heard from his boss about this party. He was telling about some of the interesting people in attendance, and one was a famous professor on Russian history—Dimitri. When an egg was stolen from the collection, my brother couldn't help but think Dimitri might have somehow been involved. He had nothing to go on other than pure conjecture.

"So, that leads me to what I was doing last night. I started parking near C.P.'s house to walk around. I would walk by the guest house, trying to figure out what might have happened there. I did wonder if the jewels were stashed in there, but it seemed so unlikely. After all these years—with different renovations and all—how was it possible? I didn't even know if they were in Bekbourg, because maybe the Count and his wife had taken them with them—why leave jewels here in Bekbourg? Then, one night, I saw Dimitri walking near the house, and I hid and watched. He stood on the sidewalk a long time looking at the guest house. He didn't go up to it. Two days later is when the first break-in occurred. I thought it might be Dimitri, but I had no proof. So, I kept walking around the neighborhood to see if I saw him again, which I never did. Then I saw Jeffrey out walking one night. He didn't stop to look at the house, but he was looking at it as he walked by.

"The night Jeffrey was killed, I had been walking over there and saw Jeffrey's car. I knew what he drove because when he stopped by the depot one day to see Kat, I saw his car out the window. Anyway, I didn't see him anywhere, and nothing looked suspicious at the guest house, so I headed back to my car. About the time I got to it, which was a couple of streets over, I heard what sounded like fire crackers or gun shots. I didn't know what it was, but if it was gun shots. I didn't want to be anywhere around, so I left.

"Last night, I walked by and saw Cheryl's car parked in front of C.P.'s house and all the lights on in the guest house. That seemed odd to me, so I squatted down behind a car and watched. This was the first time I had ever seen lights on in the guest house at night. I wondered if Cheryl and C.P. were over there, and if so, why? Then, I saw Dimitri's car drive by and slow down. He then went up the street and parked. He got out of his car and looked around. I could see all this because of the street light. He came down and jumped over the fence and went around back. He then came back around and went to the front door. He looked around like he was looking to see if anyone was around. He slowly opened the front door and eased in. That's when I thought I needed to call you.

"Why didn't you tell me all this when we talked to you the other day?" Sean asked.

"I didn't have any proof of anything. I thought you'd think I was trying to point figures at Dimitri, and it would just make me look guilty. I didn't know anything that was concrete."

"What about the box? What was in it that was so important?"

"One of the pictures showed my great-granddad standing on the platform smoking a cigarette. I think the man standing next to him was Yegor. I was concerned if someone looked close, they might see a resemblance. If Blankenship or the professor saw it, that might have put a target on my back. They might have thought I knew more about the jewels than I did."

"What were you going to do with the jewels if you found them?"

Andrian shook his head. "I really don't know. It seemed so far-fetched to think I could find them. One thought was to take them to D.C. and turn them over to the Russian embassy. I might have called the FBI. Hell, I don't know, but if you're thinking I would have kept them or sold them, that's *not* what I would have done. I wouldn't know the first thing about selling them, and what was I going to do with royal jewels other than be a target for thieves. Jewelry, even something like that, is not my thing. Besides, I likely would have been killed or charged with a crime, and that's the last thing I would want for a lot of reasons. One is what it would have done to my family if something like that would have happened."

Chapter 79

Sean had a long call with Lucky.

"Sean, that's the damnedest thing. Russian royal jewels hidden all these years in Bekbourg! Hell, had Cheryl not written that article, they may never have been discovered."

"I know, and the jewels set in motion parallels of murder eighty years apart. The Count apparently set a trap to kill the spies using the jewels as bait, and then Dimitri killed Jeffrey because he was trying to find the jewels and sell them out from under the professor."

"Blankenship was successful with the Russian egg, and Dimitri figured that out," said Lucky.

Lucky told Sean that Elias had already started to make headway with Interpol based on Sean putting them onto Dimitri. Their theory was that Dimitri was part of a small group who operated in the black market to buy and sell jewels, but they had also stolen jewels and sold them.

Sean had discussed with the county prosecutor and the federal prosecutor what to do with the necklace, which was still part of his ongoing investigation into Dimitri's death. Lucky was going to send down a team the next day to arrange the transport of the jewels to a secure vault in the Smithsonian until all the legal matters were worked out and the ownership determined.

Sean then went to the newspaper's office to see his wife. He had not yet heard how it was she knew to look in the upstairs bedrooms at the guest house.

Patti joked when he walked in, "Whatever you're here to arrest her for, all of us here know her alibis."

Sean laughed as she motioned for him to go to Cheryl's office.

Cheryl was busy working with Milton to get the story out about Dimitri's death. Sean asked, "Mind if I borrow her for a little while?"

"Not at all, Sean. It's a remarkable story we've got for this extra edition we're publishing."

Sean asked how she was feeling, and they talked for a few minutes.

He said, "I need to put on my sheriff's hat and ask you some questions."

A big smile lit up her face, "Okay, Sweetie. I'm obliged to cooperate with such a sexy, handsome lawman."

Sean could not help but grin. "So, tell me how you knew to go look in the upstairs bedroom at the guest house."

Cheryl told him the story Kat's mother, Klara, had told her. "So, I didn't know for sure, but it seemed logical. I tried to call you, but you were handling that standoff, and so I called C.P. I never dreamed we would have been in danger like we were."

"Why did Kat's mother come tell you?"

"I guess you had taken Kat to the station to question her about Jeffrey's death."

Sean nodded.

"She was petrified Kat would be charged. She thought it was the professor who had killed Jeffrey, since they were working together, and she was convinced they were here to try to find the jewels." Cheryl grinned. "I had been there the other day asking Kat about the history of the family, so she knew I had familiarity with the matter." Cheryl's grin grew wider. "After you left with Kat, she drove here. She needed help, and she told me she doesn't trust the police. In Russia, it's not good to trust the police."

Sean arched an eyebrow. "But the newspaper is trustworthy?"

Cheryl started laughing. "Of course we are."

Chapter 80

C.P.'s eyes started to flutter. He heard a woman's voice. "His blood pressure is stable but slightly lower than normal. It should return to normal soon. The other vitals look good." She leaned toward him, "Mr. Traylor. You awake?"

C.P. managed to get an eye opened. He did not know where he was or what was happening. The woman continued looking at him. "Mr. Traylor. I'm nurse Towlman. Can you hear me?"

It took an effort, but his other eye opened. "Don't try to talk, Mr. Traylor. You're in the hospital. You were shot. We're going to keep a close eye on you for a few days, but the doctor thinks you'll have a full recovery."

Pain pressed his chest and left shoulder. He felt something warm on his right hand and looked down. *Mary!* He tried to move his hand to connect better with hers, but he drifted back to sleep as she squeezed his hand, thinking he heard, "I love you, C.P."

Later in the afternoon, he woke up to find Mary still sitting beside his bed. "Mary," he whispered.

Her head flew up. "Hi, Darling," she smiled. "I've

been waiting for you to wake up."

He tried to move, but she stood and gently motioned for him to stay still. "Is there something I can get you?"

"I was trying to see you better." His mouth was dry and raspy.

"I'll stand so you can see me."

He shook his head. "That's not comfortable. I can see well enough. What happened? I remember Cheryl and I . . . Oh, God. Cheryl!"

Mary quickly put her hands on his arm. "She's fine. She wasn't shot. You fell on top of her."

"I have a lot of questions, but I'm too weak to talk right now."

"Sleep, C.P. The doctors say that's what you need now."

"You look tired. You should go home and rest."

"I will when the time is right." Sleep overcame him before she finished her sentence.

The next time he woke, Mary was still sitting by his bedside. He heard the nurse tell Mary they wanted to take him down for a scan. "If you'd like, you could go to the cafeteria and get something to eat. You've barely eaten."

"Thank you, Nurse Towlman." She turned to C.P. "I'll be back soon."

After she left, the nurse turned to him. "Okay. We're ready to move you." She went to the door and spoke to two men, who came in to start the process of moving him.

"I want to take a walk. I need to get out of this bed."

"Not until the doctor gives the okay."

"When's he going to be in here?" C.P. demanded.

"He'll be making his rounds this evening."

He watched them moving the bags and tubes. "When am I getting out of here?"

"When the doctor says it's okay."

"Any idea?"

"No. I'm going to have them bring you some soft food. You can start eating a little."

"Huh. I don't think I need all these tubes. I can walk to the bathroom."

"Maybe tomorrow."

He watched her. "You're as bad as some of those union bosses I had to deal with."

"I take that as a compliment."

The patient transporters told her they were ready

.

When Mary returned, C.P. was back in his room. "How are you doing, Darling?"

"That drill sergeant won't let me get out of this damn bed."

Mary hid a grin. "Well, I'm sure it won't be too long."

He was like a caged lion. He looked at her, "The battle-ax told me you haven't left the hospital. I'm fine— even at my age." C.P. was only in his sixties, but she knew he considered their fifteen-year age difference an issue. Her heart had sunk with fear when Bri arrived and told her what had happened to C.P. All she could think about on the drive down from Columbus, and until the doctor talked to her, was that she did not want to lose him. She took his hand. "C.P., you will never be old in my eyes. I love you, Darling."

C.P.'s eyes widened. Just then, the nurse pushed opened the door. "Mr. Traylor, the doctor ordered some more tests. We're going to take you to the third floor." She turned to Mary. "He'll probably be gone about an hour."

"Mary, go home and get some rest. The sergeant here won't let me out of her sight."

Mary smiled. "Okay. I'll be back after a while. Please try not to give Nurse Towlman too hard a time."

When he was returned to the room, Mary was not there, but she had run by his house and picked up some things. On the side table was a book, his reading glasses, and his cell phone. She had left him a note saying she had gone home and would be back in the morning, but if he needed anything, to call her. His phone was fully charged. He laid back on the pillow and fell asleep.

When the doctor made his rounds early the next morning, C.P. asked Mary to stay and listen. The doctor told them he was making progress, and they would start short walks down the hall. The chest and shoulder wounds were healing, and there was no permanent damage. He wanted to keep him in the hospital another few days and start physical therapy on his shoulder.

After the doctor left, Mary told C.P. she had to attend to something at the foundation, but she would be back in the early afternoon.

When Nurse Towlman came in, he asked her to hand him his cell phone and reading glasses. She did but told him, "The doctor says you need your rest. Don't think on my watch you're going to have long business calls."

C.P.'s eyes sparked. "Does this place have a conference room we can use?"

She ignored his jest. "Here, let me help you sit up. I'll put another pillow behind your back."

As she checked the equipment, he looked up the phone number. She started to leave, but he asked her to stay because he might need her. She stood at the foot of his bed and watched and listened, wondering what this was about. He pressed a button and put the phone to his ear. "This is C.P. Traylor. Put me through to Simon . . . . Yes, I'll wait."

"Hi, Simon. Yes. Good to talk to you. Say, I need your help on something. I need an engagement ring." The nurse's eyes popped when she heard the carat. "Yeah, I think round is good. . . . Yeah, platinum." He looked questioning at the nurse, "Oh, size? Hold on, I'll ask the nurse. . . What size do you think Mary would wear?"

She looked at her hands, which were larger. "Ms. Zimmstein is a petite woman. I would guess a five or five-and-a-half."

He repeated, "Let's go with a five-and-a-half . . . . Yeah, I'm in the hospital . . . . It's a long story, but I'll be fine once the doctor releases me. I need it tomorrow . . . . I'm in Bekbourg. It's a town in Ohio—south of

Columbus . . . . Well, put someone on a damn plane with it." C.P. relaxed his shoulders. The nurse looked at the blood pressure monitor, which was still flashing normal. "Have them bring it to the Bekbourg County Hospital. Here, the nurse can give you the address." He handed her the phone. She identified herself and gave the address and room number and handed back the phone. "Have the delivery person ask for me, but if they've taken me for a joy ride like they enjoy doing, ask for Nurse Towlman."

After he hung up, he looked at her. "It's a secret."

"When are you going to pop the question?" she asked.

"Next day or two—as soon as the ring gets here."

She had grown used to their bantering. She narrowed her eyes, "You aren't allowed to get out of bed and go down on one knee to propose."

He did not miss a comeback. "I'll have to tell Mary it's you who is the killjoy. Probably won't be a surprise to her." She nodded and turned and grinned as she walked out the door.

Sean stopped by to see C.P. to ask him some questions about what had happened at the guest house. "How are you doing, C.P.?"

"I'm coming along, Sean. I should be good as new soon."

"That's good to hear. Cheryl told me what happened—that you protected her. I appreciate what you did."

C.P. nodded. "I only did what came natural, Sean, like you would have done had you been there."

"If you're up to it, I need to ask you some questions."

"I'm up to it. You better start asking before that drill sergeant comes in."

Sean smiled. C.P. answered Sean's questions. As they were wrapping up, C.P. said, "I've kind of grown attached to that yellow crime tape around the guest house. Don't feel any rush in taking it down."

Sean laughed. "I'm glad you feel that way. I suspect Cole has a different view. It's certainly interrupted his construction project."

C.P. chuckled. "He told me he was behind schedule. I told him I thought we were probably good as long as he didn't find any more dead bodies."

Sean and C.P. laughed. Sean left C.P. to get his rest.

The following day, Nurse Towlman had C.P. sitting in a chair when Mary arrived, so he didn't have to propose from a hospital bed. Nurses and patients alike were buzzing about the happy couple when they heard Mary had accepted.

Chapter 81

Cheryl was looking through her mail and saw an envelope with a return address from Libby. When she opened it, she found a letter addressed to her with a separate paper attached. The letter read,

Dear Cheryl.

I have given much thought to Grandmother since our meeting and especially since your call informing me about the hidden necklace and the Russian agent shot by the Count in the attempted robbery. By the way, I have released all claims to the necklace. It was never Grandmother's, and my attorney advised it would be a long legal battle.

I often find myself thinking of Kat's great-grandmother, Katia, and the bravery she exhibited. One of the

unanswered questions you had was who had sent the message to the two Russian spies, and why did Yegor go to the guest house to rob the Count? I finished going through Grandmother's box and found a hand written letter—in Russian. One of our friends has a son who works for the State Department and knows Russian. He translated the letter, which I've attached. I look forward to hearing from you as to whether you think this answers your question.

I hope your friend, Mr. Traylor, is recovering nicely. My husband and I would enjoy having you and your husband as guests sometime.

Happy Thanksgiving to you and your loved ones,

Fondly,

Libby

Libby had copied the letter written in Russian as well as the translation.

Your Highness,

I fear your life in danger. Two Russians, traveling on train, placed at my home. I hear whispers and talk of jewels. I know the old ways with tea. If you invite them for a visit, my tea before may work to weaken them. Today or tomorrow good so they won't follow on train. My daughter Katia you know. For the Motherland.

Your humble servant